Dear Reader,

I can't believe that it has been over thirty years since my first Long, Tall Texans book, *Calhoun*, debuted! The series was suggested by my former editor Tara Gavin, who asked if I might like to set stories in a fictional town of my own design. Would I! And the rest is history.

As the years went by, I found more and more sexy ranchers and cowboys to add to the collection. My readers (especially Amy!) found time to gift me with a notebook listing every single one of them, along with their wives and kids and connections to other families in my own Texas town of Jacobsville. Eventually the town got a little too big for me, so I added another smaller town called Comanche Wells and began to fill it up, too.

You can't imagine how much pleasure this series has given me. I continue to add to the population of Jacobs County, Texas, and I have no plans to stop. Ever.

I hope all of you enjoy reading the Long, Tall Texans as much as I enjoy writing them. Thank you all for your kindness and loyalty and friendship. I am your biggest fan!

Love,

Diana Palmer

TEXAS PRIDE

NEW YORK TIMES BESTSELLING AUTHOR
DIANA PALMER

Two Heartfelt Stories
Coltrain and *Kingman*
(Previously published as *Coltrain's Proposal*
and *The Princess Bride*)

Harlequin
SPECIAL RELEASE

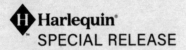
Harlequin®
SPECIAL RELEASE

Recycling programs
for this product may
not exist in your area.

ISBN-13: 978-1-335-98367-1

Texas Pride

Copyright © 2025 by Harlequin Enterprises ULC

Coltrain
First published as Coltrain's Proposal in 1995.
This edition published in 2025 with revised text.
Copyright © 1995 by Diana Palmer
Copyright © 2025 by Diana Palmer, revised text edition

Kingman
First published as The Princess Bride in 1998.
This edition published in 2025 with revised text.
Copyright © 1998 by Diana Palmer
Copyright © 2025 by Diana Palmer, revised text edition

Harlequin Enterprises ULC
22 Adelaide St. West, 41st Floor
Toronto, Ontario M5H 4E3, Canada
www.Harlequin.com

Printed in U.S.A.

CONTENTS

COLTRAIN   7

KINGMAN   187

A prolific author of more than one hundred books,
Diana Palmer got her start as a newspaper reporter.
A *New York Times* bestselling author and voted one
of the top ten romance writers in America, she has a
gift for telling the most sensual tales with charm and
humor. Diana lives with her family in Cornelia, Georgia.
Visit her website at dianapalmer.com.

Books by Diana Palmer

Long, Tall Texans

Fearless
Heartless
Dangerous
Merciless
Courageous
Protector
Invincible
Untamed
Defender
Undaunted

The Wyoming Men

Wyoming Tough
Wyoming Fierce
Wyoming Bold
Wyoming Strong
Wyoming Rugged
Wyoming Brave

Visit the Author Profile page
at Harlequin.com for more titles.

COLTRAIN

To Darlene, Cindy and Melissa

CHAPTER ONE

THE LITTLE BOY'S leg was bleeding profusely. Dr. Louise Blakely knew exactly what to do, but it was difficult to get the right pressure on the cut so that the nicked artery would stop emptying onto the brown, dead December grass.

"It hurts!" the little boy, Matt, cried. "Ow!"

"We have to stop the bleeding," she said reasonably. She smiled at him, her dark eyes twinkling in a face framed by thick, medium blond hair. "Maybe your mom could get you an ice cream after we've patched you up." She glanced at the white-faced lady beside them, who nodded enthusiastically. "Okay?"

"Well…" He grimaced, holding his leg above where Lou was putting pressure to bear.

"Only a minute more," she promised, looking around for the ambulance she'd asked a bystander to call. It was on the way. She could hear the siren. Even in a small town like Jacobsville, there was an efficient ambulance service. "You're going to get to ride in a real ambulance," she told the child. "You can tell your friends all about it on Monday at school!"

"Will I have to go back?" he asked, enthusiastic now. "Maybe I could stay in the hospital for a whole week?"

"I really think the emergency room is as far as you're

going to get this time." Lou chuckled. "Now pay attention while they're loading you up, so that you can remember everything!"

"I sure will!" he said.

She stood up as the ambulance pulled alongside the police car and two attendants jumped out. They started loading the boy onto a stretcher. Lou had a brief word with the female EMT and described the boy's injuries and gave instructions. She was on staff at the local hospital where he would be taken, and she planned to follow the ambulance in her own car.

The police officer who'd been citing the reckless driver for hitting the small boy on the bicycle came over to talk to Lou. "Good thing you were having lunch in the café," he remarked with a grin. "That was a bad cut."

"He'll be okay," Lou said as she closed her medical bag. She always had it in the car when she left the office, and this time it had paid off.

"You're Dr. Coltrain's partner, aren't you?" he asked suddenly.

"Yes." She didn't add anything to that. The expression on the officer's face said enough. Most people around Jacobsville knew that Dr. Coltrain had as little use for his partner as he had for alcohol. He'd made it all too evident in the months she'd been sharing his practice.

"He's a good man," the officer added. "Saved my wife when her lung collapsed." He smiled at the memory. "Nothing shakes him up. Nor you, either, judging by what I just saw. You're a good hand in an emergency."

"Thanks." She gave him a brief smile and went to her small gray Ford to follow the ambulance to the hospital.

THE EMERGENCY ROOM was full, as usual. It was Saturday and accidents always doubled on weekends. She nodded to a couple of her patients that she recognized, and she kept walking, right behind the trolley that was taking young Matt to a treatment room.

Dr. Coltrain was on his way back from surgery. They met in the hall. The green surgical uniform looked sloppy on some of the surgeons, but not on Coltrain. Despite the cap that hid most of his thick red hair, he looked elegant and formidable.

"Why are you here on Saturday? I'm supposed to be doing rounds today for both of us," he asked sharply.

Here he goes again, practicing Coltrain's First Law... jump to conclusions, she thought. She didn't grin, but she felt like it.

"I wound up at a car accident scene," she began.

"The hospital pays EMTs to work wrecks," he continued, glaring at her while hospital personnel came and went around them.

"I did not go out to—" she began hotly.

"Don't let this happen again, or I'll have a word with Wright, and you'll be taken off staff here. Is that clear?" he added coldly. Wright was the hospital administrator and Coltrain was medical chief of staff. He had the authority to carry out the threat.

"Will you listen?" she asked irritably. "I didn't go out with the ambulance...!"

"Doctor, are you coming?" one of the EMTs called to her.

Coltrain glanced toward the EMT and then back at Louise, irritably jerking off his cap and mask. His pale blue eyes were as intimidating as his stance. "If your social life is this stale, Doctor, perhaps you need to consider a move," he added with biting sarcasm.

She opened her mouth to reply, but he was already walking away. She threw up her hands furiously. She couldn't ever get a word in, because he kept talking, or interrupted her, and then stormed off without giving her a chance to reply. It was useless to argue with him, anyway. No matter what she said or did, she was always in the wrong.

"One day you'll break something," she told his retreating back. "And I'll put you in a body cast, so help me God!"

A passing nurse patted her on the shoulder. "There, there, Doctor, you're doing it again."

She ground her teeth together. It was a standing joke in the hospital staff that Louise Blakely ended up talking to herself every time she argued with Dr. Coltrain. That meant that she talked to herself almost constantly. Presumably he heard her from time to time, but he never gave a single indication that he had.

With a furious groan deep in her throat, she turned down the hall to join the EMT.

IT TOOK AN hour to see to the boy, who had more than one cut that needed stitches. His mother was going to have to buy him a lot of ice cream to make up for the pain, Lou thought, and she'd been wrong about another thing, too—he did have to stay overnight in the hospital. But that would only give him status among his peers, she thought, and left him smiling with a cautionary word about the proper way to ride a bicycle in town.

"No need to worry about that," his mother said

firmly. "He won't be riding his bike across city streets anymore!"

She nodded and left the emergency room, her bag in hand. She looked more like a teenager on holiday than a doctor, she mused, in her blue jeans and T-shirt and sneakers. She'd pulled her long blond hair up into its habitual bun and she wore no makeup to enhance her full mouth or her deep brown eyes. She had no man to impress, except the one she loved, and he wouldn't notice if she wore tar and feathers to the office they shared. "Copper" Coltrain had no interest in Lou Blakely, except as an efficient co-worker. Not that he ever acknowledged her efficiency; instead he found fault with her constantly. She wondered often why he ever agreed to work with her in the first place, when he couldn't seem to stand the sight of her. She wondered, too, why she kept hanging on where she wasn't wanted. The hunger her poor heart felt for him was her only excuse. And one day, even that wouldn't be enough.

Dr. Drew Morris, the only friend she had on staff, came down the hall toward her. Like Coltrain, he'd been operating, because he was wearing the same familiar green surgical clothing. But where Coltrain did chest surgery, Drew's talents were limited to tonsils, adenoids, appendices and other minor surgeries. His speciality was pediatrics. Coltrain's was chest and lungs, and many of his patients were elderly.

"What are you doing here? It's too early or too late for rounds, depending on your schedule," he added with a grin. "Besides, I thought Copper was doing them today."

Copper, indeed. Only a handful of people were priv-
ileged to call Dr. Coltrain by that nickname, and she
wasn't numbered among them.

She grimaced at him. He was about her height, although she was tall, and he had dark hair and eyes and
was a little overweight. He was the one who'd phoned
her at the Austin hospital where she was working just
after her parents' deaths, and he'd told her about the
interviews Coltrain was holding for a partner. She'd
jumped at the chance for a new start, in the hometown
where her mother and father had both been born. And
amazingly, in light of his ongoing animosity toward
her, Coltrain had asked her to join him after a ten-
minute interview.

"There was an accident in front of the café," she
said. "I was having lunch there. I haven't been to the
grocery store yet," she added with a grimace. "I hate
shopping."

"Who doesn't?" He smiled. "Doing okay?"

She shrugged. "As usual."

He stuck his hands on his hips and shook his head.
"It's my fault. I thought it would get better, but it hasn't,
has it? It's been almost a year, and he still suffers you."

She winced. She didn't quite avert her face fast
enough to hide it.

"You poor kid," he said gently. "I'm sorry. I suppose
I was too enthusiastic about getting you here. I thought
you needed a change, after…well, after your parents'
deaths. This looked like a good opportunity. Copper's
one of the best surgeons I've ever known, and you're a
skilled family practitioner. It seemed a good match of
talent, and you've taken a load off him in his regular

practice so that he could specialize in the surgery he's
so skilled at." He sighed. "How wrong can a man be?"

"I signed a contract for one year," she reminded
him. "It's almost up."

"Then what?"

"Then I'll go back to Austin."

"You could work the E.R.," he teased. It was a standing joke between them. The hospital had to contract out
the emergency room staff, because none of the local
doctors wanted to do it. The job was so demanding that
one young resident had walked out in the middle of the
unnecessary examination of a known hypochondriac
at two in the morning and never came back.

Lou smiled, remembering that. "No, thanks. I like
private practice, but I can't afford to set up and equip
an office of my own just yet. I'll go back to the drawing board. There's bound to be a practice somewhere
in Texas."

"You're fit for this one," he said shortly.

"Not to hear my partner tell it," she said curtly. "I'm
never right, didn't you know?" She let out a long breath.
"Anyway, I'm in a rut, Drew. I need a change."

"Maybe you do, at that." He pursed his lips and
smiled. "What you really need is a good social life.
I'll be in touch."

She watched him walk away with grave misgivings.
She hoped that he didn't mean what it sounded like he
meant. She wanted nothing to do with Drew in a romantic way, although she did like him. He was a kind
man, a widower who'd been in love with his wife and
was still, after five years, getting over her. Drew was
a native of Jacobsville, and knew Lou's parents. He'd

been very fond of her late mother. He'd met up with them again in Austin—that's where Lou had met him.

Lou decided not to take Drew's teasing seriously because she knew about his devotion to his wife's memory. But he'd looked very solemn when he'd remarked that her social life needed uplifting.

She was probably imagining things, she told herself. She started out to the parking lot and met Dr. Coltrain, dressed in an expensive gray vested suit, bent on the same destination. She ground her teeth together and slowed her pace, but she still reached the doors at the same time he did.

He spared her a cold glance. "You look unprofessional," he said curtly. "At least have the grace to dress decently if you're going to cruise around with the ambulance service."

She stopped and looked up at him without expression. "I wasn't cruising anywhere. I don't have a boat, so how could I cruise?"

He just looked at her. "They don't need any new EMTs…"

"You shut up!" she snapped, surprising him speechless. "Now you listen to me for a change, and don't interrupt!" she added, holding up her hand when his thin lips parted. "There was an accident in town. I was in the café, so I gave assistance. I don't need to hang out with the ambulance crew for kicks, Doctor! And how I dress on my days off is none of your—" she almost turned blue biting back the curse "—*business, Doctor!*"

He was over his shock. His hand shot out and caught the wrist of her free hand, the one that wasn't holding her black medical bag, and jerked. She caught her breath at the shock of his touch and squirmed, wrestling out of his grip. The muted violence of it brought back protective instincts that she'd almost forgotten. She stood very still, holding her breath, her eyes the size of saucers as she looked at him and waited for that hand to tighten and twist...

But it didn't. He, unlike her late father, never seemed to lose control. He released her abruptly. His blue eyes narrowed. "Cold as ice, aren't you?" he drawled mockingly. "You'd freeze any normal man to death. Is that why you never married, Doctor?"

It was the most personal thing he'd ever said to her, and one of the most insulting.

"You just think what you like," she said.

"You might be surprised at what I think," he replied.

Her own eyebrows lifted. "Really?" She laughed and walked off to her car, happy to have seen him stiffen. She walked past his Mercedes without even a glance. Take that, she thought furiously. She didn't care what he thought about her, she told herself. She spent most of her free time telling herself that. But she did care about him, far too much. That was the whole problem.

He thought she was cold, but she wasn't. It was quite the reverse where he was concerned. She always jerked away when he came too close, when he touched her infrequently. It wasn't because she found him repulsive but because his touch excited her so much. She trembled when he was too close, her breathing changed. She couldn't control her shaky legs or her shaky voice. The only solution had been to distance herself physically from him, and that was what she'd done.

There were other reasons, too, why she avoided

physical involvement. They were none of his business, or anyone else's. She did her job and avoided trouble as much as possible. But just lately, her job was becoming an ordeal.

She drove home to the small dilapidated white house on the outskirts of town. It was in a quiet neighborhood that was just beginning to go downhill. The rent was cheap. She'd spent weekends painting the walls and adding bits and pieces to the house's drab interior. She had it all but furnished now, and it reflected her own quiet personality. But there were other dimensions to the room, like the crazy cat sculpture on the mantel and the colorful serapes on the chairs, and the Indian pottery and exotic musical instruments on the bookshelf. The paintings were her own, disturbingly violent ones with reds and blacks and whites in dramatic chaos. A visitor would have found the combinations of flowers amid those paintings confusing. But, then, she'd never had a visitor. She kept to herself.

Coltrain did, too, as a rule. He had visitors to his ranch from time to time, but his invitations even when they included the medical staff invariably excluded Louise. The omission had caused gossip, which no one had been brave enough to question to his face. Louise didn't care if he never invited her to his home. After all, she never invited him to hers.

Secretly she suspected that he was grieving for Jane Parker, his old flame who'd just recently married Todd Burke. Jane was blond and blue-eyed and beautiful, a former rodeo star with a warm heart and a gentle personality.

Lou often wondered why he'd ever agreed to work

with someone he disliked so much, and on such short acquaintance. He and Dr. Drew Morris were friends, and she'd tried to question Drew about her sudden acceptance, but Drew was a clam. He always changed the subject.

Drew had known her parents in Jacobsville and he had been a student of her father's at the Austin teaching hospital where he'd interned. He'd become an ally of her mother during some really tough times, but he didn't like Lou's father. He knew too much about his home life, and how Lou and her mother were treated.

There had been one whisper of gossip at the Jacobsville hospital when she'd first gone there on cases. She'd heard one of the senior nurses remark that it must disturb "him" to have Dr. Blakely's daughter practicing at this hospital and thank God she didn't do surgery. Lou had wanted to question the nurse, but she'd made herself scarce after that and eventually had retired.

Louise had never found out who "he" was or what was disturbing about having another Blakely practice at the Jacobsville hospital. But she did begin to realize that her father had a past here.

"What did my father do at this hospital, Drew?" she'd asked him one day suddenly, while they were doing rounds at the hospital.

He'd seemed taken aback. "He was a surgeon on staff, just as I am," he said after a hesitation.

"He left here under a cloud, didn't he?" she persisted.

He shook his head. "There was no scandal, no cloud on his reputation. He was a good surgeon and well respected, right until the end. You know that. Even if he

was less than admirable as a husband and father, he
was an exceptional surgeon."

"Then why the whispers about him when I first
came here?"

"It was nothing to do with his skill as a surgeon," he
replied quietly. "It's nothing that really even concerns
you, except in a roundabout way."

"But what...?"

They'd been interrupted and he'd looked relieved.
She hadn't asked again. But she wondered more and
more. Perhaps it had affected Dr. Coltrain in some
way and that was why he disliked Lou. But wouldn't
he have mentioned it in a whole year?

She didn't ever expect to understand the so-con-
trolled Dr. Coltrain or his venomous attitude toward
her. He'd been much more cordial when she first became his partner. But about the time she realized that
she was in love with him, he became icy cold and antagonistic. He'd been that way ever since, raising eyebrows everywhere.

The remark he'd made this morning about her coldness was an old one. She'd jerked back from him at a
Christmas party, soon after she'd come to work in his
office in Jacobsville, to avoid a kiss under the mistletoe. She could hardly have admitted that even then
the thought of his hard, thin mouth on hers made her
knees threaten to buckle. Her attraction to him had
been explosive and immediate, a frightening experience to a woman whose whole life had been wrapped
around academic excellence and night upon night of
exhaustive studying. She had no social life at all—even
in high school. It had been the one thing that kept her

father's vicious sarcasm and brutality at bay, as long as she made good grades and stayed on the dean's list.

Outside achievements had been the magic key that kept the balance in her dysfunctional family. She studied and won awards and scholarships and praise, and her father basked in it. She thought that he'd never felt much for her, except pride in her ability to excel. He was a cruel man and grew crueler as his addiction climbed year after year to new heights. Drugs had caused the plane crash. Her mother had died with him. God knew, that was fitting, because she'd loved him to the point of blindness, overlooking his brutality, his addiction, his cruelty in the name of fidelity.

Lou wrapped her arms around herself, feeling the chill of fear. She'd never marry. Any woman could wake up in a relationship that damaging. All she had to do was fall in love, lose control, give in to a man's dominance. Even the best man could become a predator if he sensed vulnerability in a woman. So she would never be vulnerable, she assured herself. She would never be at a man's mercy as her mother had been.

But Copper Coltrain made her vulnerable, and that was why she avoided any physical contact with him. She couldn't give in to the feelings he roused in her, for fear of becoming a victim. Loneliness might be a disease, but it was certainly a more manageable one than love.

The ringing of the telephone caught her attention.

"Dr. Blakely?" Brenda, her office nurse, queried. "Sorry to bother you at home, but Dr. Coltrain said there's been a wreck on the north end of town and they'll be bringing the victims to the emergency room. Since he's on call, you'll have to cover the two-hour Saturday clinic at the office."

"I'll be right over," she promised, wasting no more time in conversation.

THE CLINIC WAS almost deserted. There was a football game at the local high school that night, and it was sunny and unseasonably warm outside for early December. It didn't really surprise Lou that she only needed to see a handful of patients.

"Poor Dr. Coltrain," Brenda said with a sigh as they finished the last case and closed up the office. "I'll bet he won't be in until midnight."

"It's a good thing he isn't married," Lou remarked. "He'd have no home life at all, as hard as he works."

Brenda glanced at her, but with a kind smile. "That is true. But he should be thinking about it. He's in his thirties now, and time is passing him by." She turned the key in the lock. "Pity about Miss Parker marrying that Burke man, isn't it? Dr. Coltrain was sweet on her for so many years. I always thought—I guess most people here did—that they were made for each other. But she was never more than friendly. If you saw them together, it was obvious that she didn't feel what he did."

In other words, Dr. Coltrain had felt a long and unrequited love for the lovely blond former rodeo cowgirl, Jane Parker. That much, Lou had learned from gossip. It must have hurt him very badly when she married someone else.

"What a pity that we can't love to order," Lou remarked quietly, thinking how much she'd give to be unscarred and find Dr. Coltrain as helplessly drawn to her as she was to him. That was the stuff of fantasy, however.

"Wasn't it surprising about Ted Regan and Coreen Tarleton, though?" Brenda added with a chuckle.

"Indeed it was," Lou agreed, smiling as she remembered having Ted for a patient. "She was shaking all over when she got him to me with that gored arm. He was cool. Nothing shakes Ted. But Coreen was as white as milk."

"I thought they were already married," Brenda groaned. "Well, I was new to the area and I didn't know them. I do now," she added, laughing. "I pass them at least once a week on their way to the obstetrician's office. She's due any day."

"She'll be a good mother, and Ted will certainly be a good father. Their children will have a happy life."

Brenda caught the faint bitterness in the words and glanced at Lou, but the other woman was already calling her goodbyes and walking away.

She went home and spent the rest of the weekend buried in medical journals and the latest research on the new strain of bacteria that had, researchers surmised, mutated from a deadly scarlet fever bacterium that had caused many deaths at the turn of the century.

CHAPTER TWO

MONDAY MORNING BROUGHT a variety of new cases, and Louise found herself stuck with the most routine of them, as usual. She and Coltrain were supposed to be partners, but when he wasn't operating, he got the interesting, challenging illnesses. Louise got fractured ribs and colds.

He'd been stiff with her this morning, probably because he was still fuming over the argument they'd had about his mistaken idea of her weekend activities. Accusing her of lollygagging with the EMTs for excitement; really!

She watched his white-coated back disappear into an examination room down the hall in their small building and sighed half-angrily as she went back to check an X-ray in the files. The very worst thing about unrequited love, she thought miserably, was that it fed on itself. The more her partner in the medical practice ignored and antagonized her, the harder she had to fight her dreams about him. She didn't want to get married; she didn't even want to get involved. But he made her hungry.

He'd spent a lot of time with Jane Parker until she married that Burke man, and Lou had long ago given up hope that he would ever notice her in the same way he always noticed Jane. The two of them had grown up together, though, whereas Lou had only been in partnership with him for a year. She was a native of Austin, not Jacobsville. Small towns were like extended families. Everybody knew each other, and some families had been friends for more than one generation. Lou was a true outsider here, even though she *was* a native Texan. Perhaps that was one of many reasons that Dr. Coltrain found her so forgettable.

She wasn't bad looking. She had long, thick blond hair and big brown eyes and a creamy, blemish-free complexion. She was tall and willowy, but still shorter than her colleague. She lacked his fiery temper and his authoritarian demeanor. He was tall and whipcord lean, with flaming red hair and blue eyes and a dark tan from working on his small ranch when he wasn't treating patients. That tan was odd in a redhead, although he did have a smattering of freckles over his nose and the backs of his big hands. She'd often wondered if the freckles went any farther, but she had yet to see him without his professional white coat over his very formal suit. He wasn't much on casual dressing at work. At home, she was sure that he dressed less formally.

That was something Lou would probably never know. She'd never been invited to his home, despite the fact that most of the medical staff at the local hospital had. Lou was automatically excluded from any social gathering that he coordinated.

Other people had commented on his less than friendly behavior toward her. It puzzled them, and it puzzled her, because she hadn't become his partner in any underhanded way. He had known from the day of her application that she was female, so it couldn't be that. Perhaps, she thought wistfully, he was one of those old-line dominating sort of men who thought women had no place in medicine. But he'd been instrumental in getting women into positions of authority at the hospital, so that theory wasn't applicable, either. The bottom line was that he simply did not like Louise Blakely, medical degree or no medical degree, and she'd never known why.

She really should ask Drew Morris why, she told herself with determination. It had been Drew, a surgeon and friend of her family, who'd sent word about the opening in Coltrain's practice. He'd wanted to help Lou get a job near him, so that he could give her some moral support in the terrible days following the deaths of her parents. She, in turn, had liked the idea of being in practice in a small town, one where she knew at least one doctor on the staff of the hospital. Despite growing up in Austin, it was still a big city and she was lonely. She was twenty-eight, a loner whose whole life had been medicine. She'd made sure that her infrequent dates never touched her heart, and she was innocent in an age when innocence was automatically looked on with disdain or suspicion.

Her nurse stuck her head in the doorway. "There's a call for you. Dr. Morris is on line two."

"Thanks, Brenda."

She picked up the receiver absently, her finger poised over the designated line. But when she pressed it, before she could say a word, the sentence she'd intercepted accidentally blared in her ear in a familiar deep voice.

"…told you I wouldn't have hired her in the first place, if I had known who she was related to. I did you a favor, never realizing she was Blakely's daughter. You can't imagine that I'll ever forgive her father for what he did to the girl I loved, do you? She's been a constant reminder, a constant torment!"

"That's harsh, Copper," Drew began.

"It's how I feel. She's nothing but a burden here. But to answer your question, hell no, you're not stepping on my toes if you ask her out on a date! I find Louise Blakely repulsive and repugnant, and an automaton with no attractions whatsoever. Take her with my blessing. I'd give real money if she'd get out of my practice and out of my life, and the sooner the better!" There was a click and the line, obviously open, was waiting for her.

She clicked the receiver to announce her presence and said, as calmly as she could, "Dr. Lou Blakely."

"Lou! It's Drew Morris," came the reply. "I hope I'm not catching you at a bad moment?"

"No." She cleared her throat and fought to control her scattered emotions. "No, not at all. What can I do for you?"

"There's a dinner at the Rotary Club Thursday. How about going with me?"

She and Drew occasionally went out together, in a friendly but not romantic way. She would have refused, but what Coltrain had said made her mad. "Yes, I would like to, thanks," she said.

Drew laughed softly. "Great! I'll pick you up at six on Thursday, then."

"See you then."

She hung up, checked the X-ray again meticulously, and put it away in its file. Brenda ordinarily pulled the X-rays for her, but it was Monday and, as usual, they were overflowing with patients who'd saved their weekend complaints for office hours.

She went back to her patient, her color a little high, but no disturbance visible in her expression.

She finished her quota of patients and then went into her small office. Mechanically she picked up a sheet of letterhead paper, with Dr. Coltrain's name on one side and hers on the other. Irrelevantly, she thought that the stationery would have to be replaced now.

She typed out a neat resignation letter, put it in an envelope and went to place it on Dr. Coltrain's desk. It was lunchtime and he'd already left the building. He made sure he always did, probably to insure that he didn't risk having Lou invite herself to eat with him.

Brenda scowled as her boss started absently toward the back door. "Shouldn't you take off your coat first?" she asked hesitantly.

Lou did, without a word, replaced it in her office, whipped her leather fanny pack around her waist and left the building.

It would have been nice if she'd had someone to talk to, she thought wistfully, about this latest crisis. She sat alone in the local café, drinking black coffee and picking at a small salad. She didn't mingle well with people. When she wasn't working, she was quiet and shy, and she kept to herself. It was difficult for strangers to approach her, but she didn't realize that. She stared into her coffee and remembered every word Coltrain had said to Drew Morris about her. He hated her. He couldn't possibly have made it clearer. She was repugnant, he'd said.

Well, perhaps she was. Her father had told her so, often enough, when he was alive. He and her mother were from Jacobsville but hadn't lived in the area for years. He had never spoken of his past. Not that he spoke to Lou often, anyway, except to berate her grades and tell her that she'd never measure up.

"Excuse me?"

She looked up. The waitress was staring at her. "Yes?" she asked coolly.

"I don't mean to pry, but are you all right?"

The question surprised Lou, and touched her. She managed a faint smile through her misery. "Yes. It's been a…long morning. I'm not really hungry."

"Okay." The waitress smiled again, reassuringly, and went away.

Just as Lou was finishing her coffee, Coltrain came in the front door. He was wearing the elegant gray suit that looked so good on him, and carrying a silver belly Stetson by the brim. He looked furiously angry as his pale eyes scanned the room and finally spotted Lou, sitting all alone.

He never hesitated, she thought, watching him walk purposefully toward her. There must be an emergency…

He slammed the opened envelope down on the table in front of her. "What the hell do you mean by that?" he demanded in a dangerously quiet tone.

She raised her dark, cold eyes to his. "I'm leaving," she explained and averted her gaze.

"I know that! I want to know why!"

She looked around. The café was almost empty, but the waitress and a local cowboy at the counter were glancing at them curiously.

Her chin came up. "I'd rather not discuss my private business in public, if you don't mind," she said stiffly.

His jaw clenched, and his eyes grew glittery. He stood back to allow her to get up. He waited while she paid for her salad and coffee and then followed her out to where her small gray Ford was parked.

Her heart raced when he caught her by the arm before she could get her key out of her jeans pocket. He jerked her around, not roughly, and walked her over to Jacobsville's small town square, to a secluded bench in a grove of live oak and willow trees. Because it was barely December, there were no leaves on the trees and it was cool, despite her nervous perspiration. She tried to throw off his hand, to no avail.

He only loosened his grip on her when she sat down on a park bench. He remained standing, propping his boot on the bench beside her, leaning one long arm over his knee to study her. "This is private enough," he said shortly. "Why are you leaving?"

"I signed a contract to work with you for one year. It's almost up, anyway," she said icily. "I want out. I want to go home."

"You don't have anyone left in Austin," he said, surprising her.

"I have friends," she began.

"You don't have those, either. You don't have friends at all, unless you count Drew Morris," he said flatly.

Her fingers clenched around her car keys. She looked

at them, biting into the flesh even though not a speck
of emotion showed on her placid features.

His eyes followed hers to her lap and something
moved in his face. There was an expression there that
puzzled her. He reached down and opened her rigid
hand, frowning when he saw the red marks the keys
had made in her palm.

She jerked her fingers away from him.

He seemed disconcerted for a few seconds. He
stared at her without speaking and she felt her heart
beating wildly against her ribs. She hated being helpless.

He moved back, watching her relax. He took another
step and saw her release the breath she'd been holding.
Every trace of anger left him.

"It takes time for a partnership to work," he said
abruptly. "You've only given this one a year."

"That's right," she said tonelessly. "*I've* given it a
year."

The emphasis she placed on the first word caught
his attention. His blue eyes narrowed. "You sound as
if you don't think I've given it any time at all."

She nodded. Her eyes met his. "You didn't want me
in the practice. I suspected it from the beginning, but it
wasn't until I heard what you told Drew on the phone
this morning that—"

His eyes flashed oddly. "You heard what I said?" he
asked huskily. "You heard...all of it!" he exclaimed.

Her lips trembled just faintly. "Yes," she said.

He was remembering what he'd told Drew Morris in
a characteristic outburst of bad temper. He often said
things in heat that he regretted later, but this he regret-

ted most of all. He'd never credited his cool, unflappable partner with any emotions at all. She'd backed away from him figuratively and physically since the first day she'd worked at the clinic. Her physical withdrawal had maddened him, although he'd always assumed she was frigid.

But in the past five minutes, he'd learned disturbing things about her without a word being spoken. He'd hurt her. He didn't realize she'd cared that much about his opinion. Hell, he'd been furious because he'd just had to diagnose leukemia in a sweet little boy of four. It had hurt him to do that, and he'd lashed out at Morris over Lou in frustration at his own helplessness. But he'd had no idea that she'd overheard his vicious remarks. She was going to leave and it was no less than he deserved. He was genuinely sorry. She wasn't going to believe that, though. He could tell by her mutinous expression, in her clenched hands, in the tight set of her mouth.

"You did Drew a favor and asked me to join you, probably over some other doctor you really wanted," she said with a forced smile. "Well, no harm done. Perhaps you can get him back when I leave."

"Wait a minute," he began shortly.

She held up a hand. "Let's not argue about it," she said, sick at knowing his opinion of her, his real opinion. "I'm tired of fighting you to practice medicine here. I haven't done the first thing right, according to you. I'm a burden. Well, I just want out. I'll go on working until you can replace me." She stood up.

His hand tightened on the brim of his hat. He was

losing this battle. He didn't know how to pull his irons out of the fire.

"I had to tell the Dawes that their son has leukemia," he said, hating the need to explain his bad temper. "I say things I don't mean sometimes."

"We both know that you meant what you said about me," she said flatly. Her eyes met his levelly. "You've hated me from almost the first day we worked together. Most of the time, you can't even be bothered to be civil to me. I didn't know that you had a grudge against me from the outset…"

She hadn't thought about that until she said it, but there was a subtle change in his expression, a faint distaste that her mind locked on.

"So you heard that, too." His jaw clenched on words he didn't want to say. But maybe it was as well to say them. He'd lived a lie for the past year.

"Yes." She gripped the wrought-iron frame of the park bench hard. "What happened? Did my father cause someone to die?"

His jaw tautened. He didn't like saying this. "The girl I wanted to marry got pregnant by him. He performed a secret abortion and she was going to marry me anyway." He laughed icily. "A fling, he called it. But the medical authority had other ideas, and they invited him to resign."

Lou's fingers went white on the cold wrought iron. Had her mother known? What had happened to the girl afterward?

"Only a handful of people knew," Coltrain said, as if he'd read her thoughts. "I doubt that your mother did. She seemed very nice—hardly a fit match for a man like that."

"And the girl?" she asked levelly.

"She left town. Eventually she married." He rammed his hands into his pockets and glared at her. "If you want the whole truth, Drew felt sorry for you when your parents died so tragically. He knew I was looking for a partner, and he recommended you so highly that I asked you. I didn't connect the name at first," he added on a mocking note. "Ironic, isn't it, that I'd choose as a partner the daughter of a man I hated until the day he died."

"Why didn't you tell me?" she asked irritably. "I would have resigned!"

"You were in no fit state to be told anything," he replied with reluctant memories of her tragic face when she'd arrived. His hands clenched in his pockets. "Besides, you'd signed a one-year contract. The only way out was if you resigned."

It all made sense immediately. She was too intelligent not to understand why he'd been so antagonistic. "I see," she breathed. "But I didn't resign."

"You were made of stronger stuff than I imagined," he agreed. "You wouldn't back down an inch. No matter how rough it got, you threw my own bad temper back at me." He rubbed his fingers absently over the car keys in his pocket while he studied her. "It's been a long time since anyone around here stood up to me like that," he added reluctantly.

She knew that without being told. He was a holy terror. Even grown men around Jacobsville gave him a wide berth when he lost his legendary temper. But Lou never had. She stood right up to him. She wasn't fiery by nature, but her father had been viciously cruel to her. She'd learned early not to show fear or back down, because it only made him worse. The same rule seemed to apply to Coltrain. A weaker personality wouldn't have lasted in his office one week, much less one year, male or female.

She knew now that Drew Morris had been doing what he thought was a good deed. Perhaps he'd thought it wouldn't matter to Coltrain after such a long time to have a Blakely working for him. But he'd obviously underestimated the man. Lou would have realized at once, on the shortest acquaintance, that Coltrain didn't forgive people.

He stared at her unblinkingly. "A year. A whole year, being reminded every day I took a breath what your father cost me. There were times when I'd have done anything to make you leave. Just the sight of you was painful." He smiled wearily. "I think I hated you, at first."

That was the last straw. She'd loved him, against her will and all her judgment, and he was telling her that all he saw when he looked at her was an ice woman whose father had betrayed him with the woman he loved. He hated her.

It was too much all at once. Lou had always had impeccable control over her emotions. It had been dangerous to let her father know that he was hurting her, because he enjoyed hurting her. And now here was the one man she'd ever loved telling her that he hated her because of her father.

What a surprise it would be for him to learn that

her father, at the last, had been little more than a high-class drug addict, stealing narcotics from the hospital where he worked in Austin to support his growing habit. He'd been as high as a kite on narcotics, in fact, when the plane he was piloting went down, killing himself and his wife.

Tears swelled her eyelids. Not a sound passed her lips as they overflowed in two hot streaks down her pale cheeks.

He caught his breath. He'd seen her tired, impassive, worn-out, fighting mad, and even frustrated. But he'd never seen her cry. His lean hand shot out and touched the track of tears down one cheek, as if he had to touch them to make sure they were real.

She jerked back from him, laughing tearfully. "So that was why you were so horrible to me." She choked out the words. "Drew never said a word...no wonder you suffered me! And I was silly enough to dream...!" The laughter was harsher now as she dashed away the tears, staring at him with eyes full of pain and loss. "What a fool I've been," she whispered poignantly. "What a silly fool!"

She turned and walked away from him, gripping the car keys in her hand. The sight of her back was as eloquently telling as the words that haunted him. She'd dreamed...what?

FOR THE NEXT few days, Lou was polite and remote and as courteous as any stranger toward her partner. But something had altered in their relationship. He was aware of a subtle difference in her attitude toward him, in a distancing of herself that was new. Her eyes had always followed him, and he'd been aware of it at some subconscious level. Perhaps he'd been aware of more than covert glances, too. But Lou no longer watched him or went out of her way to seek him out. If she had questions, she wrote them down and left them for him on his desk. If there were messages to be passed on, she left them with Brenda.

The one time she did seek him out was Thursday afternoon as they closed up.

"Have you worked out an advertisement for someone to replace me?" she asked him politely.

He watched her calm dark eyes curiously. "Are you in such a hurry to leave?" he asked.

"Yes," she said bluntly. "I'd like to leave after the Christmas holidays." She turned and would have gone out the door, but his hand caught the sleeve of her white jacket. She slung it off and backed away. "At the first of the year."

He glared at her, hating the instinctive withdrawal that came whenever he touched her. "You're a good doctor," he said flatly. "You've earned your place here."

High praise for a man with his grudges. She looked over her shoulder at him, her eyes wounded. "But you hate me, don't you? I heard what you said to Drew, that every time you looked at me you remembered what my father had done and hated me all over again."

He let go of her sleeve, frowning. He couldn't find an answer.

"Well, don't sweat it, Doctor," she told him. "I'll be gone in a month and you can find someone you like to work with you."

She laughed curtly and walked out of the office.

SHE DRESSED SEDATELY that evening for the Rotary Club
dinner, in a neat off-white suit with a pink blouse. But
she left her blond hair long around her shoulders for
once, and used a light dusting of makeup. She didn't
spend much time looking in the mirror. Her appearance had long ago ceased to matter to her.

Drew was surprised by it, though, and curious. She
looked strangely vulnerable. But when he tried to hold
her hand, she drew away from him. He'd wanted to ask
her for a long time if there were things in her past that
she might like to share with someone. But Louise was
an unknown quantity, and she could easily shy away.
He couldn't risk losing her altogether.

Drew held her arm as they entered the hall, and Lou
was disconcerted to find Dr. Coltrain there. He almost
never attended social functions unless Jane Parker was
in attendance. But a quick glance around the room as-
certained that Jane wasn't around. She wondered if
the doctor had brought a date. It didn't take long to
have that question answered, as a pretty young bru-
nette came up beside him and clung to his arm as if it
was the ticket to heaven.

Coltrain wasn't looking at her, though. His pale,
narrow eyes had lanced over Lou and he was watching
her closely. He hadn't seen her hair down in the year
they'd worked together. She seemed more approach-
able tonight than he'd ever noticed, but she was Drew's
date. Probably Drew's woman, too, he thought bitterly,
despite her protests and reserve.

But trying to picture Lou in Drew's bed was more
difficult than he'd thought. It wasn't at all in character.
She was rigid in her views, just as she was in her mode

of dress and her hairstyle. Just because she'd loosened that glorious hair tonight didn't mean that she'd suddenly become uninhibited. Nonetheless, the change disturbed him, because it was unexpected.

"Copper's got a new girl, I see," Drew said with a grin. "That's Nickie Bolton," he added. "She works as a nurse's aide at the hospital."

"I didn't recognize her out of uniform," Lou murmured.

"I did," he said. "She's lovely, isn't she?"

She nodded amiably. "Very young, too," she added with an indulgent smile.

He took her hand gently and smiled down at her. "You aren't exactly over the hill yourself," he teased.

She smiled up at him with warm eyes. "You're a nice man, Drew."

Across the room, a redheaded man's grip tightened ominously on a glass of punch. For over a year, Louise had avoided even his lightest touch. A few days ago, she'd thrown off his hand violently. But there she stood not only allowing Drew to hold her hand, but actually smiling at him. She'd never smiled at Coltrain that way; she'd never smiled at him any way at all.

His companion tapped him on the shoulder.

"You're with me, remember?" she asked with a pert smile. "Stop staring daggers at your partner. You're off duty. You don't have to fight all the time, do you?"

He frowned slightly. "What do you mean?"

"Everyone knows you hate her," Nickie said pleasantly. "It's common gossip at the hospital. You rake her over the coals and she walks around the corridors, red in the face and talking to herself. Well, most of the

time, anyway. Once, Dr. Simpson found her crying in
the nursery. But she doesn't usually cry, no matter how
bad she hurts. She's pretty tough, in her way. I guess
she's had to be, huh? Even if there are more women
in medical school these days, you don't see that many
women doctors yet. I'll bet she had to fight a lot of
prejudice when she was in medical school."

That came as a shock. He'd never seen Lou cry until
today, and he couldn't imagine her being upset at any
temperamental display of his. Or was it, he pondered
uneasily, just that she'd learned how not to show her
wounds to him?

CHAPTER THREE

AT DINNER, Lou sat with Drew, as far away from Coltrain and his date as she could get. She listened attentively to the speakers and whispered to Drew in the spaces between speakers. But it was torture to watch Nickie's small hand smooth over Coltrain's, to see her flirt with him. Lou didn't know how to flirt. There were a lot of things she didn't know. But she'd learned to keep a poker face, and she did it very well this evening. The one time Coltrain glanced down the table toward her, he saw nothing on her face or in her eyes that could tell him anything. She was unreadable.

After the meeting, she let Drew hold her hand as they walked out of the restaurant. Behind them, Coltrain was glaring at her with subdued fury.

When they made it to the parking lot, she found that the other couple had caught up with them.

"Nice bit of surgery this morning, Copper," Drew remarked. "You do memorable stitches. I doubt if Mrs. Blake will even have a scar to show around."

He managed a smile and held Nickie's hand all the tighter. "She was adamant about that," he remarked. "It seems that her husband likes perfection."

"He'll have a good time searching for it in this imperfect world," Drew replied. "I'll see you in the morning. And I'd like your opinion on my little strep-throat patient. His mother wants the whole works taken out, tonsils and adenoids, but he doesn't have strep often and I don't like unnecessary surgery. Perhaps she'd listen to you."

"Don't count on it," Copper said dryly. "I'll have a look if you like, though."

"Thanks."

"My pleasure." He glanced toward Lou, who hadn't said a word. "You were ten minutes late this morning," he added coldly.

"Oh, I overslept," she replied pleasantly. "It wears me out to follow the EMTs around looking for work."

She gave him a cool smile and got into the car before he realized that she'd made a joke, and at his expense.

"Be on time in the morning," he admonished before he walked away with Nickie on his arm.

"On time," Lou muttered beside Drew in the comfortable Ford he drove. Her hands crushed her purse. "I'll give him on time! I'll be sitting in *his* parking spot at eight-thirty on the dot!"

"He does it on purpose," he told her as he started the car. "I think he likes to make you spark at him."

"He's overjoyed that I'm leaving," she muttered. "And so am I!"

He gave her a quick glance and hid his smile. "If you say so."

She twisted her small purse in her lap, fuming, all the way back to her small house.

"I haven't been good company, Drew," she said as he walked her to the door. "I'm sorry."

He patted her shoulder absently. "Nothing wrong

with the company," he said, correcting her. He smiled down at her. "But you really do rub Copper the wrong way, don't you?" he added thoughtfully. "I've noticed that antagonism from a distance, but tonight is the first time I've seen it at close range. Is he always like that?"

She nodded. "Always, from the beginning. Well, not quite," she confessed, remembering. "From last Christmas."

"What happened last Christmas?"

She studied him warily.

"I won't tell him," he promised. "What happened?"

"He tried to kiss me under the mistletoe and I, well, I sort of ducked and pulled away." She flushed. "He rattled me. He does, mostly. I get shaky when he comes too close. He's so forceful, and so physical. Even when he wants to talk to me, he's forever trying to grab me by the wrist or a sleeve. It's as if he knows how much it disturbs me, so he does it on purpose, just to make me uncomfortable."

He reached down and caught her wrist very gently, watching her face distort and feeling the instinctive, helpless jerk of her hand.

He let go at once. "Tell me about it, Lou."

With a wan smile, she rubbed her wrist. "No. It's history."

"It isn't, you know. Not if it makes you shaky to have people touch you…"

"Not everyone, just him," she muttered absently.

His eyebrows lifted, but she didn't seem to be aware of what she'd just confessed.

She sighed heavily. "I'm so tired," she said, rubbing

the back of her neck. "I don't usually get so tired from even the longest days."

He touched her forehead professionally and frowned. "You're a bit warm. How do you feel?"

"Achy. Listless." She grimaced. "It's probably that virus that's going around. I usually get at least one every winter."

"Go to bed and if you aren't better tomorrow, don't go in," he advised. "Want me to prescribe something?"

She shook her head. "I'll be okay. Nothing does any good for a virus, you know that."

He chuckled. "Not even a sugarcoated pill?"

"I can do without a placebo. I'll get some rest. Thanks for tonight. I enjoyed it."

"So did I. I haven't done much socializing since Eve died. It's been five long years and I still miss her. I don't think I'll ever get over her enough to start a new relationship with anyone. I only wish we'd had a child. It might have made it easier."

She was studying him, puzzled. "It's said that many people marry within months of losing a mate," she began.

"I don't fit that pattern," he said quietly. "I only loved once. I'd rather have my memories of those twelve years with Eve than a hundred years with someone else. I suppose that sounds old-fashioned."

She shook her head. "It sounds beautiful," she said softly. "Lucky Eve, to have been loved so much."

He actually flushed. "It was mutual."

"I'm sure it was, Drew. I'm glad to have a friend like you."

"That works both ways." He smiled ruefully. "I'd

like to take you out occasionally, so that people will stop thinking of me as a mental case. The gossip is beginning to get bad."

"I'd love to go out with you," she replied. She smiled. "I'm not very worldly, you know. It was books and exams and medicine for eight long years, and then internship. I was an honor student. I never had much time for men." Her eyes darkened. "I never wanted to have much time for them. My parents' marriage soured me. I never knew it could be happy or that people could love each other enough to be faithful—" She stopped, embarrassed.

"I knew about your father," he said. "Most of the hospital staff did. He liked young girls."

"Dr. Coltrain told me," she said miserably.

"He what?"

She drew in a long breath. "I overheard what he said to you on the telephone the other day. I'm leaving. My year is up after New Year's, anyway," she reminded him. "He told me what my father had done. No wonder he didn't want me here. You shouldn't have done it, Drew. You shouldn't have forced him to take me on."

"I know. But it's too late, isn't it? I thought I was helping, if that's any excuse." He searched her face. "Maybe I hoped it would help Copper, too. He was infatuated with Jane Parker. She's a lovely, sweet woman, and she has a temper, but she was never a match for Copper. He's the sort who'd cow a woman who couldn't stand up to him."

"Just like my father," she said shortly.

"I've never mentioned it, but one of your wrists looks as if it's suffered a break."

She flushed scarlet and drew back. "I have to go in now. Thanks again, Drew."

"If you can't talk to me, you need to talk to someone," he said. "Did you really think you could go through life without having the past affect the future?"

She smiled sweetly. "Drive carefully going home."

He shrugged. "Okay. I'll drop it."

"Good night."

"Good night."

She watched him drive away, absently rubbing the wrist he'd mentioned. She wouldn't think about it, she told herself. She'd go to bed and put it out of her mind.

Only it didn't work that way. She woke up in the middle of the night in tears, frightened until she remembered where she was. She was safe. It was over. But she felt sick and her throat was dry. She got up and found a pitcher, filling it with ice and water. She took a glass along with her and went back to bed. Except for frequent trips to the bathroom, she finally slept soundly.

THERE WAS A LOUD, furious knock at the front door. It kept on and on, followed by an equally loud voice. What a blessing that she didn't have close neighbors, she thought drowsily, or the police would be screaming up the driveway.

She tried to get up, but surprisingly, her feet wouldn't support her. She was dizzy and weak and sick at her stomach. Her head throbbed. She lay back down with a soft groan.

A minute later, the front door opened and a furious redheaded man in a lab coat came in the bedroom door.

"So this is where you are," he muttered, taking in her condition with a glance. "You couldn't have called?"

She barely focused on him. "I was up most of the night…"

"With Drew?"

She couldn't even manage a glare. "Being sick," she corrected. "Have you got anything on you to calm my stomach? I can't keep down anything to stop the nausea."

"I'll get something."

He went back out, grateful that she kept a key under the welcome mat. He didn't relish having to break down doors, although he had in the past to get to a patient.

He got his medical bag and went back into the bedroom. She was pale and she had a fever. He turned off the electronic thermometer and checked her lungs. Clear, thank God.

Her pulse was a little fast, but she seemed healthy enough. "A virus," he pronounced.

"No!" she exclaimed with weak sarcasm.

"You'll live."

"Give me the medicine, please," she asked, holding out a hand.

"Can you manage?"

"If you'll get me to the bathroom, sure."

He helped her up, noticing the frailty of her body. She didn't seem that thin in her clothing, but she was wearing silky pajamas that didn't conceal the slender lines of her body. He supported her to the door, and watched the door close behind her.

Minutes later, she opened the door again and let him help her back into bed.

He watched her for a minute and then, with reso-
lution, he picked up the telephone. He punched in a
number. "This is Dr. Coltrain. Send an ambulance out
to Dr. Blakely's home, 23 Brazos Lane. That's right.
Yes. Thank you."

She glared at him. "I will not…!"

"Hell, yes, you will," he said shortly. "I'm not leaving you out here alone to dehydrate. At the rate you're
losing fluids, you'll die in three days."

"What do you care if I die?" she asked furiously.

He reached down to take her pulse again. This time,
he caught the left wrist firmly, but she jerked it back.
His blue eyes narrowed as he watched her color. Drew
had been holding her right hand. At the table, it was her
right hand he'd touched. But most of the time, Copper
automatically reached for the left one…

He glanced down to where it lay on the coverlet and
he noticed what Drew had; there was a definite break
there, one which had been set but was visible.

She clenched her fist. "I don't want to go to the
hospital."

"But you'll go, if I have to carry you."

She glared at him. It did no good at all. He went
into the kitchen to turn off all the appliances except
the refrigerator. On his way back, he paused to look
around the living room. There were some very disturbing paintings on her walls, side by side with beautiful pastel drawings of flowers. He wondered who'd
done them.

The ambulance arrived shortly. He watched the
paramedics load her up and he laid the small bag she'd
asked him to pack on the foot of the gurney.

"Thank you so much," she said with her last lucid breath. The medicine was beginning to take effect, and it had a narcotic in it to make her sleep.

"My pleasure, Dr. Blakely," he said. He smiled, but it didn't reach his eyes. They were watchful and thoughtful. "Do you paint?" he asked suddenly.

Her dark eyes blinked. "How did you know?" she murmured as she drifted off.

SHE AWOKE HOURS later in a private room, with a nurse checking her vital signs. "You're awake!" the nurse said with a smile. "Feeling any better?"

"A little." She touched her stomach. "I think I've lost weight."

"No wonder, with so much nausea. You'll be all right now. We'll take very good care of you. How about some soup and Jell-O and tea?"

"Coffee?" she asked hopefully.

The nurse chuckled. "Weak coffee, perhaps. We'll see." She charted her observations and went to see about supper.

It was modest fare, but delicious to a stomach that had hardly been able to hold anything. Imagine being sent to the hospital with a twenty-four-hour virus, Lou thought irritably, and wanted to find Dr. Coltrain and hit him.

Drew poked his head in the door while he was doing rounds. "I told you you felt feverish, didn't I?" he teased, smiling. "Better?"

She nodded. "But I would have been just fine at home."

"Not to hear your partner tell it. I expected to find

your ribs sticking through your skin," he told her,
chuckling. "I'll check on you later. Stay put."

She groaned and lay back. Patients were stacking
up and she knew that Brenda had probably had to deal
with angry ones all day, since Dr. Coltrain would have
been operating in the morning. Everyone would be
sitting in the waiting room until long after dark, mut-
tering angrily.

It was after nine before he made rounds. He looked
worn, and she felt guilty even if it couldn't be helped.

"I'm sorry," she said irritably when he came to the
bedside.

He cocked an eyebrow. "For what?" He reached
down and took her wrist—the right one—noticing that
she didn't react while he felt her pulse.

"Leaving you to cope with my patients as well as
your own," she said. The feel of his long fingers was
disturbing. She began to fidget.

He leaned closer, to look into her eyes, and his hand
remained curled around her wrist. He felt her pulse jump
as his face neared hers and suddenly a new thought
leaped into his shocked mind and refused to be banished.

She averted her gaze. "I'm all right," she said. She
sounded breathless. Her pulse had gone wild under his
searching fingers.

He stood up, letting go of her wrist. But he noticed
the quick rise and fall of her chest with new interest.
What an odd reaction for a woman who felt such antagonism toward him.

He picked up her chart, still frowning, and read
what was written there. "You've improved. If you're

doing this well in the morning, you can go home. Not to work," he added firmly. "Drew's going to come in and help me deal with the backlog in the morning while he has some free time."

"That's very kind of him."

"He's a kind man."

"Yes. *He* is."

He chuckled softly. "You don't like me, do you?" he asked through pursed lips. "I've never given you any reason to. I've been alternately hostile and sarcastic since the day you came here."

"Your normal self, Doctor," she replied.

His lips tugged up. "Not really. You don't know me."

"Lucky me."

His blue eyes narrowed thoughtfully. She'd reacted to him from the first as if he'd been contagious. Every approach he'd made had been met with instant withdrawal. He wondered why he'd never questioned her reactions. It wasn't revulsion. Oh, no. It was something much more disturbing on her part. She was vulnerable, and he'd only just realized it, when it was too late. She would leave before he had the opportunity to explore his own feelings.

He stuck his hands into his pockets and his eyes searched her pale, worn face. She wasn't wearing a trace of makeup. Her eyes held lingering traces of fever and her hair was dull, lackluster, disheveled by sleep. But even in that condition, she had a strange beauty.

"I know how I look, thanks," she muttered as she saw how he was looking at her. "You don't need to rub it in."

"Was I?" He studied her hostile eyes.

She dropped her gaze to her slender hands on the sheets. "You always do." Her eyes closed. "I don't need you to point out my lack of good looks, Doctor. My father never missed an opportunity to tell me what I was missing."

Her father. His expression hardened as the memories poured out. But even as they nagged at his mind, he began to remember bits and pieces of gossip he'd heard about the way Dr. Fielding Blakely treated his poor wife. He'd dismissed it at the time, but now he realized that Mrs. Blakely had to be aware of her husband's affairs. Had she not minded? Or was she afraid to mind...

He had more questions about Lou's family life than he had answers, and he was curious. Her reticence with him, her broken wrist, her lack of self-esteem—they began to add up.

His eyes narrowed. "Did your mother know that your father was unfaithful to her?" he asked.

She stared at him as if she didn't believe what she'd heard. "What?"

"You heard me. Did she know?"

She drew the sheet closer to her collarbone. "Yes." She bit off the word.

"Why didn't she leave him?"

She laughed bitterly. "You can't imagine."

"Maybe I can." He moved closer to the bed. "Maybe I can imagine a lot of things that never occurred to me before. I've looked at you for almost a year and I've never seen you until now."

She fidgeted under the cover. "Don't strain your

imagination, Doctor," she said icily. "I haven't asked for your attention. I don't want it."

"Mine, or any other man's, right?" he asked gently.

She felt like an insect on a pin. "Will you stop?" she groaned. "I'm sick. I don't want to be interrogated."

"Is that what I'm doing? I thought I was showing a belated interest in my partner," he said lazily.

"I won't be your partner after Christmas."

"Why?"

"I've resigned. Have you forgotten? I even wrote it down and gave it to you."

"Oh. That. I tore it up."

Her eyes popped. "You what?"

"Tore it up," he said with a shrug. "I can't do without you. You have too many patients who won't come back if they have to see me."

"You had a fine practice…"

"Too fine. I never slept or took vacations. You've eased the load. You've made yourself indispensable. You have to stay."

"I do not." She shot her reply back instantly. "I hate you!"

He studied her, nodding slowly. "That's healthy. Much healthier than withdrawing like a frightened clam into a shell every time I come too close."

She all but gasped at such a blunt statement. "I do not…!"

"You do." He looked pointedly at her left wrist. "You've kept secrets. I'm going to worry you to death until you tell me every last one of them, beginning with why you can't bear to have anyone hold you by the wrist."

She couldn't get her breath. She felt her cheeks becoming hot as he stared down at her intently. "I'm not telling you any secrets," she assured him.

"Why not?" he replied. "I don't ever tell what I know."

She knew that. If a patient told him anything in confidence, he wouldn't share it.

She rubbed the wrist absently, wincing as she remembered how it had felt when it was broken, and how.

Coltrain, watching her, wondered how he could ever have thought her cold. She had a temper that was easily the equal of his own, and she never backed away from a fight. She'd avoided his touch, but he realized now that it was the past that made her afraid, not the present.

"You're mysterious, Lou," he said quietly. "You hold things in, keep things back. I've worked with you for a year, but I know nothing about you."

"That was your choice," she reminded him coolly. "You've treated me like a leper in your life."

He started to speak, took a breath and finally, nodded. "Yes. Through no fault of your own, I might add. I've held grudges."

She glanced at his hard, lean face. "You were entitled," she admitted. "I didn't know about my father's past. I probably should have realized there was a reason he never went back to Jacobsville, even to visit, while his brother was still alive here. Afterward, there wasn't even a cousin to write to. We all lost touch. My mother never seemed to mind that we didn't come back." She looked up at him. "She probably knew…" She flushed and dropped her eyes.

"But she stayed with him," he began.

"She had to!" The words burst out. "If she'd tried to leave, he'd have…" She swallowed and made a futile gesture with her hand.

"He'd have what? Killed her?"

She wouldn't look at him. She couldn't. The memories came flooding back, of his violence when he used narcotics, of the threats, her mother's fear, her own. The weeping, the cries of pain…

She sucked in a quick breath, and all the suffering was in the eyes she lifted to his when he took her hand.

His fingers curled hard around hers and held them, as if he could see the memories and was offering comfort.

"You'll tell me, one day," he said abruptly, his eyes steady on her own. "You'll tell me every bit of it."

She couldn't understand his interest. She searched his eyes curiously and suddenly felt a wave of feeling encompass her like a killing tide, knocking her breathless. Heat surged through her slender body, impaling her, and in his hard face she saw everything she knew of love, would ever know of it.

But he didn't want her that way. He never would. She was useful to the practice, but on a personal level, he was still clutching hard at the past; at the girl her father had taken from him, at Jane Parker. He was sorry for her, as he would be for anyone in pain, but it wasn't a personal concern.

She drew her hand away from his slowly and with a faint smile. "Thanks," she said huskily. "I… I think too hard sometimes. The past is long dead."

"I used to think so," he said, watching her. "Now, I'm not so sure."

She didn't understand what he was saying. It was just as well. The nurse came in to do her round and any personal conversation was banished at once.

CHAPTER FOUR

THE NEXT DAY, Lou was allowed to go home. Drew had eaten breakfast with her and made sure that she was well enough to leave before he agreed with Copper that she was fit. But when he offered to drive her home, Coltrain intervened. His partner, he said, was his responsibility. Drew didn't argue. In fact, when they weren't looking, he grinned.

Copper carried her bag into the house and helped her get settled on the couch. It was lunchtime and he hesitated, as if he felt guilty about not offering to take her out for a meal.

"I'm going to have some soup later," she murmured without looking at him. "I'm not hungry just yet. I expect you are."

"I could eat." He hesitated again, watching her with vague irritation. "Will you be all right?"

"It was only a virus," she said, making light of it. "I'm fine. Thank you for your concern."

"You might as well enjoy it, for novelty value if nothing else," he said without smiling. "It's been a long time since I've given a damn about a woman's comfort."

"I'm just a colleague," she replied, determined to show him that she realized there was nothing personal in their relationship. "It isn't the same thing."

"No, it isn't," he agreed. "I've been very careful to keep our association professional. I've never even asked you to my home, have I?"

He was making her uneasy with that unblinking stare. "So what? I've never asked you to mine," she replied. "I wouldn't presume to put you in such an embarrassing situation."

"Embarrassing? Why?"

"Well, because you'd have to find some logical excuse to refuse," she said.

He searched her quiet face and his eyes narrowed thoughtfully. "I don't know that I'd refuse. If you asked me."

Her heart leaped and she quickly averted her eyes. She wanted him to go, now, before she gave herself away. "Forgive me, but I'm very tired," she said.

She'd fended him off nicely, without giving offense. He wondered how many times over the years she'd done exactly that to other men.

He moved closer to her, noticing the way she tensed, the telltale quickening of her breath, the parting of her soft lips. She was affected by his nearness and trying valiantly to hide it. It touched him deeply that she was so vulnerable to him. He could have cursed himself for the way he'd treated her, for the antagonism that made her wary of any approach now.

He stopped when there was barely a foot of space between them, with his hands in his pockets so that he wouldn't make her any more nervous.

He looked down at her flushed oval face with curious pleasure. "Don't try to come in tomorrow if you don't feel like it. I'll cope."

"All right," she said in a hushed tone.

"Lou."

He hadn't called her by her first name before. It surprised her into lifting her eyes to his face.

"You aren't responsible for anything your father did," he said. "I'm sorry that I've made things hard for you. I hope you'll reconsider leaving."

She shifted uncomfortably. "Thank you. But I think I'd better go," she said softly. "You'll be happier with someone else."

"Do you think so? I don't agree." His hand lowered slowly to her face, touching her soft cheek, tracing it down to the corner of her mouth. It was the first intimate contact she'd ever had with him, and she actually trembled.

Her reaction had an explosive echo in his own body. His breath jerked into his throat and his teeth clenched as he looked at her mouth and thought he might die if he couldn't have it. But it was too soon. He couldn't…!

He drew back his hand as if she'd burned it. "I have to go," he said tersely, turning on his heel. Her headlong response had prompted a reaction in him that he could barely contain at all. He had to distance himself before he reached for her and ruined everything.

Lou didn't realize why he was in such a hurry to leave. She assumed that he immediately regretted that unexpected caress and wanted to make sure that she didn't read anything into it.

"Thank you for bringing me home," she said formally.

He paused at the door and looked back at her, his eyes fiercely intent on her slender body in jeans and sweatshirt, on her loosened blond hair and exquisite complexion and dark eyes. "Thank your lucky stars that I'm leaving in time." He bit off the words.

He closed the door on her puzzled expression. He was acting very much out of character lately. She didn't know why, unless he was sorry he'd tried to talk her out of leaving the practice. Oh, well, she told herself, it was no longer her concern. She had to get used to the idea of being out of his life. He had nothing to offer her, and he had good reason to hate her, considering the part her father had played in his unhappy past.

She went into the kitchen and opened a can of tomato soup. She'd need to replenish her body before she could get back to work.

The can slipped in her left hand and she grimaced. Her dreams of becoming a surgeon had been lost overnight in one tragic act. A pity, her instructor had said, because she had a touch that few surgeons ever achieved, almost an instinctive knowledge of the best and most efficient way to sever tissue with minimum loss of blood. She would have been famous. But alas, the tendon had been severed with the compound fracture. And the best efforts of the best orthopedic surgeon hadn't been able to repair the damage. Her father hadn't even been sorry....

She shook her head to clear away the memories and went back to her soup. Some things were better forgotten.

SHE WAS BACK at work the day after her return home, a bit shaky, but game. She went through her patients efficiently, smiling at the grievance of one small boy whose stitches she'd just removed.

"Dr. Coltrain doesn't like little kids, does he?" he muttered. "I showed him my bad place and he said he'd seen worse!"

"He has," she told the small boy. She smiled at him. "But you've been very brave, Patrick my boy, and I'm giving you the award of honor." She handed him a stick of sugarless chewing gum and watched him grin. "Off with you, now, and mind you don't fall down banks into any more creeks!"

"Yes, ma'am!"

She handed his mother the charge sheet and was showing them out the door of the treatment cubicle just as Coltrain started to come into it. The boy glowered at him, smiled at Lou and went back to his waiting mother.

"Cheeky brat," he murmured, watching him turn the corner.

"He doesn't like you," she told him smugly. "You didn't sympathize with his bad place."

"Bad place." He harrumphed. "Two stitches. My God, what a fuss he made."

"It hurt," she informed him.

"He wouldn't let me take the damn stitches out, either. He said that I didn't know how to do it, but you did."

She grinned to herself at that retort while she dealt with the mess she'd made while working with Patrick.

"You don't like children, do you?" she asked.

He shrugged. "I don't know much about them, except what I see in the practice," he replied. "I deal mostly with adults since you came."

He leaned against the doorjamb and studied her with his hands in the pockets of his lab coat, a stethoscope draped around his neck. His eyes narrowed as he watched her work.

She became aware of the scrutiny and turned, her eyes meeting his and being captured there. She felt her heart race at the way he looked at her. Her hands stilled on her preparations for the next patient as she stood helplessly in thrall.

His lips compressed. He looked at her mouth and traced the full lower lip, the soft bow of the upper, with her teeth just visible where her lips parted. The look was intimate. He was wondering how it would feel to kiss her, and she knew it.

Muffled footsteps caught them unawares, and Brenda jerked open the sliding door of the cubicle. "Lou, I've got the wrong... Oh!" She bumped into Coltrain, whom she hadn't seen standing there.

"Sorry," he muttered. "I wanted to ask Lou if she'd seen the file on Henry Brady. It isn't where I left it."

Brenda grimaced as she handed it to him. "I picked it up mistakenly. I'm sorry."

"No harm done." He glanced back at Lou and went out without another word.

"Not another argument," Brenda groaned. "Honestly, partners should get along better than this."

Lou didn't bother to correct that assumption. It was much less embarrassing than what had really happened. Coltrain had never looked at her in that particular way before. She was glad that she'd resigned; she wasn't sure that she could survive any physical teasing from him. If he started making passes, she'd be a lot safer in Austin than she would be here.

After all he was a confirmed bachelor and there was no shortage of women on his arm at parties. Nickie was the latest in a string of them. And according to rumor, before Nickie, apparently he'd been infatuated with Jane Parker. He might be nursing a broken heart as well, since Jane's marriage.

Lou didn't want to be anybody's second-best girl. Besides, she never wanted to marry. It had been better when Coltrain treated her like the enemy. She wished he'd go back to his former behavior and stop looking at her mouth that way. She still tingled remembering the heat in his blue eyes. A man like that would be just plain hell to be loved by. He would be addictive. She had no taste for addictions and she knew already that Coltrain would break her heart if she let him. No, it was better that she leave. Then she wouldn't have the anguish of a hopeless relationship.

THE ANNUAL HOSPITAL Christmas party was scheduled for Friday night, two weeks before Christmas so that the staff wouldn't be too involved with family celebrations to attend.

Lou hadn't planned to go, but Coltrain cornered her in his office as they prepared to leave that afternoon for the weekend.

"The Christmas party is tonight," he reminded her.

"I know. I'm not going."

"I'll pick you up in an hour," he said, refusing to listen when she tried to protest. "I know you still tire easily after the virus. We won't stay long."

"What about Nickie?" she asked irritably. "Won't she mind if you take your partner to a social event?"

Her antagonism surprised him. He lifted an indignant eyebrow. "Why should she?" he asked stiffly.

"You've been dating her."

"I escorted her to the Rotary Club meeting. I haven't proposed to her. And whatever you've heard to the contrary, she and I are not an item."

"You needn't bite my head off!" She shot the words at him.

His eyes dropped to her mouth and lingered there. "I know something I'd like to bite," he said deep in his throat.

She actually gasped, so stunned by the remark that she couldn't even think of a reply.

His eyes flashed back up to catch hers. He was a bulldozer, she thought, and if she didn't stand up to him, he'd run right over her.

She stiffened her back. "I'm not going to any hospital dance with you," she said shortly. "You've given me hell for the past year. Do you think you can just walk in here and wipe all that out with an invitation? Not even an invitation, at that—a command!"

"Yes, I do," he returned curtly. "We both belong to the hospital staff, and nothing will start gossip quicker than having one of us stay away from an annual event. I do not plan to have any gossip going around here at my expense. I had enough of that in the past, thanks to your philandering father!"

She gripped her coat, furious at him. "You just got through saying that you didn't blame me for what he did."

"And I don't!" he said angrily. "But you're being blind and stupid."

"Thank you. Coming from you, those are compliments!"

He was all but vibrating with anger. He stared at her, glared at her, until her unsteady movement made him realize that she'd been ill.

He became less rigid. "Ben Maddox is going to be there tonight. He's a former colleague of ours from Canada. He's just installed a massive computer system with linkups to medical networks around the world. I think it's too expensive for our purposes, but I agreed to hear him out about it. You're the high-tech expert," he added with faint sarcasm. "I'd like your opinion."

"My opinion? I'm honored. You've never asked for it before."

"I've never given a damn about it before," he retorted evenly. "But maybe there's something to this electronic revolution in medicine." He lifted his chin in a challenge. "Or so you keep telling me. Put your money where your mouth is, Doctor. Convince me."

She glared at him. "I'll drive my own car and see you there."

It was a concession, of sorts. He frowned slightly. "Why don't you want to ride with me? What are you afraid of?" he taunted softly.

She couldn't admit what frightened her. "It wouldn't look good to have us arrive together," she said. "It would give people something to talk about."

He was oddly disappointed, although he didn't quite know why. "All right, then."

She nodded, feeling that she'd won something. He

nodded, too, and quietly left her. It felt like a sort of truce. God knew, they could use one.

BEN MADDOX WAS TALL, blond and drop-dead gorgeous. He was also married and the father of three. He had photographs, which he enjoyed showing to any of his old colleagues who were willing to look at them. But in addition to those photographs, he had information on a networking computer system that he used extensively in his own practice. It was an expensive piece of equipment, but it permitted the user instant access to medical experts in every field. As a diagnostic tool and a means of getting second opinions from recognized authorities, it was breathtaking. But so was the price.

Lou had worn a black silk dress with a lace overlay, a demure rounded neckline and see-through sleeves. Her hairstyle, a topknot with little tendrils of blond hair slipping down to her shoulders, looked sexy. So did her long, elegant legs in high heels, under the mid-knee fitted skirt. She wore no jewelry at all, except for a strand of pearls with matching earrings.

Watching her move, Coltrain was aware of old, un-wanted sensations. At the party a year ago, she'd worn something a little more revealing, and he'd deliberately maneuvered her under the mistletoe out of mingled curiosity and desire. But she'd evaded him as if he had the plague, then and since. His ego had suffered a sharp blow. He hadn't felt confident enough to try again, so antagonism and anger had kept her at bay. Not that his memories of her father's betrayal hadn't added to his enmity.

She was animated tonight, talking to Ben about the

computer setup as if she knew everything there was to know about the machines.

"Copper, you've got a savvy partner here," Ben remarked when he joined them. "She's computer literate!"

"She's the resident high-tech expert," Copper replied. "I like old-fashioned, hands-on medicine. She'd rather reach for a machine to make diagnoses."

"High tech is the way of the future," Ben said coaxingly.

"It's also the reason medical costs have gone through the roof," came the predictable reply. "The money we spend on these outrageously expensive machines has to be passed on to the patients. That raises our fees, the hospital's fees, the insurance companies' fees…"

"Pessimist!" Ben accused.

"I'm being realistic," Copper told him, lifting his highball glass in a mock toast. He drained it, feeling the liquor.

Ben frowned as his old colleague made his way past the dancers back to the buffet table. "That's odd," he remarked. "I don't remember ever seeing Copper take more than one drink."

Neither did Lou. She watched her colleague pour himself another drink and she frowned.

Ben produced a card from the computer company for her, and while he was explaining the setup procedure, she noticed Nickie going up to Coltrain. She was wearing an electric blue dress that could have started a riot. The woman was pretty anyway, but that dress certainly revealed most of her charms.

Nickie laughed and dragged Coltrain under the mistletoe, looking up to indicate it there, to the amusement of the others standing by. Coltrain laughed softly, whipped a lean arm around Nickie's trim waist and pulled her against his tall body. He bent his head, and the way he kissed her made Lou go hot all over. She'd never been in his arms, but she'd dreamed about it. The fever in that thin mouth, the way he twisted Nickie even closer, made her breath catch. She averted her eyes and flushed at the train of her own thoughts.

"Leave it to Coltrain to draw the prettiest girls." Ben chuckled. "The gossip mill will grind on that kiss for a month. He's not usually so uninhibited. He must be over his limit!"

She could have agreed. Her hand clenched around the piña colada she was nursing. "This computer system, is it reliable?" she asked through tight lips, forcing a smile.

"Yes, except in thunderstorms. Always unplug it, regardless of what they tell you about protective spikes. One good hit, and you could be down for days."

"I'll remember, if we get it."

"The system I have is expensive," Ben agreed, "but there are others available that would be just right for a small practice like yours and Copper's. In fact…"

His voice droned on and Lou tried valiantly to pay attention. She was aware at some level that Coltrain and Nickie were dancing and making the rounds of guests together. It was much later, and well into her second piña colada, when the lavish mistletoe began to get serious workouts.

Lou wasn't in the mood to dance. She refused Ben's offer, and several others. A couple of hours had passed and it felt safe to leave now, before her spirit was totally crushed by being consistently ignored by Coltrain. She put down her half-full glass. "I really do have to go," she told Ben. "I've been ill and I'm not quite back up to par yet." She shook his hand. "It was very nice to have met you."

"Same here. I wonder why Drew Morris didn't show up? I had hoped to see him again while I was here."

"I don't know," she said, realizing that she hadn't heard from Drew since she was released from the hospital. She had no idea where he was, and she hadn't asked.

"I'll check with Copper. He's certainly been elusive this evening. Not that I can blame him, considering his pretty companion over there." He raised his hand to catch the other man's eyes, to Lou's dismay.

Coltrain joined them with Nickie hanging on his arm. "Still here?" he asked Lou with a mocking smile. "I thought you'd be out the door and gone by now."

"I'm just about to leave. Do you know where Drew is?"

"He's in Florida at that pediatric seminar. Didn't Brenda tell you?"

"She was so busy she probably forgot," she said.

"So that's where the old devil has gone," Ben said ruefully. "I'm sorry I missed him."

"I'm sure he will be, too," Lou said. The sight of Nickie and Coltrain together was hurting her. "I'd better be off—"

"Oh, not yet," Copper said with glittery blue eyes. "Not before you've been kissed under the mistletoe, Doctor."

She flushed and laughed nervously. "I'll forgo that little ritual, I think."

"No, you won't." He sounded pleasant enough, but the expression on his face was dangerous. He moved away from Nickie and his lean arm shot around Lou's waist, maneuvering her under a low-hanging sprig of mistletoe tied with a red velvet bow. "You're not getting away this time," he said huskily.

Before she could think, react, protest, his head bent and his thin, cruel mouth fastened on hers with fierce intent. He didn't close his eyes when he kissed, she thought a bit wildly, he watched her all through it. His arm pressed her closer to the length of his muscular body, and his free hand came up so that his thumb could rub sensuously over her mouth while he kissed it, parting her lips, playing havoc with her nerves.

She gasped at the rough pleasure, and inadvertently gave him exactly what he wanted. His open mouth ground into hers, pressing her lips apart. She tasted him in an intimacy that she'd never shared with a man, in front of the amused hospital staff, while his cold eyes stared straight into hers.

She made a faint sound and he lifted his head, looking down at her swollen lips. His thumb traced over them with much greater tenderness than his mouth had given her, and he held her shocked eyes for a long moment before he reluctantly let her go.

"Merry Christmas, Dr. Blakely," he said in a mocking tone, although his voice was husky.

"And you, Dr. Coltrain," she said shakily, not quite meeting his eyes. "Good night, Ben... Nickie."

She slid away from them toward the door, on shaky legs, with a mouth that burned from his cold, fierce kiss. She barely remembered getting her coat and saying goodbye to the people she recognized on her way to the car park.

Coltrain watched her go with feelings he'd never encountered in his life. He was burning up with desire, and he'd had enough whiskey to threaten his control.

Nickie tugged on his sleeve. "You didn't kiss me like that," she protested, pouting prettily. "Why don't you take me home and we can…"

"I'll be back in a minute," he said, shaking her off.

She glared at him, coloring with embarrassment when she realized that two of the staff had overheard her. Rejection in private was one thing, but it hurt to have him make it so public. He hadn't called her since the night of the Rotary Club meeting. He'd just kissed her very nicely, but it looked different when he'd done it with his partner. She frowned. Something was going on. She followed at a distance. She was going to find out what.

Coltrain, unaware of her pursuit, headed after Lou with no real understanding of his own actions. He couldn't get the taste of her out of his head. He was pretty sure that she felt the same way. He couldn't let her leave until he knew…

Lou kept walking, but she heard footsteps behind her as she neared her car. She knew them, because she heard them every day on the slick tile of the office floor. She walked faster, but it did no good. Coltrain reached her car at the same time she reached it.

His hand came around her, grasping her car key and her fingers, pulling, turning her. She was pressed completely against the car by the warm weight of his body, and she looked up into a set, shadowy face while his mouth hovered just above her own in the starlit darkness.

"It wasn't enough," he said roughly. "Not nearly enough."

He bent and his mouth found hers expertly. His hands smoothed into hers and linked with her fingers. His hips slid sensuously over hers, seductive, refusing to entertain barriers or limits. His mouth began to open, brushing in soft strokes over her lips until they began to part, but she stiffened.

"Don't you know how to kiss?" he whispered, surprised. "Open your mouth, little one. Open it and fit it to mine... Yes, that's it."

She felt his tongue dance at the opening he'd made, felt it slowly ease into her mouth and penetrate, teasing, probing, tasting. Her fingers clutched helplessly at his and she shivered. It was so intimate, so...familiar! She moaned sharply as his hips began to caress hers. She felt him become aroused and her whole body vibrated.

His mouth grew more insistent then. He released one of her hands and his fingers played with her mouth, as they had inside, but now there was the heat and the magic they were generating, and it was no cold, clinical experiment. He groaned against her mouth and she felt his body go rigid all at once.

He bit her lower lip, hard, when her teeth clenched at the soft probing of his tongue. Suddenly she came to her senses and realized what was happening. He tasted blatantly of whiskey. He'd had too much to drink and he'd forgotten which woman he was with. Did he think she was Nickie? she wondered dizzily. Was that why he was making love to her? And that was what it was, she realized with a shock. Only a lover would take such intimacy for granted, be so blind to surroundings and restraint.

CHAPTER FIVE

DESPITE THE PLEASURE she felt, the whiskey on his breath brought back unbearable memories of another man who drank; memories not of kisses, but of pain and fear. Her hands pressed against his warm shirtfront under the open dinner jacket and she pushed, only vaguely aware of thick hair under the silkiness of the fabric.

"No," she whispered into his insistent mouth.

He didn't seem to hear her. His mouth hardened and a sound rumbled out of the back of his throat. "For God's sake, stop fighting me," he whispered fiercely.

The fear in her voice got through the intoxication. His mouth stilled against her cheek, but his body didn't withdraw. She could feel it against every inch of her like a warm, steely brand. His breathing wasn't steady, and over her breasts, his heart was beating like a frenzied bass drum.

It suddenly dawned on him what he was doing, and with whom.

"My God!" he whispered fiercely. His hands tightened for an instant before they fell away from her. A faint shudder went through his powerful body as he slowly, so slowly, pushed himself away from her, balancing his weight on his hands against the car doorframe.

She felt his breath on her swollen mouth as he fought for control. He was still too close.

"You haven't used my given name before," he said as he levered farther away from her. "I didn't know you knew it."

"It's…on our contract," she said jerkily.

He removed his hands from the car and stood upright, dragging in air. "I've had two highballs," he said on an apologetic laugh. "I don't drink. It hit me harder than I realized."

He was apologizing, she thought dazedly. That was unexpected. He wasn't that kind of man. Or was he? She hadn't thought he was the type to get drunk and kiss women in that intimate, fierce way, either. Especially her.

She tried to catch her own breath. Her mouth hurt from the muted violence of his kisses and her legs felt weak. She leaned back against the car, only now noticing its coldness. She hadn't felt it while he was kissing her. She touched her tongue to her lips and she tasted him on them.

She eased away from the car a little, shy now that he was standing back from her.

She was so shaky that she wondered how she was going to drive home. Then she wondered, with even more concern, how *he* was going to drive home.

"You shouldn't drive," she began hesitantly.

In the faint light from the hospital, she saw him smile sardonically. "Worried about me?" he chided.

She shouldn't have slipped like that. "I'd worry about anyone who'd had too much to drink," she began.

"All right, I won't embarrass you. Nickie can drive. She doesn't drink at all."

Nickie. Nickie would take him home and she'd probably stay to nurse him, too, in his condition. God only knew what might happen, but she couldn't afford to interfere. He'd had too much to drink and he'd kissed her, and she'd let him. Now she was ashamed and embarrassed.

"I have to go," she said stiffly.

"Drive carefully," he replied.

"Sure."

She found her keys where they'd fallen to the ground when he kissed her and unlocked the car door. She closed it once she was inside and started it after a bad fumble. He stood back from it, his hands in his pockets, looking dazed and not quite sober.

She hesitated, but Nickie came out the door, calling him. When he turned and raised a hand in Nickie's direction and answered her, laughing, Lou came to her senses. She lifted a hand toward both of them and drove away as quickly as she could. When she glanced back in the rearview mirror, it was to see Nickie holding Coltrain's hand as they went toward the building again.

So much for the interlude, she thought miserably. He'd probably only just realized who he'd kissed and was in shock.

THAT WAS CLOSE to the truth. Coltrain's head was spinning. He'd never dreamed that a kiss could be so explosive or addictive. There was something about Lou Blakely that made his knees buckle. He had no idea why he'd reacted so violently to her that he couldn't even let her leave. God knew what would have happened if she hadn't pushed him away when she did.

Nickie held on to him as they went back inside. "You've got her lipstick all over you," she accused.

He paused, shaken out of his brooding. Nickie was pretty, he thought, and uncomplicated. She already knew that he wasn't going to get serious however long they dated, because he'd told her so. It made him relax. He smiled down at her. "Wipe it off."

She pulled his handkerchief out of his pocket and did as he asked, smiling pertly. "Want to sample mine again?"

He tapped her on the nose. "Not tonight," he said. "We'd better leave. It's getting late."

"I'm driving," she told him.

"Yes, you are," he agreed.

She felt better. At least she was the one going home with him, not Lou. She wasn't going to give him up without a struggle, not when he was the best thing that had ever happened to her. Wealthy bachelor surgeons didn't come along every day of the week.

Lou DROVE HOME in a similar daze, overcome by the fervor of Coltrain's hard kisses. She couldn't understand why a man who'd always seemed to hate her had suddenly become addicted to her mouth; so addicted, in fact, that he'd followed her to her car. It had been the sweetest night of her life, but she had to keep her head and realize that it was an isolated incident. If Coltrain hadn't been drinking, it would never have happened. Maybe by Monday, she thought, he'd have convinced himself that it hadn't. She wished she could. She was

more in love with him than ever, and he was as far out
of her reach as he had ever been. Except that now he'd
probably go even farther out of reach, because he'd lost
his head and he wouldn't like remembering it.

She did her usual housework and answered emergency calls. She got more than her share because Dr.
Coltrain had left word with their answering service
that he was going to be out of town until Monday and
Dr. Blakely would be covering for him.

Nice of him to ask her first, she thought bitterly, and
tell her that he was going to be out of town. But perhaps he'd been reluctant to talk to her after what had
happened. If the truth were known, he was more than
likely as embarrassed as she was and just wanted to
forget the whole thing.

She did his rounds and hers at the hospital, noticing absently that she was getting more attention than
usual. Probably, she reasoned, because people were
remembering the way Coltrain had kissed her. Maybe
they thought something was going on between them.

"How's it going?" Drew asked on Sunday afternoon,
grinning at her. "I hear I missed a humdinger of a kiss
at the Christmas party," he added wickedly.

She blushed to her hairline. "Lots of people got
kissed."

"Not like you did. Not so that he followed you out
to the parking lot and damn near made love to you on
the hood of your car." He chuckled.

"Who...?"

"Nickie," he said, confirming her worst nightmare.
"She was watching, apparently, and she's sweet on
Copper. I guess she thought it might turn him off you

if there was a lot of gossip about what happened. Rumors fly, especially when they're about two doctors who seem to hate each other."

"He'll walk right into it when he comes back," she said uneasily. "What can I do?"

"Nothing, I'm afraid."

Her eyes narrowed. "That's what you think."

She turned on her heel and went in search of Nickie. She found her in a patient's room and waited calmly while the girl, nervous and very insecure once she saw Lou waiting for her, finished the chore she was performing.

She went out into the hall with Lou, and she looked apprehensive.

Lou clutched a clipboard to her lab jacket. She didn't smile. "I understand you've been feeding the rumor mill. I'll give you some good advice. Stop it while you can."

By now, Nickie's face had gone puce. "I never meant... I was kidding!" she burst out. "That's all, just kidding!"

Lou studied her without emotion. "I'm not laughing. Dr. Coltrain won't be laughing, either, when he hears about it. And I'll make sure he knows where it came from."

"That's spiteful!" Nickie cried. "I'm crazy about him!"

"No, you aren't," Lou said shortly. "You'd never subject him to the embarrassment you have with all this gossip if you really cared."

Nickie's hands locked together. "I'm sorry," she said on a long sigh. "I really am. I was just jealous," she confessed, avoiding Lou's eyes. "He wouldn't even kiss me good-night, but he'd kiss you that way, and he hates you."

"Try to remember that he'd had too much to drink," Lou said quietly. "Only a fool would read anything into a kiss under the mistletoe."

"I guess so," Nickie said, but she wasn't really convinced. "I'm sorry. You won't tell him it was me, will you?" she added worriedly. "He'll hate me. I care so much, Dr. Blakely!"

"I won't tell him," Lou said. "But no more gossip!"

"Yes, ma'am!" Nickie brightened, grinned and went off down the hall, irrepressibly young and optimistic. Watching her, Lou felt ancient.

THE NEXT MORNING was Monday, and Lou went into the office to come face-to-face with a furious partner, who blocked her doorway and glared at her with blue eyes like arctic ice.

"Now what have I done?" she asked before he could speak, and slammed her bag down on her desk, ready to do battle.

"You don't know?" he taunted.

She folded her arms over her breasts and leaned back against the edge of the desk. "There's a terrible rumor going around the hospital," she guessed.

His eyebrow jerked, but the ice didn't leave his eyes. "Did you start it?"

"Of course," she agreed furiously. "I couldn't wait to tell everybody on staff that you bent me back over the hood of my car and ravished me in the parking lot!"

Brenda, who'd started in the door, stood there with

her mouth open, intercepted a furious glare from two pairs of eyes, turned on her heel and got out.

"Could you keep your voice down?" Coltrain snapped.

"Gladly, when you stop making stupid accusations!"

He glared at her and she glared back.

"I was drinking!"

"That's it, announce it to everyone in the waiting room, why don't you, and see how many patients run for their cars!" she raged.

He closed her office door, hard, and leaned back against it. "Who started the rumor?" he asked.

"That's more like it," she replied. "Don't accuse until you ask. I didn't start it. I have no wish to become the subject of gossip."

"Not even to force me to do something about the rumors?" he asked. "Such as announce our engagement?"

Her eyes went saucer-wide. "Please! I've just eaten!"

His jaw went taut. "I beg your pardon?"

"And so you should!" she said enthusiastically. "Marry you? I'd rather chain myself to a tree in an alligator swamp!"

He didn't answer immediately. He stared at her instead while all sorts of impractical ideas sifted through his mind.

A buzzer sounded on her desk. She reached over and pressed a button. "Yes?"

"What about the patients?" Brenda prompted.

"He doesn't *have* any patience," Lou said without thinking.

"Excuse me?" Brenda stammered.

"Oh. That sort of patients. Send my first one in, will you, Brenda? Dr. Coltrain was just leaving."

"No, he wasn't," he returned when her finger left the intercom button. "We'll finish this discussion after office hours."

"After office hours?" she asked blankly.

"Yes. But, don't get your hopes up about a repeat of Friday evening," he said with a mocking smile. "After all, I'm not drunk today."

Her eyes flashed murderously and her lips compressed. But he was already out the door.

LOU WAS NEVER sure afterward how she'd managed to get through her patients without revealing her state of mind. She was furiously angry at Coltrain for his accusations and equally upset with Brenda for hearing what she'd said in retaliation. Now it would be all over the office as well as all over the hospital that she and Coltrain had something going. And they didn't! Despite Lou's helpless attraction to him, it didn't take much imagination to see that Coltrain didn't feel the same. Well, maybe physically he felt something for her, but emotionally he still hated her. A few kisses wouldn't change that!

She checked Mr. Bailey's firm, steady heartbeat, listened to his lungs and pronounced him over the pneumonia she'd been treating him for.

As she started to go, leaving Brenda to help him with his shirt, he called to her.

"What's this I hear about you and Doc Coltrain?" he teased. "Been kissing up a storm at the hospital

Christmas party, they say. Any chance we'll be hearing wedding bells?"

He didn't understand, he told Brenda on his way out, why Dr. Blakely had suddenly screamed like that. Maybe she'd seen a mouse, Brenda replied helpfully.

When the office staff went home, Coltrain was waiting at the front entrance for Lou. He'd stationed himself there after checking with the hospital about a patient, and he hadn't moved, in case Lou decided to try to sneak out.

He was wearing the navy blue suit that looked so good on him, lounging against the front door with elegant carelessness, when she went out of her office. His red hair caught the reflection of the overhead light and seemed to burn like flames over his blue, blue eyes. They swept down over her neat gray pantsuit to her long legs encased in slacks with low-heeled shoes.

"That color looks good on you," he remarked.

"You don't need to flatter me. Just say what's on your mind, please, and let me go home."

"All right." His eyes fell to her soft mouth and lingered there. "Who started the rumors about us?"

She traced a pattern on her fanny pack. "I promised I wouldn't tell."

"Nickie," he guessed, nodding at her shocked expression.

"She's young and infatuated," she began.

"Not that young," he said with quiet insinuation.

Her eyes flashed before she could avert them. Her hand dug into the fanny pack for her car keys. "It's a nine-days wonder," she continued. "People will find something else to talk about."

"Nothing quite this spicy has happened since Ted Regan went chasing off to Victoria after Coreen Tarleton and she came home wearing his engagement ring."

"There's hardly any comparison," she said, "considering that everyone knows how we feel about each other!"

"How *do* we feel about each other, Lou?" he replied quietly, and watched her expression change.

"We're enemies," she returned instantly.

"Are we?" He searched her eyes in a silence that grew oppressive. His arms fell to his sides. "Come here, Lou."

She felt her breathing go wild. That could have been an invitation to bypass him and leave the building. But the look in his eyes told her it wasn't. Those eyes blazed like flames in his lean, tanned face, beckoning, promising pleasures beyond imagination.

He lifted a hand. "Come on, coward," he chided softly, and his lips curled at the edges. "I won't hurt you."

"You're sober," she reminded him.

"Cold sober," he agreed. "Let's see how it feels when I know what I'm doing."

Her heart stopped, started, raced. She hesitated, and he laughed softly and started toward her, with that slow, deliberate walk that spoke volumes about his intent.

"You mustn't," she spoke quickly, holding up a hand.

He caught the hand and jerked her against him, imprisoning her there with a steely arm. "I must," he corrected her, letting his eyes fall to her mouth. "I *have* to know." He bit off the words against her lips.

She never found out what he had to know, because the instant she felt his lips probing her mouth, she went under in a blaze of desire unlike anything she'd felt before. She gasped, opened her lips, yielded to his enveloping arms without a single protest. If anything, she pushed closer into his arms, against that steely body that was instantly aroused by the feel of her.

She tried to speak, to protest, but he pushed his tongue into her mouth with a harsh groan, and his arms lifted her so that she fit perfectly against him from breast to thigh. She fought, frightened by the intimacy and the sensations kindled in her untried body.

Her frantic protest registered at once. He remembered she'd had the same reaction the night of the Christmas party. His mouth lifted, and his searching eyes met hers.

"You couldn't be a virgin," he said, making it sound more like an accusation than a statement of fact.

She bit her lip and dropped her eyes, shamed and embarrassed. "Rub it in," she growled.

"My God." He eased her back onto her feet and held her by the upper arms so that she wouldn't fall. "My God! How old are you, thirty?"

"Twenty-eight," she said unsteadily, gasping for breath. Her whole body felt swollen. Her dark eyes glowered up at him as she pushed back her disheveled hair. "And you needn't look so shocked, you of all people should know that some people still have a few principles! You're a doctor, after all!"

"I thought virgins were a fairy tale," he said flatly. "Damn it!"

Her chin lifted. "What's wrong, Doctor, did you see me as a pleasant interlude between patients?"

His lips compressed. He rammed his hands into his trouser pockets, all too aware of a throbbing arousal that wouldn't go away. He turned to the door and jerked it open. All weekend he'd dreamed of taking Louise Blakely home with him after work and seducing her in his big king-size bed. She was leaving anyway, and the hunger he felt for her was one he had to satisfy or go mad. It had seemed so simple. She wanted him; he knew she did. People were already talking about them, so what would a little more gossip matter? She'd be gone at the first of the year, anyway.

But now he had a new complication, one he'd never dreamed of having. She was no young girl, but it didn't take an expert to know why she backed away from intimacy like a repressed adolescent. He'd been baiting her with that accusation of virginity, but she hadn't realized it. She'd taken it at face value and she'd given him a truth he didn't even want. She was innocent. How could he seduce her now? On the other hand, how was he going to get rid of this very inconvenient and noticeable desire for her?

Watching him, Lou was cursing her own headlong response. She hated having him know how much she wanted him.

"Any man could have made me react that way!" she flared defensively, red-faced. "Any experienced man!"

His head turned and he stared at her, seeing through the flustering words to the embarrassment.

"It's all right," he said gently. "We're both human. Don't beat your conscience to death over a kiss, Lou."

She went even redder and her hands clenched at her sides. "I'm still leaving!"

"I know."

"And I won't let you seduce me!"

He turned. "I won't try," he said solemnly. "I don't seduce virgins."

She bit her lip and tasted him on it. She winced.

"Why?" he asked quietly.

She glared at him.

"Why?" he persisted.

Her eyes fell under that piercing blue stare. "Because I don't want to end up like my mother," she said huskily.

Of all the answers he might have expected, that was the last. "Your mother? I don't understand."

She shook her head. "You don't need to. It's personal. You and I are business partners until the end of the month, and then nothing that happened to me will be any concern of yours."

He didn't move. She looked vulnerable, hurt. "Counseling might be of some benefit," he said gently.

"I don't need counseling."

"Tell me how your wrist got broken, Lou," he said matter-of-factly.

She stiffened.

"Oh, a layman wouldn't notice, it's healed nicely. But surgery is my business. I know a break when I see one. There are scars, too, despite the neat stitching job. How did it happen?"

She felt weak. She didn't want to talk to him, of all people, about her past. It would only reinforce what he already thought of her father, though God only knew why she should defend such a man.

She clasped her wrist defensively, as if to hide what had been done to it. "It's an old injury," she said finally.

"What sort of injury? How did it happen?"

She laughed nervously. "I'm not your patient."

He absently jingled the change in his pocket, watching her. It occurred to him that she was a stranger. Despite their heated arguments over the past year, they'd never come close to discussing personal matters. Away from the office, they were barely civil to each other. In it, they never discussed anything except business. But he was getting a new picture of her, and not a very reassuring one. This was a woman with a painful past, so painful that it had locked her up inside an antiseptic prison. He wondered if she'd ever had the incentive to fight her way out, or why it should matter to him that she hadn't.

"Can you talk to Drew about it?" he asked suddenly.

She hesitated and then shook her head. Her fingers tightened around her wrist. "It doesn't matter, I tell you."

His hand came out of his pocket and he caught the damaged wrist very gently in his long fingers, prepared for her instinctive jerk. He moved closer, drawing that hand to his chest. He pressed it gently into the thick fabric of his vest.

"There's nothing you can't tell me," he said solemnly. "I don't carry tales, or gossip. Anything you say to me will remain between the two of us. If you want to talk, ever, I'll listen."

She bit her bottom lip. She'd never been able to tell anyone. Her mother knew, but she defended her husband, trying desperately to pretend that Lou had imagined it, that it had never happened. She excused her husband's affairs, his drinking bouts, his drug addiction, his brutality, his sarcasm…everything, in the name of love, while her marriage disintegrated around her and her daughter turned away from her. Obsessive love, one of her friends had called it—blind, obsessive love that refused to acknowledge the least personality flaw in the loved one.

"My mother was emotionally crippled," she said, thinking aloud. "She was so blindly in love with him that he could do no wrong, no wrong at all…" She remembered where she was and looked up at him with the pain still in her eyes.

"Who broke your wrist, Lou?" he asked gently.

She remembered aloud. "He was drinking and I tried to take the bottle away from him, because he'd hit my mother. He hit my wrist with the bottle, and it broke," she added, wincing at the memory of the pain. "And all the while, when they operated to repair the damage, he kept saying that I'd fallen through a glass door, that I'd tripped. Everyone believed him, even my mother. I told her that he did it, and she said that I was lying."

"He? Who did it, Lou?"

She searched his curious eyes. "Why…my father," she said simply.

CHAPTER SIX

COLTRAIN SEARCHED HER dark eyes, although the confession didn't really surprise him. He knew too much about her father to be surprised.

"So that was why the whiskey on my breath bothered you Friday night," he remarked quietly.

She averted her head and nodded. "He was a drunkard at the last, and a drug addict. He had to stop operating because he almost killed a patient. They let him retire and act in an advisory capacity because he'd been such a good surgeon. He was, you know," she added. "He might have been a terrible father, but he was a wonderful surgeon. I wanted to be a surgeon, to be like him." She shivered. "I was in my first year of medical school when it happened. I lost a semester and afterward, I knew I'd never be able to operate. I decided to become a general practitioner."

"What a pity," he said. He understood the fire for surgical work because he had it. He loved what he did for a living.

She smiled sadly. "I'm still practicing medicine. It isn't so bad. Family practice has its place in the scheme of things, and I've enjoyed the time I've spent in Jacobsville."

"So have I," he admitted reluctantly. He smiled at

her expression. "Surprised? You've been here long enough to know how a good many people react to me. I'm the original bad boy of the community. If it hadn't been for the scholarship one of my teachers helped me get, I'd probably be in jail by now. I had a hard childhood and I hated authority in any form. I was in constant trouble with the law."

"You?" she asked, aghast.

He nodded. "People aren't always what they seem, are they?" he continued. "I was a wild boy. But I loved medicine and I had an aptitude for it and there were people who were willing to help me. I'm the first of my family to escape poverty, did you know?"

She shook her head. "I don't know anything about your family," she said. "I wouldn't have presumed to ask anyone something so personal about you."

"I've noticed that," he returned. "You avoid sharing your feelings. You'll fight back, but you don't let people close, do you?"

"When people get too close, they can hurt you," she said.

"A lesson your father taught you, no doubt."

She wrapped her arms around her chest. "I'm cold," she said dully. "I want to go home."

He searched her face. "Come home with me."

She hesitated warily.

He made a face. "Shame on you for what you're thinking. You should know better. You're off the endangered list. I'll make chili and Mexican corn bread and strong coffee and we can watch a Christmas special. Do you like opera?"

Her eyes brightened. "Oh, I love it."

His own eyes brightened. "Pavarotti?"

"And Domingo." She looked worried. "But people will talk…"

"They're already talking. Who cares?" he asked. "We're both single adults. What we do together is nobody's business."

"Yes, well, the general consensus of opinion is that we're public property, or didn't you hear what Mr. Bailey said?"

"I heard you scream," he mused.

She cleared her throat. "Well, it was the last straw."

He caught her hand, the undamaged one, and locked her fingers into his, tugging her out the door.

"Dr. Coltrain," she began.

He locked the office door. "You know my name."

She looked wary. "Yes."

He glanced at her. "My friends call me Copper," he said softly, and smiled.

"We're not friends."

"I think we're going to be, though, a year too late." He tugged her toward his car.

"I can drive mine," she protested.

"Mine's more comfortable. I'll drive you home, and give you a lift to work in the morning. Is it locked?"

"Yes, but…"

"Don't argue, Lou. I'm tired. It's been a long day and we've still got to make rounds at the hospital later."

We. He couldn't know the anguish of hearing him link them together when she had less than two weeks left in Jacobsville. He'd said that he'd torn up her resignation, but she was levelheaded enough to know that she had to go. It would be pure torment to be around him all the time and have him treat her as a friend and nothing more. She couldn't have an affair with him, either, so what was left?

He glanced down at her worried face and his fingers contracted. "Stop brooding. I promised not to seduce you."

"I know that!"

"Unless you want me to," he chided, chuckling at her expression. "I'm a doctor," he added in a conspiratorial whisper. "I know how to protect you from any consequences."

"Damn you!"

She jerked away from him, furiously. He laughed at her fighting stance.

"That was wicked," he acknowledged. "But I do love to watch you lose that hot temper. Are you Irish, by any chance?"

"My grandfather was," she muttered. She dashed a strand of blond hair out of her eyes. "You stop saying things like that to me!"

He unlocked her door, still smiling. "All right. No more jokes."

She slid into the leather seat and inhaled the luxurious scent of the upholstery while he got in beside her and started the car. It was dark. She sat next to him in perfect peace and contentment as they drove out to his ranch, not breaking the silence as they passed by farms and ranches silhouetted against the flat horizon.

"You're very quiet," he remarked when he pulled up in front of the Spanish-style adobe house he called home.

"I'm happy," she said without thinking.

He was quiet, then. He helped her out and they walked a little apart on the flagstone walkway that led to the front porch. It was wide and spacious, with gliders and a porch swing.

"It must be heaven to sit out here in the spring," she remarked absently.

He glanced at her curiously. "I never pictured you as the sort to enjoy a porch swing."

"Or walks in the woods, or horseback riding, or baseball games?" she asked. "Because I like those things, too. Austin does have suburbs, and I had friends who owned ranches. I know how to ride and shoot, too."

He smiled. She'd seemed like such a city girl. He'd made sure that he never looked too closely at her, of course. Like father, like daughter, he'd always thought. But she was nothing like Fielding Blakely. She was unique.

He unlocked the door and opened it. The interior was full of Spanish pieces and dark furniture with creams and beiges and browns softened by off-white curtains. It had the look of professional decorating, which it probably was.

"I grew up sitting on orange crates and eating on cracked plates," he commented as she touched a bronze sculpture of a bronc rider. "This is much better."

She laughed. "I guess so. But orange crates and cracked plates wouldn't be so bad if the company was pleasant. I hate formal dining rooms and extravagant place settings."

Now he was getting suspicious. They really couldn't have that much in common! His eyebrow jerked. "Full

of surprises, aren't you? Or did you just take a look
at my curriculum vitae and tell me what I wanted to
hear?" he added in a crisp, suspicious tone.

Her surprise was genuine, and he recognized it immediately. She searched his face. "This was a mistake,"
she said flatly. "I think I'd like to go…"

He caught her arm. "Lou, I'm constantly on the
defensive with women," he said. "I never know, you
see…" He hesitated.

"Yes, I understand," she replied. "You don't have
to say it."

"All that, and you read minds, too," he said with
cool sarcasm. "Well, well."

She drew away from him. She seemed to read his
mind quite well, she thought, because she usually knew
what he was going to say.

That occurred to him, too. "It used to make me mad
as hell when you handed me files before I asked for
them," he told her.

"It wasn't deliberate," she said without thinking.

"I know." His jaw firmed as he looked at her. "We
know too much about each other, don't we, Lou? We
know things we shouldn't, without ever saying them."

She looked up, feeling the bite of his inspection all
the way to her toes. "We can't say them," she replied.
"Not ever."

He only nodded. His eyes searched hers intently.
"I don't believe in happily ever after," he said. "I did,
once, until your father came along and shattered all
my illusions. She wouldn't let me touch her, you see.
But she slept with him. She got pregnant by him. The
hell of it was that she was going to marry me with-

out telling me anything." He sighed. "I lost my faith in women on the spot, and I hated your father enough to beat him to his knees. When you came here, and I found out who you were…" He shook his head. "I almost decked Drew for not telling me."

"I didn't know, either," she said.

"I realize that." He smiled. "You were an asset, after I got over the shock. You never complained about long hours or hard work, no matter how much I put on you. And I put a lot on you, at first. I thought I could make you quit. But the more I demanded, the more you gave. After a while, it occurred to me that I'd made a good bargain. Not that I liked you," he added sardonically.

"You made that perfectly clear."

"You fought back," he said. "Most people don't. They knuckle under and go home and fume about it, and think up things they wish they'd said. You just jump in with both feet and give it all you've got. You're a hell of an adversary, Lou. I couldn't beat you down."

"I always had to fight for things," she recalled. "My father was like you." Her face contorted and she turned away.

"I don't get drunk as a rule, and I've never hurt a woman!" he snapped.

"I didn't mean that," she said quickly. "It's just that you're forceful. You demand, you push. You don't ever give up or give in. Neither did he. If he thought he was right, he'd fight the whole world to prove it. But he fought the same when he was wrong. And in his later years, he drank to excess. He wouldn't admit he had a problem. Neither would my mother. She was his slave," she added bitterly. "Even her daughter was dispensable if the great man said so."

"Didn't she love you?"

"Who knows? She loved him more. Enough to lie for him. Even to die for him. And she did." She turned, her face hard. "She got into a plane with him, knowing that he was in no condition to fly. Maybe she had a premonition that he would go down and she wanted to go with him. I'm almost sure that she still would have gone with him if she'd known he was going to crash the plane. She loved him that much."

"You sound as if you can't imagine being loved that much."

"I can't," she said flatly, lifting her eyes. "I don't want that kind of obsessive love. I don't want to give it or receive it."

"What do you want?" he persisted. "A lifetime of loneliness?"

"That's what you're settling for, isn't it?" she countered.

He shrugged. "Maybe I am," he said after a minute. His blue eyes slid over her face and then averted. "Can you cook?" he asked on the way into the kitchen. Like the rest of the house, it was spacious and contained every modern device known to man.

"Of course," she said.

He glanced at her with a grin. "How well do you do chili?" he persisted.

"Well…"

"I've won contests with mine," he said smugly. He slid out of his jacket and vest and tie, opened the top buttons of his shirt and turned to the stove. "You can make the coffee."

"Trusting soul, aren't you?" she murmured as he acquainted her with the coffeemaker and the location of filters, coffee and measuring spoons.

"I always give a fellow cook the benefit of the doubt once," he replied. "Besides, you drink coffee all the time, just like I do. That means you must know how to make it."

She laughed. "I like mine strong," she warned.

"So do I. Do your worst."

Minutes later, the food was on the small kitchen table, steaming and delicious. Lou couldn't remember when she'd enjoyed a meal more.

"That's good chili," she had to admit.

He grinned. "It's the two-time winner of the Jacobsville Chili Cookoff."

"I'm not surprised. The corn bread was wonderful, too."

"The secret to good corn bread is to cook it in an iron skillet," he confessed. "That's where the crispness comes from."

"I don't own a single piece of iron cookware. I'll have to get a pan."

He leaned back, balancing his coffee mug in one hand as he studied her through narrow eyes. "It hasn't all been on my side," he remarked suddenly.

Her eyes lifted to his. "What hasn't?"

"All that antagonism," he said. "You've been as prickly as I have."

Her slender shoulders rose and fell. "It's instinctive

to recoil from people when we know they don't like us. Isn't it?"

"Maybe so." He checked his watch and finished his coffee. "I'll get these things in the dishwasher, then we'd better get over to the hospital and do rounds before the Christmas concert comes on the educational channel."

"I don't have my car," she said worriedly.

"We'll go together."

"Oh, that will certainly keep gossip down," she said on a sigh.

He smiled at her. "Damn gossip."

"Was that an adjective or a verb?"

"A verb. I'll rinse, you stack."

They loaded the dishes and he started the dishwasher. He slid back into his jacket, buttoned his shirt and fixed his tie. "Come on. We'll get the chores out of the way."

THE HOSPITAL WAS CROWDED, and plenty of people noticed that Drs. Coltrain and Blakely came in together to make rounds. Lou tried not to notice as she went from patient to patient, checking charts and making conversation.

But when she finished, Coltrain was nowhere in sight. She glanced out the window into the parking lot. His car was still there in his designated space. She went to the doctors' lounge looking for him, and turned the corner just in time to see him with a devastating blond woman in a dress that Lou would love to have been able to afford.

Coltrain saw Lou and he looked grim. He turned toward her with his hands in his pockets, and Lou no-

ticed that the woman was clutching one of his arms
tightly in both hands.

"This is my partner," he said, without giving her
name. "Lou, this is Dana Lester, an old…friend."

"His ex-fiancée." The woman corrected him in a
sweet tone. "How nice to meet you! I've just accepted
an appointment as nursing director here, so we'll be
seeing a lot of each other!"

"You're a nurse?" Lou asked politely, while she
caved in inside.

"A graduate nurse," she said, nodding. "I've been
working in Houston, but this job came open and was
advertised in a local paper. I applied for it, and here I
am! How lovely it will be to come home. I was born
here, you know."

"Oh, really?" Lou said.

"Darling," she told Copper, "you didn't tell me your
partner's name."

"It's Blakely," he said evenly. "Dr. Louise Blakely."

"Blakely?" the woman queried, her blue eyes pen-
sive. "Why does that name sound so familiar…?" She
suddenly went pale. "No," she said, shaking her head.
"No, that would be too coincidental."

"My father," Lou said coolly, "was Dr. Fielding
Blakely. I believe you…knew him?" she added pointedly.

Dana's face looked like rice paper. She drew away
from Coltrain. "I… I must fly, darling," she said.
"Things to do while I get settled! I'll have you over
for supper one night soon!"

She didn't speak to Lou again, not that it was expected. Lou watched her go with cold, angry eyes.

"You didn't want to tell her my name," Lou accused softly.

His face gave away nothing. "The past is best left alone."

"Did you know about her job here?"

His jaw clenched. "I knew there was an opening. I didn't know she'd been hired. If Selby Wills hadn't just retired as hospital administrator, she wouldn't have gotten the job."

She probed into the pocket of her lab coat without really seeing it. "She's pretty."

"She's blond, too, isn't that what you're thinking?"

She raised her face. "So," she added, "is Jane Parker."

"Jane Burke, now," he corrected her darkly. "I like blondes."

His tone dared her to make another remark. She lifted a shoulder and turned. "Some men do. Just don't expect me to welcome her with open arms. I'm sure that my mother suffered because of her. At least my father was less careless with women in his later years."

"It was over a long time ago," Copper said quietly. "If I can overlook your father, you can overlook her."

"Do you think so?"

"What happened between them was nothing to do with you," he persisted.

"He betrayed my mother with her, and it's nothing to do with me?" she asked softly.

He rammed his hands into his pockets, his face set and cold. "Are you finished here?"

"Oh, yes, I'm finished here," she agreed fervently.

"If you'll drop me off at my car, I'd like to go home now. We'll have to save the TV Special for another time."

He hesitated, but only for a minute. Her expression told him everything he needed to know, including the futility of having an argument with her right now.

"All right," he agreed, nodding toward the exit. "Let's go."

He stopped at her car in the office parking lot and let her out.

"Thanks for my supper," she said politely.

"You're welcome."

She closed the door and unlocked her own car. He didn't drive away until she was safely inside and heading out toward home.

DANA LESTER'S ARRIVAL in town was met with another spate of gossip, because there were people in Jacobsville who remembered the scandal very well. Lou tried to pay as little attention to it as possible as she weathered the first few days with the new nursing supervisor avoiding her and Coltrain barely speaking to her.

It was, she told herself, a very good thing that she was leaving after the first of January. The situation was strained and getting worse. She couldn't work out if Dana was afraid of her or jealous of her. Gossip about herself and Coltrain had been lost in the new rumors about his ex-fiancée's return, which did at least spare Lou somewhat. She couldn't help but see that Dana spent a fair amount of time following Coltrain around the hospital, and once or twice she phoned him at the office. Lou pretended not to notice and not to mind, but it was cutting her up inside.

The night she'd had supper with her taciturn partner had been something of a beginning. But Dana's arrival had nipped it all in the bud. He'd turned his back on Lou and now he only spoke to her when it was necessary and about business. If he'd withdrawn, so had she. Poor Brenda and the office receptionist worked in an armed camp, walking around like people on eggshells. Coltrain's temper strained at the bit, and every time he flared up, Lou flared right back.

"We hear that Nickie and Dana almost came to blows the other night about who got to take Dr. Coltrain a file," Brenda remarked a few days later.

"Too bad someone didn't have a hidden camera, isn't it?" Lou remarked. She sipped her coffee.

Brenda frowned. "I thought… Well, it did seem that you and the doctor were getting along better."

"A temporary truce, nothing more," she returned. "I'm still leaving after the first of the year, Brenda. Nothing's really changed except that Coltrain's old flame has returned."

"She was poison," Brenda said. "I heard all about her from some of the older nurses at the hospital. Did you know that at least two threatened to quit when they knew she was taking over as head nurse at the hospital? One of the nurses she worked with in Houston has family here. They said she was about to be fired when she grabbed this job. Her credentials look impressive, but she's not a good administrator, regardless of her college background, and she plays favorites. They'll learn that here, the hard way."

"It's not my problem."

"Isn't it?" Brenda muttered. "Well, they also say that her real purpose in applying for this job was to see if Copper was willing to take her back and try again. She's looking for a husband and he's number one on her list."

"Lucky him," she said blithely. "She's very pretty."

"She's a blond tarantula," she said hotly. "She'll suck him dry!"

"He's a big boy, Brenda," Lou returned imperturbably. "He can take care of himself."

"No man is immune to a beautiful face and figure and having a woman absolutely worship him. You take my word for it, there's going to be trouble."

"I won't be here to see it," Lou reminded her. And for the first time, she was glad. Nickie and Dana could fight over Coltrain and may the best woman win, she thought miserably. At least she wouldn't have to watch the struggle. She'd always known that Coltrain wasn't for her. She might as well accept defeat with good grace and get out while she could.

She went back to work, all too aware of Coltrain's deep voice in one of the cubicles she passed. She wondered how her life was going to feel when this was all a bad memory, and she wouldn't hear his voice again.

Drew invited her out to eat and she went, gratefully, glad for the diversion. But the restaurant he chose, Jacobsville's best, had two unwelcome diners: Coltrain and his ex-fiancée.

"I'm sorry," Drew said with a smile and a grimace

of apology. "I didn't know they'd be here or I'd have chosen another place to take you for supper."

"Oh, I don't mind," she assured him. "I have to see them at the hospital every day, anyway."

"Yes, *see* them being the key word here," he added knowingly. "I understand that they both avoid you."

"God knows why," she agreed. "She's anywhere I'm not when I need to ask her a question, and he only talks to me about patients. I'm glad I'm leaving, Drew. And with all respect to you, I'm sorry I came."

He smiled ruefully. "I'm sorry I got you into this," he said. "Nothing went as I planned."

"What exactly did you plan?" she asked probingly.

He lifted his water glass and took a sip. "Well, I had hoped that Copper would see something in you that he hadn't found anywhere else. You're unique, Lou. So is he, in some respects. You seemed like a match."

She glared at him. "We're chalk and cheese," she said, ignoring the things she and the redheaded doctor did have in common. "And we can't get along for more than five minutes."

"So I see." He looked around and made a face. "Oh, God, more complications!"

She followed his gaze. A determined Nickie, in a skintight dress cut almost to the navel, was dragging an embarrassed intern to a table right beside Coltrain and Dana's.

"That won't do," she remarked, watching Coltrain's blue eyes start to glitter. "He won't like that. And if she thinks he'll forgo a scene, she's very wrong. Any minute now he's going to get up and walk out."

When he did exactly that, leaving an astonished Dana at one table and a shocked Nickie at the other, Drew whistled through his teeth and gave Lou a pointed stare.

"You know him very well," was all he said, though.

"I know him," Lou said simply. "He says I read his mind. Maybe I do, on some level."

He frowned. "Do you realize how rare a rapport that is?"

She shrugged. "Not really. He seems to read my mind, too. I shouldn't feel sorry for him, but I do. Imagine shuffling two women in one restaurant."

He didn't add that it was really three, and that Copper had been watching Lou surreptitiously ever since she and Drew entered the restaurant. But of the three women, Lou was the only one who wasn't blatantly chasing him.

"He's paying the check," he remarked. "And, yes, there he goes, motioning to Dana. Good thing they'd finished dessert, wasn't it? Poor Nickie. She won't forget this in a while."

"I told her she was pushing too hard," Lou remarked. "Too bad. She's so young. I suppose she hasn't learned that you can chase a man too relentlessly and lose him."

"Some women never chase a man at all," he said.

She looked up and saw the teasing expression on his face. She laughed. "Drew, you are a dear," she said genuinely.

He chuckled. "My wife always said that I was," he agreed. "What are you going to do?"

"Me? What do you mean? What am I going to do about what?"

"About Copper."

"Nothing," she replied. "Right after the holidays, I leave for Austin."

He pursed his lips as he lifted his coffee cup. "You know," he said, "I have a feeling you'll never get out of town."

CHAPTER SEVEN

SATURDAY MORNING, Lou woke to the sound of some-one hammering on her front door. Half-asleep, with a pale pink satin robe whipped around her slender body and her hair disheveled, she made her way to open it.

The sight that met her eyes was shocking. Coltrain was standing there, dressed in jeans and boots and a faded cotton shirt under a fleece-lined jacket, with a weather-beaten gray Stetson in one lean hand.

She blinked. "Are we filming a new series called 'Cowboy Doctor'?"

"Cute," he remarked, but he wasn't smiling. "I have to talk to you."

She opened the door, still drowsy. "Come on in. I'll make coffee," she said, stifling a yawn as she shuffled toward the kitchen. She could have gone immediately to change, but she was more than adequately covered and he was a doctor. Besides, she reminded herself, he had two women chasing him relentlessly anyway.

"I'll make the coffee. How about some toast to go with it?"

"Plain or cinnamon?"

"Suit yourself."

She got out butter and cinnamon and, just as the coffee finished brewing, she had the toast ready—piping hot from the oven.

He watched her moving about the kitchen. He was sitting leaning back in one of her kitchen chairs with one booted foot on the floor and the chair propped against the wall. He looked out of humor and wickedly handsome all at the same time.

In the position he was occupying, his jeans clung closely to every powerful line of his long legs. He was muscular without being exaggerated, and with his faded shirt unbuttoned at the throat and his red hair disheveled from the hat, he looked more relaxed than she'd ever seen him.

It occurred to her that this was the way he usually was, except when he was working. It was like a private look into his secret life, and she was unexpectedly pleased to have been given it before she left town for good.

"Here." She put the toast on the table, handed him a plate, put condiments on the spotless white tablecloth and then poured coffee into two cups.

"The Christmas concert was nice," he remarked.

"Was it?" she replied. "I went to bed."

"I had nothing to do with getting Dana down here," he said flatly. "In case you wondered."

"It's none of my business."

"Yes, I know," he said heavily. He sipped coffee and munched toast, but he was preoccupied. "Nickie and Dana are becoming an embarrassment."

"Leave it to you to be irritated when two lovely women compete for your attention," she remarked dryly.

His eyes narrowed on her face. "Irritation doesn't quite cover it. I feel like the stud of the month," he said disgustedly.

She burst out laughing. "Oh, I'm sorry!" she said when he glared at her. "It was the way you said it."

He was ruffled, and looked it. He sipped more coffee. "I wasn't trying to make a joke."

"I know. It must be difficult, especially when you have to make rounds at the hospital, with both of them working there."

"I understand you're having some problems of your own in that regard."

"You might say that," she agreed. "I can't find Dana or Nickie when I need them. I seem to have the plague."

"You know that it can't continue?"

"Of course I do," she assured him. "And when I leave, things will settle down, I'm sure."

He scowled. "What do you mean, when you leave? How will that help? Anyway, we'd already agreed that you were staying."

"We agreed on nothing," she returned. "I gave you my resignation. If you tore it up, that's your problem. I consider it binding."

He stared down into his coffee cup, deep in thought. "I had no idea that you meant it."

"Amazing," she mused, watching him. "You have such a convenient memory, Dr. Coltrain. I can't forget a single word you said to Drew about me, and you can't remember?"

His face hardened. "I didn't know you were listening."

"That makes everything all right?" she asked with mock solemnity.

He ran a hand through his already disheveled hair. "Things came to a head," he replied. "I'd just had to diagnose leukemia in a child who should have had years of happiness to look forward to. I'd had a letter from my father asking for money…"

She shifted against the table. "I didn't know that your parents were still alive."

"My mother died ten years ago," he replied. "My father lives in Tucson. He wrangles horses, but he likes to gamble. When he gets in too deep, he always comes to me for a grubstake." He said it with utter contempt.

"Is that all you mean to him? Money?" she asked gently.

"It was all I ever meant to him." He lifted cold blue eyes to hers. He smiled unpleasantly. "Who do you think put me up to breaking and entering when I was a teenager? I was a juvenile, you know. Juveniles don't go to jail. Oh, we didn't do it here," he added. "Not where he lived. We always went to Houston. He cased the houses and sent me in to do the actual work."

Her gasp was audible. "He should have been arrested!"

"He was," he replied. "He served a year and got probation. We haven't spent any time together since I was placed with a foster family when I was thirteen, long before I started medical school. I put all that behind me. Apparently so did he. But now that I'm making a comfortable living, he doesn't really see any good reason not to ask me for help when he needs it."

What sort of family life had *he* grown up in? she wondered. It was, in some ways, like her own upbringing. "What a pity that we can't choose our parents," she remarked.

"Amen." His broad shoulders shifted against the wall. "I was in a temper already, and Drew's phone call was the last straw. It irritated the hell out of me that you liked him, but you jerked away from my slightest touch as if I might contaminate you."

She hadn't thought he'd noticed. He took her reaction as a sign of her distaste for him, when it was a fierce, painful attraction. It was ironic.

She lowered her eyes. "You said when I first came to work with you that we would have a business relationship."

"So I did. But that didn't mean you should treat me like a leper," he remarked. Oddly, he didn't seem to be concerned about it anymore. He smiled, in fact, his blue eyes sparkling. "But I wouldn't have had you overhear what I told Drew for all the world, Lou. It shamed me when you asked to end our partnership."

She toyed with a fingernail. "I thought it would make you happy."

Her choice of words delighted him. He knew exactly what she felt for him. He'd had suspicions for a while now, but he hadn't been certain until he kissed her. He couldn't let her leave until he was sure about what he felt for her. But how was he going to stop her? His blue eyes ran searchingly over her face and a crazy idea popped into his mind. "If you and I were engaged," he mused aloud, "Dana and Nickie would give up."

The words rambled around in her mind like marbles as she stared at him. The sun was out. It was a nice December day. Her Christmas decorations lined the windows and the tinsel on the Christmas tree in the living room caught the sun through the curtains and glittered.

"Did you hear me?" he asked when she didn't react.

Her cheeks burned. "I don't think that's very funny," she remarked, turning away.

He got to his feet with an audible thud and before she could move three feet, he had her by the waist from behind. Steely hands pulled her back against him and when she caught them, she felt their warm strength under her cool fingers. She felt his breath against her hair, felt it as his chest moved at her back.

"Shall we stop dancing around it?" he asked roughly. "You're in love with me. I've pretended not to see it, but we both know it's why you're leaving."

She gasped aloud. Frozen in his arms, she hadn't even a comeback, a face-saving reply. She felt his hands contract under hers, as if he thought she might pull away and run for it.

"Don't panic," he said quietly. "Dodging the issue won't solve it."

"I…didn't realize you could tell," she whispered, her pride in ashes at his feet.

His lean arms contracted, bringing her soft warmth closer to his taut body. "Take it easy. We'll deal with it."

"You don't have to deal with anything," she began huskily. "I'm going to…"

He turned her while she was speaking and his mouth was on hers before she could finish. She fought him for an instant, as he anticipated. But he was slow and very gentle, and she began to melt into him like ice against a flame.

He brought her closer, aware of her instant response

when she felt his body harden. He made a rough sound
against her mouth and deepened the kiss.

Her fingers caught in the cool flames of his hair,
holding on for dear life as his ardor burned high and
wild. He kissed her as he'd kissed Nickie at the party,
not an inch of space between their bodies, no quarter
in the thin lips devouring her open mouth. This time
when his tongue penetrated, she didn't pull away. She
accepted the intimate contact without a protest, shivering a little as it ignited new fires in her own taut
body. The sensation was unlike anything she'd known.
She held on tight, moaning, aware somewhere in the
back of her mind that his hand was at the base of her
spine, rubbing her against him, and that she should
say something.

She was incapable of anything except blind response.

She didn't resist even when he eased her back onto
her feet and, still kissing her hungrily, slid his hand
under her robe against the soft, tight curve of her
breast. He felt her heartbeat run away. With a groan,
he fought his way under the gown, against the petal-
soft warmth of her skin, and cupped her tenderly, dragging his thumb against the small hardness he found.
She shivered again. Reeling, he traced the tight nub
with his thumb and forefinger, testing its hardness.
She sobbed against his mouth. Probably, he thought
dizzily, she'd never had such a caress. And he could
give her something more; another pleasure that she
didn't know yet.

His mouth left hers and found its way down past her
collarbone to the softness under his hand. It opened

on her body, and he drank in the scented warmth of her while his tongue took the place of his thumb. She gasped and struggled, but he began to suckle her, his arms swallowing her, and she shuddered once and gave in. He felt her body go lax in his arms, so that if he hadn't supported her, she would have fallen. She caressed his nape with trembling hands, gasping a little as he increased the pressure, but clinging, not pushing.

When he thought he might explode from the pleasure it was giving him, he forced his mouth to release her and he stood erect, pulling her up abruptly.

His face was ruddy with high color, his eyes blazing as they met her half-open, dazed ones. She was oblivious to everything except the taste of him. Her lips were swollen. Even her tongue felt swollen. She couldn't say a word.

He searched over her face and then dropped his eyes to her bodice. He moved it out of the way and looked at the small, firm breast he'd been tasting. She looked like a rosebud there, the nipple red from his mouth.

He traced around it lazily and then looked back up at the shocked pleasure in her dark, dark eyes.

"I could have you on the kitchen table, right now," he said in a deep, quiet tone. "And you think you're leaving in two weeks?"

She blinked. It was all so unreal. He'd all but seduced her. His hand was still on her breast and he'd pulled the robe and gown aside. He was looking at her…!

She gasped, horrified, jerking back from him. Her hands grappled with the unruly fabric before she finally got her body covered. She backed away, blushing, glaring at him accusingly.

He didn't move, except to lean back against the kitchen counter and cross his long legs. That action drew her eyes to something she'd felt earlier, and she blushed scarlet before she managed to look away. What had she done? What had she let him do?

"You look outraged," he mused. "I think I like having you blush when I look at you."

"Would you leave, please?" she asked tightly.

"No, I don't think so," he said pleasantly. "Get dressed. Wear jeans and boots. I'm taking you riding."

"I don't want to go anywhere with you!"

"You want to go to bed with me," he corrected, smiling gently. "I can't think of anything I'd enjoy more, but I saddled the horses and left them in the stable before I came over here."

She huddled in her robe, wincing as it rubbed against her body.

"Breast sore?" he asked softly. "I'm sorry. I lost my head a little."

She flushed more and the robe tightened. "Dr. Coltrain…"

"Copper," he reminded her. "Or you can call me Jeb, if you like." He pursed his lips and his eyes were hot and possessive. "You'd really better get dressed, Lou," he murmured. "I'm still pretty hot, and aroused men are devious."

She moved back. "I have things to do…"

"Horseback riding or…?" He moved toward her.

She turned and ran for the bedroom. She couldn't believe what had just happened, and he'd said something about them becoming engaged. She must be losing her mind. Yes, that was it, she'd worried over leaving so much that she was imagining things. The whole thing had probably been a hallucination.

HE'D CLEARED AWAY the breakfast things by the time she washed, dressed, pulled her hair back into a ponytail with a blue ribbon and came into the kitchen with a rawhide jacket on.

He smiled. "You look like a cowgirl."

She'd felt a bit uneasy about facing him after that torrid interlude, but apparently he wasn't embarrassed. She might as well follow his lead. She managed a smile in return. "Thanks. But I may not quite merit the title. I haven't ridden in a long time."

"You'll be all right. I'll look after you."

He opened the door and let her out, waiting for her to lock it. Then he helped her into the Jaguar and drove her to his ranch.

THE WOODS WERE LOVELY, despite their lack of leaves. The slow, easy rhythm of the horses was relaxing, even if the company wasn't. She was all too aware of Coltrain beside her, tall and elegant even on horseback. With the Stetson pulled low over his eyes, he looked so handsome that he made her toes tingle.

"Enjoying yourself?" he asked companionably.

"Oh, yes," she admitted. "I haven't been riding in a long time."

"I do more of it than I like sometimes," he confessed. "This isn't a big ranch, but I run about fifty head of pedigree cattle. I have two married cowhands who help out."

"Why do you keep cattle?" she asked.

"I don't know. It was always a dream of mine, I guess, from the time I was a boy. My grandfather had one old milk cow and I'd try to ride her." He chuckled. "I fell off a lot."

She smiled. "And your grandmother?"

"Oh, she was a cook of excellent proportions," he replied. "She made cakes that were the talk of the county. When my dad went wrong, it broke her heart, and my grandfather's. I think they took it harder because he lured me into it with him." He shook his head. "When a kid goes bad, everyone blames it on the upbringing. But my grandparents were kind, good people. They were just poor. A lot of people were…still are."

She'd noticed that he had a soft spot for his needy patients. He made extra time for them, acting as counselor and even helping them get in touch with the proper government agencies when they needed help. At Christmas, he was the first to pledge a donation to local charities and contribute to parties for children who wouldn't otherwise have presents. He was a good man, and she adored him.

"Do you want children, eventually?" she asked.

"I'd like a family," he said noncommittally. He glanced at her. "How about you?"

She grimaced. "I don't know. It would be hard for me to juggle motherhood and medicine. I know plenty of people do, but it seems like begging from Peter to pay Paul, you know? Children need a lot of care. I think plenty of social problems are caused by parents who can't get enough time off from work to look after their children. And good day care is a terrible financial headache. Why isn't day care free?" she asked abruptly. "It should be. If women are going to have to work, companies should provide access to day care for them. I know of hospitals and some companies that do it for their employees. Why can't every big company?"

"Good question. It would certainly take a burden off working parents."

"All the same, if I had kids, I'd want to be with them while they were young. I don't know if I could give up practice for so long...."

He reined in his horse and caught her bridle, bringing her horse gently around so that they were facing each other at the side. "That's not the reason. Talk to me," he said quietly. "What is it?"

She huddled into her jacket. "I hated being a child," she muttered. "I hated my father and my mother and my life."

His eyebrows lifted. "Do you think a child would hate me?"

She laughed. "Are you kidding? Children love you. Except that you don't do stitches as nicely as I do," she added.

He smiled ruefully. "Thanks for small favors."

"The secret is the chewing gum I give them afterward."

"Ah, I see. Trade a few stitches for a few cavities."

"It's sugarless gum," she said smugly.

He searched her face with warm eyes. "Touché."

He wheeled his horse and led her off down a pasture path to where the big barn was situated several hundred yards away from the house. He explained the setup, and how he'd modernized his small operation.

"I'm not as up-to-date as a lot of ranchers are, and this is peanut scale," he added. "But I've put a lot of work and time into it, and I'm moderately proud of what I've accomplished. I have a herd sire who's mentioned in some of the bigger cattle magazines."

"I'm impressed. Do I get to see him?"

"Do you want to?"

"You sound surprised. I like animals. When I started out, it was a toss-up between being a doctor and being a vet."

"What swayed you?"

"I'm not really sure. But I've never regretted my choice."

He swung out of the saddle and waited for her to dismount. He tied the horses to the corral rail and led the way into the big barn.

It was surprisingly sanitary. The walkway was paved, the stalls were spacious with metal gates and fresh hay. The cows were sleek and well fed, and the bull he'd mentioned was beautiful even by bovine standards.

"Why, he's gorgeous," she enthused as they stood at the gate and looked at him. He was red-coated, huge, streamlined and apparently docile, because he came up to let Coltrain pet his muzzle.

"How are you, old man?" he murmured affectionately. "Had enough corn, have you?"

"He's a Santa Gertrudis, isn't he?" she asked curiously.

His hand stilled on the bull's nose. "How did you know that?" he asked.

"Ted Regan is one of my patients. He had a breeder's edition of some magazine with him one day, and he left it behind. I got a good idea of coat colors, at least. We have a lot of cattlemen around here," she added. "It never hurts to know a little bit about a good bull."

"Why, Lou," he mused. "I'm impressed."

"That's a first."

He chuckled. His blue eyes twinkled down at her as he propped one big boot on the low rail of the gate. "No, it's not. You impressed me the first week you were here. You've grown on me."

"Good heavens, am I a wart?"

He caught a strand of her hair and wound it around his finger. "You're a wonder," he corrected, searching her eyes. "I didn't realize we had so much in common. Funny, isn't it? We've worked together for a year, but I've found out more about you in the past two weeks than I ever knew."

"That goes for me, too."

She dropped her eyes to his chest, where the faded shirt clung to the hard muscles. She loved the way he stood, the way he walked, the way he looked with that hat tilted rakishly over one eye. She remembered the feel of his warm arms around her and she felt suddenly cold.

Her expressions fascinated him. He watched them change, saw the hunger filter into her face.

She drew a wistful breath and looked up at him with a wan smile.

He frowned. Without understanding why, he held out a lean arm.

She accepted the invitation without question. Her

body went against his, pressing close. Her arms went under his and around him, so that her hands could flatten on the muscles of his long back. She closed her eyes and laid her cheek against his chest, and listened to his heart beat.

He was surprised, yet he wasn't. It felt natural to have Lou in his arms. He drew her closer, in a purely nonsexual way, and absently stroked her hair while he watched his bull eat corn out of the trough in his pen.

"Next week is Christmas," he said above her head.

"Yes, I know. What do you do for Christmas? Do you go to friends, or invite people over?"

He laughed gently. "I used to have it with Jane, before she married," he recalled, feeling her stiffen without really thinking much about it. "But last year, since she married, I cooked a TV dinner and watched old movies all day."

She didn't answer for a minute. Despite what she'd heard about Coltrain and Jane Parker in the past year, she hadn't thought that he and Jane had been quite so close. But it seemed that they were. It depressed her more than anything had in recent weeks.

He wasn't thinking about Christmases past. He was thinking about the upcoming one. His hand explored her hair strand by strand. "Where are we going to have Christmas dinner, and who's going to cook it?" he asked matter-of-factly.

That was encouraging, that he wanted to spend Christmas with her. She couldn't refuse, even out of hurt pride. "We could have it at my house," she offered.

"I'll help cook it."

She smiled. "It would be nice to have someone to eat it with," she confessed.

"I'll make sure we're on call Christmas Eve, not Christmas Day," he promised. His arm slid down her back and drew her closer. He was aware of a kind of contentment he'd never experienced before, a belonging that he hadn't known even with Jane. Funny, he thought, until Lou came along, it had never occurred to him that he and Jane couldn't have had a serious relationship even if Todd Burke hadn't married her.

It was a sobering thought. This woman in his arms had come to mean a lot to him, without his realizing it until he'd kissed her for the first time. He laid his cheek against her head with a long sigh. It was like coming home. He'd been searching all his life for something he'd never found. He was closer to it than he'd ever been right now.

Her arms tightened around his lean waist. She could feel the wall of his chest hard against her breasts, the buckle of his belt biting into her. But it still wasn't quite close enough. She moved just a little closer, so that her legs brushed his.

He moved to accommodate her, sliding one boot higher on the fence so that she could fit against him more comfortably. But the movement aroused him and he caught his breath sharply.

"Sorry," she murmured and started to step away.

But his hand stayed her hips. "I can't help that," he said at her temple, secretly delighted at his headlong physical response to her. "But it isn't a threat."

"I didn't want to make you uncomfortable."

He smiled lazily. "I wouldn't call it that." He brushed

a kiss across her forehead. "Relax," he whispered. "It's pretty public here, and I'm sure you know as well as I do that making love in a hay barn is highly unsanitary."

She laughed at his humor. "Oh, but this barn is very clean."

"Not that clean," he murmured dryly. "Besides," he added, "it's been a long, dry spell. When I'm not in the market for a companion, I don't walk around prepared for sweet interludes."

She lifted her face and searched his mocking eyes demurely. "A long, dry spell? With Nickie prancing around half-naked to get your attention?"

He didn't laugh, as she expected him to. He traced her pert nose. "I don't have affairs," he said. "And I'm the soul of discretion in my private life. There was a widow in a city I won't name. She and I were good friends, and we supplied each other with something neither of us was comfortable spreading around. She married year before last. Since then, I've concentrated on my work and my cattle. Period."

She was curious. "Can you…well, do it…without love?"

"I was fond of her," he explained. "She was fond of me. We didn't have to be in love."

She moved restlessly.

"It would have to be love, for you, wouldn't it, Lou?" he asked. "Even desperate desire wouldn't be enough." He traced her soft lips with deliberation. "But you and I are an explosive combination. And you do love me."

She laid her forehead at his collarbone. "Yes," she admitted. "I love you. But not enough to be your mistress."

"I know that."

"Then it's hopeless."

He laughed mirthlessly. "Is it? I thought I mentioned that we could get engaged."

"Engaged isn't married," she began.

He put a finger over her lips, and he looked solemn. "I know that. Will you let me finish? We can be engaged until the first of the year, when I can afford to take a little time off for a honeymoon. We could have a New Year's wedding."

CHAPTER EIGHT

"You mean, get married? Us?" she echoed blankly.

He tilted up her chin and searched her dark, troubled eyes. "Sex doesn't trouble you half as much as marriage does, is that it? Marriage means commitment, and to you, that's like imprisonment."

She grimaced. "My parents' marriage was horrible. I don't want to become like my mother."

"So you said." He traced her cheek. "But I'm not like your father. I don't drink. Well," he murmured with a sheepish grin, "maybe just once, and I had justification for that. You were letting Drew hold your hand, when you always jerked back if I touched you at all."

She was surprised. She smiled. "Was *that* why?"

He chuckled. "Yes, that was why."

"Imagine that!"

"Take one day at a time, okay?" he asked. "Let's rock along for a couple of weeks, and spend Christmas together. Then we'll talk about this again."

"All right."

He bent and kissed her softly. She pressed up against him, but he stepped back.

"None of that," he said smartly. "We're going to get to know each other before we let our glands get in the way."

"Glands!"

"Don't you remember glands, Doctor?" He moved toward her threateningly. "Let me explain them to you."

"I think I've got the picture," she said on a laugh. "Keep away, you lecher!"

He laughed, too. He caught her hand and tangled her fingers with his as they walked back to where the horses were tied. He'd never been quite this interested in marriage, even if he'd once had it in the back of his mind when he'd dated Jane. But when he'd had Lou close in his arms, in the barn, he'd wanted it with a maddening desire. It wasn't purely physical, although she certainly attracted him that way. But despite the way she felt about him, he had a feeling that she'd have to be carefully coaxed down the aisle. She was afraid of everything marriage stood for because of her upbringing. Their marriage wouldn't be anything like her parents', but he was going to have to convince her of that first.

THEY MADE ROUNDS together the next morning at the hospital, and as usual, Dana was lying in wait for Coltrain.

But this time, he deliberately linked Lou's hand in his as he smiled at her.

"Good morning," he said politely.

Dana was faintly startled. "Good morning, doctors," she said hesitantly, her eyes on their linked hands.

"Lou and I became engaged yesterday," he said.

Dana's face paled. She drew a stiff breath and managed the semblance of a smile. "Oh, did you? Well, I suppose I should offer my congratulations!" She laughed. "And I had such high hopes that you and I might regain something of the past."

"The past is dead," he said firmly, his blue eyes steady on her face. "I have no inclination whatsoever to revive it."

Dana laughed uncomfortably. "So I see." She glanced at Lou's left hand. "Quite a sudden engagement, was it?" she added slyly. "No ring yet?"

Lou's hand jerked in his, but he steadied it. "When Lou makes up her mind what sort she wants, I'll buy her one," he said lazily. "I'd better get started. Wait for me in the lounge when you finish, sweet," he told Lou and squeezed her fingers before he let them go.

"I will," she promised. She smiled at Dana carelessly and went down the hall to begin her own rounds.

Dana followed her. "Well, I hope you fare better than I did," she muttered. "He's had the hots for Jane Parker for years. He asked me to marry him because he wanted me and I wouldn't give in, but even so, I couldn't compete with dear Jane," she said bitterly. "Your father was willing, so I indulged in a stupid affair, hoping I might make him jealous. That was the lunatic act of the century!"

"So I heard," Lou said stiffly, glaring at the other woman.

"I guess you did," the older woman said with a grimace. "He hated me for it. There's one man who doesn't move with the times, and he never forgets a wrong you do him." Her eyes softened as she looked at Lou's frozen face. "Your poor mother must have hated me. I know your father did. He was livid that I'd been

so careless, and of course, I ruined his chances of staying here. But he didn't do so bad in Austin."

Lou had different memories of that. She couldn't lay
it all at Dana's door, however. She paused at her first
patient's door. "What do you mean about Jane Parker?"
she asked solemnly.

"You must have heard by now that she was his first
love, his only love, for years. I gave up on him after
my fling with your father. I thought it was surely over
between them until I came back here. She's married,
you know, but she still sees Copper socially." Her eyes
glittered. "They say he sits and stares at her like an oil
painting when they're anywhere together. You'll find
that out for yourself. I should be jealous, but I don't
think I am. I feel sorry for you, because you'll always
be his second choice, even if he marries you. He may
want you, but he'll never stop loving Jane."

She walked away, leaving a depressed, worried Lou
behind. Dana's former engagement to Coltrain sounded
so much like her own "engagement" with him that it
was scary. She knew that he wanted her, but he didn't
show any signs of loving her. Did he still love Jane? If
he did, she couldn't possibly marry him.

Nickie came up the hall when Lou had finished her
rounds and was ready to join Coltrain in the lounge.

"Congratulations," she told Lou with a resigned
smile. "I guess I knew I was out of the running when
I saw him kiss you in the car park. Good luck. From
what I hear, you'll need it." She kept walking.

Lou was dejected. It was in her whole look when
she went into the doctors' lounge, where Coltrain had

just finished filling out a form at the table near the window. He looked up, frowning.

"What is it?" he asked curtly. "Have Dana and Nickie been giving you a hard time?"

"Not at all," she said. "I'm just a little tired." She touched her back and winced, to convince him. "Horseback riding takes some getting used to, doesn't it?"

He smiled, glad that he'd mistaken soreness for depression. "Yes, it does. We'll have to do more of it." He picked up the folder. "Ready to go?"

"Yes."

He left the form at the nurses' station, absorbing more congratulations from the nurses, and led Lou out to his Jaguar.

"We'll take some time off this afternoon for lunch and shop for a ring," he said.

"But I don't need…"

"Of course you do," he said. "We can't let people think I'm too miserly to buy you an engagement ring!"

"But what if…?"

"Lou, it's my money," he declared.

She grimaced. Well, if he wanted to be stuck with a diamond ring when she left town, that was his business. The engagement, as far as she was concerned, was nothing more than an attempt to get his life back on an even keel and discourage Nickie and Dana from hounding him.

She couldn't forget what had been said about Jane Parker, Jane Burke now, and she was more worried than ever. She knew how entangled he'd been with Jane, all right, because she'd considered her a rival until the day Jane married Todd Burke. Coltrain's manner even when he spoke to the woman was tender, solicitous, almost reverent.

He'd proposed. But even though he knew Lou loved him, he'd never mentioned feeling anything similar for her. He was playing make-believe. But she wondered what would happen if Jane Burke suddenly became a free woman. It would be a nightmare to live with a man who was ever yearning for someone else, someone he'd loved most of his life. Jane was a habit he apparently couldn't break. She was married. But could that fact stop him from loving her?

"You're very quiet," he remarked.

"I was thinking about Mr. Bailey," she hedged. "He really needs to see a specialist about that asthma. What do you think of referring him to Dr. Jones up in Houston?"

He nodded, diverted. "A sound idea. I'll give you the number."

THEY WORKED IN harmony until the lunch hour. Then, despite her arguments, they drove to a jewelry shop in downtown Jacobsville. As bad luck would have it, Jane Burke was in there, alone, making a purchase.

She was so beautiful, Lou thought miserably. Blond, blue-eyed, with a slender figure that any man would covet.

"Why hello!" Jane said enthusiastically, and hugged Copper as if he was family.

He held her close and kissed her cheek, his smile tender, his face animated. "You look terrific," he said huskily. "How's the back? Still doing those exercises?"

"Oh, yes," she agreed. She held him by the arms

and searched his eyes. "You look terrific yourself."
She seemed only then to notice that he wasn't alone.
She glanced at Lou. "Dr. Blakely, isn't it?" she asked
politely, and altered the smile a little. "Nice to see you
again."

"What are you doing here?" Coltrain asked her.

"Buying a present for my stepdaughter for Christmas. I thought she might like a nice strand of pearls.
Aren't these lovely?" she asked when the clerk had
taken them out of the case to show them. "I'll take
them," she added, handing him her credit card.

"Is she staying with you and Todd all the time now?"

She nodded. "Her mother and stepfather and the
baby are off to Africa to research his next book," she
said with a grin. "We're delighted to have her all to
ourselves."

"How's Todd?"

Lou heard the strained note in his voice with miserable certainty that Dana had been telling the truth.

"He's as impossible as ever." Jane chuckled. "But
we scratch along, me with my horses and my clothing
line and he with his computer business. He's away so
much these days that I feel deserted." She lifted her
eyes to his and grinned. "I don't guess you'd like to
come to supper tonight?"

"Sure I would," he said without thinking. Then he
made a sound. "I can't. There's a hospital board meeting."

"Oh, well," she muttered. "Another time, then." She
glanced at Lou hesitantly. "Are you two out Christmas
shopping—together?" she added as if she didn't think
that was the case.

Coltrain stuck his hands deep into his pockets. "We're shopping for an engagement ring," he said tersely.

Her eyes widened. "For whom?"

Lou wanted to sink through the floor. She flushed to the roots of her hair and clung to her shoulder bag as if it were a life jacket.

"For Lou," Coltrain said. "We're engaged."

He spoke reluctantly, which only made Lou feel worse.

Jane's shocked expression unfroze Lou's tongue. "It's just for appearances," she said, forcing a smile. "Dana and Nickie have been hounding him."

"Oh, I see!" Jane's face relaxed, but then she frowned. "Isn't that a little dishonest?"

"It was the only way, and it's just until my contract is up, the first of the year," Lou forced herself to say. "I'll be leaving then."

Coltrain glared at her. He wasn't certain what he'd expected, but she made the proposal sound like a hoax. He hadn't asked her to marry him to ward off the other women; he'd truly wanted her to be his wife. Had she misunderstood totally?

Jane was as startled as Coltrain was. She knew that Copper wasn't the sort of man to give an engagement ring lightly, although Lou seemed to think he was. Since Dana's horrible betrayal, Copper had been impervious to women. But even Jane had heard about the hospital Christmas party and the infamous kiss. She'd hoped that Copper had finally found someone to love, although it was surprising that it would be the partner with whom he fought with so enthusiastically. Now, looking at them together, she was confused. Lou looked as if she were being tortured. Copper was taciturn and frozen. And they said it was a sham. Lou didn't love him. She couldn't, and be so lighthearted about it. Copper looked worn.

Jane glared at Lou and put a gentle hand on Coltrain's arm. "This is a stupid idea, Copper. You'll be the butt of every joke in town when Lou leaves, don't you realize it? It could even damage your reputation, hurt your practice," she told Copper intently.

His jaw tautened. "I appreciate your concern," he said gently, even as it surprised him that Jane should turn on Lou, who was more an innocent bystander than Coltrain's worst enemy.

That got through to Lou, too. She moved restlessly, averting her gaze from the diamond rings in the display case. "She's right. It *is* stupid. I can't do this," she said suddenly, her eyes full of torment. "Please, excuse me, I have to go!"

She made it out the door before the tears were visible, cutting down an alley and ducking into a department store. She went straight to the women's rest room and burst into tears, shocking a store clerk into leaving.

In the jewelry store, Coltrain stood like a statue, unspeakably shocked at Lou's rash departure and furious at having her back out just when he'd got it all arranged.

"For God's sake, did you have to do that?" Coltrain asked harshly. He rammed his hands into his pockets. "It's taken me days just to get her to agree on any pretext…!"

Jane realized, too late, what she'd done. She winced.

"I didn't know," she said miserably. "It's my fault that she's bolted," Jane said quickly. "Copper, I'm sorry!"

"Not your fault," he said stiffly. "I used Dana and Nickie to accomplish this engagement, but she was reluctant from the beginning." He sighed heavily. "I guess she'll go, now, in spite of everything."

"I don't understand what's going on."

He moved a shoulder impatiently. "She's in love with me," he said roughly, and rammed his hands deeper into his pockets.

"Oh, dear." Jane didn't know what to say. She'd lashed out at the poor woman, and probably given Lou a false picture of her relationship with Copper to boot. They were good friends, almost like brother and sister, but there had been rumors around Jacobsville for years that they were secret lovers. Until she married Todd, that was. Now, she wondered how much Lou had heard and if she'd believed it. And Jane had brazenly invited him to supper, ignoring Lou altogether.

She grimaced. "I've done it now, haven't I? I would have included her in my invitation if I'd had any idea. I thought she was just tagging along with you on her lunch hour!"

"I'd better go after her," he said reluctantly.

"It might be best if you didn't," she replied. "She's hurt. She'll want to be alone for a while, I should think."

"I can't strand her in town." He felt worse than he could ever remember feeling. "Maybe you're both right, and this whole thing was a stupid idea."

"If you don't love her, it certainly was," she snapped at him. "What are you up to? Is it really just to protect you from a couple of lovesick women? I'm shocked. A few years ago, you'd have cussed them both to a fare-thee-well and been done with it."

He didn't reply. His face closed up and his blue eyes glittered at her. "My reasons are none of your business," he said, shutting her out.

Obviously Lou had to mean something to him. Jane felt even worse. She made a face. "We were very close once. I thought you could talk to me about anything."

"Anything except Lou," he said shortly.

"Oh." Her eyes were first stunned and then amused.

"You can stop speculating, too," he added irritably, turning away.

"She sounds determined to leave."

"We'll see about that."

Despite Jane's suggestion, he went off toward the department store where Lou had vanished and strode back to the women's rest room. He knew instinctively that she was there. He caught the eye of a female clerk.

"Could you ask Dr. Blakely to come out of there, please?"

"Dr. Blakely?"

"She's so high—" he indicated her height with his hand up to his nose "—blond hair, dark eyes, wearing a beige suit."

"Oh, her! She's a doctor? Really? My goodness, I thought doctors never showed their emotions. She was crying as if her heart would break. Sure, I'll get her for you."

He felt like a dog. He'd made her cry. The thought of Lou, so brave and private a person, with tears in her eyes made him hurt inside. And it had been so unnecessary. If Jane had only kept her pretty mouth shut! She was like family, and she overstepped the bounds sometimes with her comments about how Coltrain should live his life. He'd been more than fond of her once, and he still had a soft spot for her, but it was Lou who was disrupting his whole life.

He leaned against the wall, his legs and arms crossed, and waited. The female clerk reappeared, smiled reassuringly, and went to wait on a customer.

A minute later, a subdued and dignified Lou came out of the small room, her chin up. Her eyes were slightly red, but she didn't look as if she needed anyone's pity.

"I'm ready to go if you are," she said politely.

He searched her face and decided that this wasn't the time for a row. They still had to get lunch and get back to the office.

He turned, leaving her to follow. "I'll stop by one of the hamburger joints and we can get a burger and fries."

"I'll eat mine at the office, if you don't mind," she said wearily. "I'm not in the mood for a crowd."

Neither was he. He didn't argue. He opened the car door and let her in, then he went by the drive-in window of the beef place and they carried lunch back.

Lou went directly into her office and closed the door. She hardly tasted what she was eating. Her heart felt as if it had been burned alive. She knew what Dana meant now. Jane Parker was as much a part of Coltrain's life as his cattle, his practice. No woman, no matter how much she loved him, could ever compete with his love for the former rodeo star.

She'd been living in a fool's paradise, but fortu-

nately there was no harm done. They could say that
the so-called "engagement" had been a big joke. Surely
Coltrain could get Nickie and Dana out of his hair by
simply telling them the truth, that he wasn't interested.
God knew, once he got started, he wasn't shy about ex-
pressing his feelings any other time, regardless of who
was listening. Which brought to mind the question of
why he'd asked her to marry him. He wasn't in love
with her. He wanted her. Had that been the reason?
Was he getting even with Jane because she'd married
and deserted him? She worried the question until she
finished eating. Then her patients kept her occupied
for the rest of the day, so that she had no time to think.

JANE HAD WONDERED if she could help undo the damage she'd already done to Copper's life, and at last she
came up with a solution. She decided to give a farewell
party for Lou. She called Coltrain a few days later to
tell him the news.

"Christmas is next week," he said shortly. "And I
doubt if she'd come. She only speaks to me when she
has to. I can't get near her anymore."

That depressed Jane even more. "Suppose I phone
her?" she asked.

"Oh, I know she won't talk to you." He laughed
without humor. "We're both in her bad books."

Jane sighed. "Then who can we have talk to her?"

"Try Drew Morris," he said bitterly. "She likes him."

That note in his voice was disturbing. Surely he
knew that Drew was still mourning his late wife. If he
and Lou were friends, it was nothing more than that,
despite any social outings together.

"You think she'd listen to Drew?" she asked.

"Why not?"

"I'll try, then."

"Don't send out any invitations until she gives you an answer," he added. "She's been hurt enough, one way or the other."

"Yes, I know," Jane said gently. "I had no idea, Copper. I really meant well."

"I know that. She doesn't."

"I guess she's heard all the old gossip, too."

He hadn't considered that. "What old gossip?"

"About us," she persisted. "That we had something going until I married Todd."

He smoothed his fingers absently over the receiver. "She might have, at that," he said slowly. "But she must know that—" He stopped dead. She'd have heard plenty from Dana, who had always considered Jane, not her affair with Fielding Blakely, the real reason for their broken engagement. Others in the hospital knew those old rumors, too, and Jane had given Lou the wrong impression of their relationship in the jewelry store.

"I'm right, aren't I?" Jane asked.

"You might be."

"What are you going to do?"

"What can I do?" he asked shortly. "She doesn't really want to marry anyone."

"You said she loves you," she reminded him.

"Yes, and she does. It's the only thing I'm sure of. But she doesn't want to marry me. She's so afraid that she'll become like her mother, blindly accepting faults and abuse without question, all in the name of love."

"Poor girl," she said genuinely. "What a life she must have had."

"I expect it was worse than we'll ever know," he agreed. "Well, call Drew and see if he can get through to her."

"If he can, will you come, too?"

"It would look pretty bad if I didn't, wouldn't it?" he asked dryly. "They'd say we were so antagonistic toward each other that we couldn't even get along for a farewell party. And coming on the heels of our 'engagement,' they'd really have food for thought."

"I'd be painted as the scarlet woman who broke it up, wouldn't I?" Jane groaned. "Todd would love that! He's still not used to small-town life."

"Maybe Drew can reach her. If he can't, you'll have to cancel it. We can't embarrass her."

"I wouldn't dream of it."

"I know that. Jane, thanks."

"For what?" she asked. "I'm the idiot who got you into this mess in the first place. The least I owe is to try to make amends for what I said to her. I'll let you know what happens."

"Do that."

He went back to work, uncomfortably aware of Lou's calm demeanor. She didn't even look ruffled after all the turmoil. Of course, he remembered that she'd been crying like a lost child in the department store after Jane's faux pas. But that could have been so much more than a broken heart.

She hadn't denied loving him, but could love survive a year of indifference alternating with vicious antagonism, such as he'd given her? Perhaps loving him

was a sort of habit that she'd finally been cured of.
After all, he'd given her no reason to love him, even
to like him. He'd missed most of his chances there.
But if Drew could convince her to come to a farewell
party, on neutral ground, Coltrain had one last chance
to change her mind about him. That was his one hope;
the only one he had.

CHAPTER NINE

DREW INVITED LOU to lunch the next day. It was Friday, the week before the office closed for Christmas holidays. Christmas Eve would be on a week from Saturday night, and Jane had changed her mind about dates. She wanted to give the farewell party the following Friday, the day before New Year's Eve. That would, if Lou didn't reconsider her decision, be Lou's last day as Coltrain's partner.

"I'm surprised," Lou told him as they ate quiche at a local restaurant. "You haven't invited me to lunch in a long time. What's on your mind?"

"It could be just on food."

She laughed. "Pull the other one."

"Okay. I'm a delegation of one."

She held her fork poised over the last morsel of quiche on her plate. "From whom?"

"Jane Burke."

She put the fork down, remembering. Her expression hardened. "I have nothing to say to her."

"She knows that. It's why she asked me to talk to you. She got the wrong end of the stick and she's sorry. I'm to make her apologies to you," he added. "But she also wants to do something to make up for what she said to you. She wants to give you a farewell party on the day before New Year's Eve."

She glared at Drew. "I don't want anything to do with any parties given by that woman. I won't go!"

His eyebrows lifted. "Well! You are miffed, aren't you?"

"Accusing me of trying to ruin Jebediah's reputation and destroy his privacy…how dare she! I'm not the one who's being gossiped about in connection with him! And she's married!"

He smiled wickedly. "Lou, you're as red as a beet."

"I'm mad," she said shortly. "That…woman! How dare she!"

"She and Copper are friends. Period. That's all they've ever been. Are you listening?"

"Sure, I'm listening. Now," she added, leaning forward, "tell me he wasn't ever in love with her. Tell me he isn't still in love with her."

He wanted to, but he had no idea of Coltrain's feelings for Jane. He knew that Coltrain had taken her marriage hard, and that he seemed sometimes to talk about her to the exclusion of everyone else. But things had changed in the past few weeks, since the hospital Christmas dance the first week of December.

"You see?" she muttered. "You can't deny it. He may have proposed to me, but it was…"

"Proposed?"

"Didn't you know?" She lifted her coffee cup to her lips and took a sip. "He wanted me to pretend to be engaged to him, just to get Nickie and Dana off his back. Then he decided that we might as well get married for real. He caught me at a weak moment," she added, without details, "and we went to buy an engagement ring. But Jane was there. She was rude to me," she said miserably, "and Jebediah didn't say a word to stop her. In fact, he acted as if I wasn't even there."

"And that was what hurt most, wasn't it?" he queried gently.

"I guess it was. I have no illusions about him, you know," she added with a rueful smile. "He likes kissing me, but he's not in love with me."

"Does he know how you feel?"

She nodded. "I don't hide things well. It would be hard to miss."

He caught her hand and held it gently. "Lou, isn't he worth taking a chance on?" he asked. "You could let Jane throw this party for you, because she badly wants to make amends. Then you could talk to Copper and get him to tell you exactly why he wants to marry you. You might be surprised."

"No, I wouldn't. I know why he wants to marry me," she replied. "But I don't want to get married. I'm crazy about him, that's the truth, but I've seen marriage. I don't want it."

"You haven't seen a good marriage," he emphasized. "Lou, I had one. I had twelve years of almost ethereal happiness. Marriage is what you make of it."

"My mother excused every brutal thing my father did," she said shortly.

"That sort of love isn't love," he said quietly. "It's a form of domination. Don't you know the difference? If she'd loved your father, she'd have stood up to him and tried to help him stop drinking, stop using drugs."

She felt as if her eyes had suddenly been opened.

She'd never seen her parents' relationship like that. "But he was terrible to her..."

"Codependence," he said to her. "You must have studied basic psychology in college. Don't you remember any of it?"

"Yes, but they were my parents!"

"Your parents, anybody, can be part of a dysfunctional family." He smiled at her surprise. "Didn't you know? You grew up in a dysfunctional family, not a normal one. That's why you have such a hard time accepting the idea of marriage." He smoothed her hand with his fingers and smiled. "Lou, I had a normal upbringing. I had a mother and father who doted on me, who supported me and encouraged me. I was loved. When I married, it was a good, solid, happy marriage. They are possible, if you love someone and have things in common, and are willing to compromise."

She studied the wedding ring on Drew's left hand. He still wore it even after being widowed.

"It's possible to be happily married?" she asked, entertaining that possibility for the first time.

"Of course."

"Coltrain doesn't love me," she said.

"Make him."

She laughed. "That's a joke. He hated me from the beginning. I never knew it was because of my father, until I overheard him talking to you. I was surprised later when he was so cool to Dana, because he'd been bitter about her betrayal. But when I found out how close he was to Jane Burke, I guess I gave up entirely. You can't fight a ghost, Drew." She looked up. "And you know it, because no woman will ever be able to come between you and your memories. How would you feel if you found out some woman was crazily in love with you right now?"

He was stunned by the question. "Well, I don't know. I guess I'd feel sorry for her," he admitted.

"Which is probably how Coltrain feels about me, and might even explain why he offered to be engaged to me," she added. "It makes sense, doesn't it?"

"Lou, you don't propose to people out of pity."

"Coltrain might. Or out of revenge, to get back at Jane for marrying someone else. Or to get even with Dana."

"Coltrain isn't that scatty."

"Men are unpredictable when they're in love, aren't they?" she mused. "I wish he loved me, Drew. I'd marry him, with all my doubts and misgivings, in a minute if I thought there was half a chance that he did. But he doesn't. I'd know if he did feel that way. Somehow, I'd know."

He dropped his gaze to their clasped hands. "I'm sorry."

"Me, too. I've been invited to join a practice in Houston. I'm going Monday to speak with them, but they've tentatively accepted me." She lifted her sad face. "I understand that Coltrain is meeting some prospects, too. So I suppose he's finally taken me at my word that I want to leave."

"Don't you know?"

She shrugged. "We don't speak."

"I see." So it was that bad, he thought. Coltrain and Lou had both withdrawn, afraid to take that final step to commitment. She had good reasons, but what were

Copper's? he wondered. Did he really feel pity for Lou and now he was sorry he'd proposed? Or was Lou right, and he was still carrying a torch for Jane?

"Jane is a nice woman," he said. "You don't know her, but she isn't the kind of person who enjoys hurting other people. She feels very unhappy about what she said. She wants to make it up to you. Let her. It will be a nice gesture on your part and on hers."

"Dr. Coltrain will come," she muttered.

"He'd better," he said, "or the gossips will say he's glad to be rid of you."

She shook her head. "You can't win for losing."

"That's what I've been trying to tell you. Let Jane give the party. Lou, you'd like her if you got to know her. She's had a hard time of it since the wreck that took her father's life. Just being able to walk again at all is a major milestone for her."

"I remember," she said. And she did, because Coltrain had been out at the ranch every waking minute looking after the woman.

"Will you do it?"

She took a long breath and let it out. "All right."

"Great! I'll call Jane the minute I get home and tell her. You won't regret it. Lou, I wish you'd hold off about that spot in Houston."

She shook her head. "No, I won't do that. I have to get away. A fresh start is what I need most. I'm sure I won't be missed. After all, Dr. Coltrain didn't want me in the first place."

He grimaced, because they both knew her present

circumstances were Drew's fault. Saying again that he meant well wouldn't do a bit of good.

"Thanks for lunch," she said, remembering her manners.

"That was my pleasure. You know I'll be going to Maryland to have Christmas with my in-laws, as usual. So Merry Christmas, if I don't see you before I leave."

"You, too, Drew," she said with genuine affection.

IT WASN'T UNTIL the next Thursday afternoon that the office closed early for Christmas holidays—if Friday and Monday, added to the weekend, qualified as holidays—that Coltrain came into Lou's office. Lou had been to Houston and formally applied for a position in the family practitioner group. She'd also been accepted, but she hadn't been able to tell Coltrain until today, because he'd been so tied up with preholiday surgeries and emergencies.

He looked worn-out, she thought. There were new lines in his lean face, and his eyes were bloodshot from lack of sleep. He looked every year of his age.

"You couldn't just tell me, you had to put it in writing?" he asked, holding up the letter she'd written him.

"It's legal this way," she said politely. "I'm very grateful for the start you gave me."

He didn't say anything. He looked at the letter from the Houston medical group. It was written on decaledge bond, very expensive, and the lettering on the letterhead was embossed.

"I know this group," he said. "They're high-powered city physicians, and they practice supermarket medicine. Do you realize what that means? You'll be ex-

pected to spend five minutes or less with every patient.
A buzzer will sound to alert you when that time is up.
As the most junior partner, you'll get all the dirty jobs,
all the odd jobs, and you'll be expected to stay on call
on weekends and holidays for the first year. Or until
they can get another partner, more junior than you are."

"I know. They told me that." They had. It had depressed her no end.

He folded his arms across his chest and leaned back
against the wall, his stethoscope draped around his
neck. "We haven't talked."

"There's nothing to say," she replied, and she smiled
kindly. "I notice that Nickie and Dana have become
very businesslike, even to me. I'd say you were over
the hump."

"I asked you to marry me," he said. "I was under
the impression that you'd agreed and that was why we
were picking out a ring."

The memory of that afternoon hurt. She lowered
her eyes to the clipboard she held against her breasts.
"You said it was to get Nickie and Dana off your back."

"You didn't want to get married at all," he reminded
her.

"I still don't."

He smiled coldly. "And you're not in love with me?"

She met his gaze levelly. This was no time to back
down. "I was infatuated with you," she said bluntly.
"Perhaps it was because you were out of reach."

"You wanted me. Explain that."

"I'm human," she told him, blushing a little. "You
wanted me, too, so don't look so superior."

"I hear you're coming to Jane's party."

"Drew talked me into it." She smoothed her fingers over the cold clipboard. "You and Jane can't help it," she said. "I understand."

"Damn it! You sound just like her husband!"

She was shocked at the violent whip of his deep voice. He was furious, and it showed.

"Everyone knows you were in love with her," she faltered.

"Yes, I was," he admitted angrily, and for the first time. "But she's married now, Lou."

"I know. I'm sorry," she said gently. "I really am. It must be terrible for you...."

He threw up his hands. "My God!"

"It's not as if you could help it, either of you," she continued sadly.

He just shook his head. "I can't get through to you, can I?" he asked with a bite in his deep voice. "You won't listen."

"There's really nothing to say," she told him. "I hope you've found someone to replace me when I go."

"Yes, I have. He's a recent graduate of Johns Hopkins. He wanted to do some rural practice before he made up his mind where he wanted to settle." He gazed at her wan face. "He starts January 2."

She nodded. "That's when I start, in Houston." She tugged the clipboard closer.

"We could spend Christmas together," he suggested.

She shook her head. She didn't speak. She knew words would choke her.

His shoulders rose and fell. "As you wish," he said quietly. "Have a good Christmas, then."

"Thanks. You, too."

She knew that she sounded choked. She couldn't help herself. She'd burned her bridges. She hadn't meant to. Perhaps she had a death wish. She'd read and studied about people who were basically self-destructive, who destroyed relationships before they could begin, who found ways to sabotage their own success and turn it to failure. Perhaps she'd become such a person, due to her upbringing. Either way, it didn't matter now. She'd given up Coltrain and was leaving Jacobsville. Now all she had to do was survive Jane's little going-away party and get out of town.

Coltrain paused in the doorway, turning his head back toward her. His eyes were narrow, curious, assessing. She didn't look as if the decision she'd made had lifted her spirits any. And the expression on her face wasn't one of triumph or pleasure.

"If Jane hadn't turned up in the jewelry store, would you have gone through with it?" he asked abruptly.

Her hands tightened on the clipboard. "I'll never know."

He leaned against the doorjamb. "You don't want to hear this, but I'm going to say it. Jane and I were briefly more than friends. It was mostly on my side. She loves her husband and wants nothing to do with anyone else. Whatever I felt for her is in the past now."

"I'm glad, for your sake," she said politely.

"Not for yours?" he asked.

She bit her lower lip, worriedly.

He let his blue gaze fall to her mouth. It lingered there so long that her heart began to race, and she couldn't quite breathe properly. His gaze lifted then, to catch hers, and she couldn't break it. Her toes curled

inside her sensible shoes, her heart ran wild. She had
to fight the urge to go to him, to press close to his lean,
fit body and beg him to kiss her blind.

"You think you're over me?" he drawled softly, so
that his voice didn't carry. "In a pig's eye, Doctor!"

He pushed away from the door and went on his way,
whistling to himself as he went down the corridor to
his next patient.

Lou, having given herself away, muttered under her
breath and went to read the file on her next patient. But
she waited until her hands stopped shaking before she
opened the examining room door and went in.

THEY CLOSED UP the office. Coltrain had been called
away at the last minute to an emergency at the hospital, which made things easier for Lou. She'd be bound
to run into him while she was making her rounds, but
that was an occupational hazard, and there would be
plenty of other people around. She wouldn't have to
worry about being alone with him. Or so she thought.

When she finished her rounds late in the afternoon,
she stopped by the nurses' station to make sure they'd
been able to contact a new patient's husband, who had
been out of town when she was admitted.

"Yes, we found him," the senior nurse said with a
smile. "In fact, he's on his way over here right now."

"Thanks," she said.

"No need. It goes with the job," she was assured.

She started back down the hall to find Coltrain coming from the emergency room. He looked like a thundercloud, all bristling bad temper. His red hair flamed under
the corridor lights, and his blue eyes were sparking.

He caught Lou's arm, turned and drew her along with him without saying a word. People along the corridor noticed and grinned amusedly.

"What in the world are you doing?" she asked breathlessly.

"I want you to tell a—" he bit off the word he wanted to say "—*gentleman* in the emergency room that I was in the office all morning."

She gaped at him, but he didn't stop or even slow down. He dragged her into a cubicle where a big, angry-looking blond man was sitting on the couch having his hand bandaged.

Coltrain let Lou go and nodded curtly toward the other man. "Well, tell him!" He shot the words at Lou.

She gave him a stunned glance, but after a minute, she turned back to the tall man and said, "Dr. Coltrain was in the office all morning. He couldn't have escaped if he'd wanted to, because we had twice our usual number of patients, anticipating that we'd be out of the office over the holidays."

The blond man relaxed a little, but he was still glaring at Coltrain when there was a small commotion in the corridor and Jane Burke came in the door, harassed and frightened.

"Todd! Cherry said that you'd had an accident and she had to call an ambulance…!" She grabbed the blond man's hand and fought tears. "I thought you were killed!"

"Not hardly," he murmured. He drew her head to his shoulder and held her gently. "Silly woman." He chuckled. "I'm all right. I slammed the car door on my hand. It isn't even broken, just cut and bruised."

Jane looked at Coltrain. "Is that true?"

He nodded, still irritated at Burke.

Jane looked from him to Lou and back to her husband. "Now what's wrong?" she asked heavily.

Todd just glowered. He didn't say anything.

"You and I had been meeting secretly this morning at your house, while he and Cherry were away," Coltrain informed her. "Because the mailman saw a gray Jaguar sitting in your driveway."

"Yes, he did," Jane said shortly. "It belongs to the new divisional manager of the company that makes my signature line of leisure wear. *She* has a gray Jaguar exactly like Copper's."

Burke's hard cheekbones flushed a little.

"That's why you slammed the door on your hand, right?" she muttered. "Because the mailman is our wrangler's sister and he couldn't wait to tell you what your wife was doing behind your back! He'll be lucky if I don't have him for lunch!"

The flush got worse. "Well, I didn't know!" Todd snapped.

Coltrain slammed his clipboard down hard on the examination couch at Burke's hip. "That does it, by God," he began hotly.

He looked threatening and Burke stood up, equally angry.

"Now, Copper," Jane interrupted. "This isn't the place."

Burke didn't agree, but he'd already made a fool of himself once. He wasn't going to try for twice. He glanced at Lou, who looked as miserable as he felt. "They broke up your engagement, I understand," he added. "Pity they didn't just marry each other to begin with!"

Lou studied his glittery eyes for a moment, oblivious to the other two occupants of the cubicle. It was amazing how quickly things fell into place in her mind, and at once. She leaned against the examination couch. "Dr. Coltrain is the most decent man I know," she told Todd Burke. "He isn't the sort to do things in an underhanded way, and he doesn't sneak around. If you trusted your wife, Mr. Burke, you wouldn't listen to old gossip or invented tales. Small towns are hotbeds of rumor, that's normal. But only an idiot believes everything he hears."

Coltrain's eyebrows had arched at the unexpected defense.

"Thanks, Lou," Jane said quietly. "That's more than I deserve from you, but thank you." She turned back to her husband. "She's absolutely right," Jane told her husband. She was mad, too, and it showed. "I married you because I loved you. I still love you, God knows why! You won't even listen when I tell you the truth. You'd rather cling to old gossip about Copper and me."

Lou blushed scarlet, because she could have been accused of the same thing.

She wouldn't look at Coltrain at all.

"Well, here's something to take your mind off your foul suspicions," Jane continued furiously. "I was going to wait to tell you, but you can hear it now. I'm pregnant! And, no, it isn't Copper's!"

Burke gasped. "Jane!" He exploded, his injured hand forgotten as he moved forward to pull her hungrily into his arms. "Jane, is it true?"

"Yes, it's true," she muttered. "Oh, you idiot! You idiot…!"

He was kissing her, so she had to stop talking. Lou, a little embarrassed, edged out of the cubicle and moved away, only to find Coltrain right beside her as she left the emergency room.

"Maybe that will satisfy him," he said impatiently. "Thank you for the fierce defense," he added. "Hell of a pity that you didn't believe a word you were saying!"

She stuck her hands into her slacks pockets. "I believe she loves her husband," she said quietly. "And I believe that there's nothing going on between the two of you."

"Thanks for nothing."

"Your private life is your own business, Dr. Coltrain, none of mine," she said carelessly. "I'm already a memory."

"By your own damn choice."

The sarcasm cut deep. They walked through the parking lot to the area reserved for physicians and surgeons, and she stopped beside her little Ford.

"Drew loved his wife very much," she said. "He never got over losing her. He still spends holidays with his in-laws because he feels close to her that way, even though she's dead. I asked him how he'd feel if he knew that a woman was in love with him. Know what he said? He said that he'd pity her."

"Do you have a point?" he asked.

"Yes." She turned and looked up at him. "You haven't really gotten over Jane Burke yet. You have nothing to offer anyone else until you do. That's why I wouldn't marry you."

His brows drew together while he searched her face. He didn't say a word. He couldn't.

"She's part of your life," she continued. "A big part of it. You can't let go of the past, even if she can. I understand. Maybe someday you'll come to terms with it. Until you do, it's no good trying to be serious about anyone else."

He jiggled the change in his pockets absently. His broad shoulders rose and fell. "She was just starting into rodeo when I came back here as an intern in the hospital. She fell and they brought her to me. We had an instant rapport. I started going to watch her ride, she went out with me when I was free. She was special. Her father and I became friends as well, and when I bought my ranch, he helped me learn the ropes and start my herd. Jane and I have known each other a long, long time."

"I know that." She studied a button on his dark jacket. "She's very pretty, and Drew says she has a kind nature."

"Yes."

Her shoulders rose and fell. "I have to go."

He put out a lean hand and caught her shoulder, preventing her from turning away. "I never told her about my father."

She was surprised. She didn't think he had any secrets from Jane. She lifted her eyes and found him staring at her intently, as if he were trying to work out a puzzle.

"Curious, isn't it?" he mused aloud. "There's another curious thing, but I'm not ready to share that just yet."

He moved closer and she wanted to move away, to

stop him… No, she didn't. His head bent and his mouth closed on hers, brushing, lightly probing. She yielded without a protest, her arms sliding naturally around his waist, her mouth opening to the insistence of his lips. He kissed her, leaning his body heavily on hers, so that she could feel the metal of the car at her back and his instant, explosive response to her soft warmth.

She made a sound, and he smiled against her lips.

"What?" He bit off the words against her lips.

"It's…very…public," she breathed.

He lifted his head and looked around. The parking lot was dotted with curious onlookers. So was the emergency room ramp.

"Hell," he said irritably, drawing away from her. "Come home with me," he suggested, still breathing roughly.

She shook her head before her willpower gave out. "I can't."

"Coward," he drawled.

She flushed. "All right, I want to," she said fiercely. "But I won't, so there. Damn you! It isn't fair to play on people's weaknesses!"

"Sure it is," he said, correcting her. He grinned at her maddeningly. "Come on, be daring. Take a chance! Risk everything on a draw of the cards. You live like a scientist, every move debated, planned. For once in your life, be reckless!"

"I'm not the reckless sort," she said as she fought to get her breath back. "And you shouldn't be, either." She glanced ruefully toward the emergency room exit, where a tall blond man and a pretty blond woman were standing, watching. "Was it for her benefit?" she added, nodding toward them.

He glanced over her shoulder. "I didn't know they were there," he said genuinely.

She laughed. "Sure." She pulled away from him, unlocked her car, got in and drove off. Her legs were wobbly, but they'd stop shaking eventually. Maybe the rest of her would, too. Coltrain was driving her crazy. She was very glad that she'd be leaving town soon.

CHAPTER TEN

IT DIDN'T HELP that the telephone rang a few minutes after Lou got home.

"Still shaky, are we?" Coltrain drawled.

She fumbled to keep from dropping the receiver. "What do you want?" she faltered.

"An invitation to Christmas dinner, of course," he said. "I don't want to sit in front of the TV all day eating TV dinners."

She was still angry at him for making a public spectacle of them for the second time. The hospital would buzz with the latest bit of gossip for weeks. At least she wouldn't have long to put up with it.

"TV dinners are good for you," she said pointedly.

"Home cooking is better. I'll make the dressing and a fruit salad if you'll do turkey and rolls."

She hesitated. She wanted badly to spend that day with him, but in the long run, it would make things harder.

"Come on," he coaxed in a silky tone. "You know you want to. If you're leaving town after the first, it will be one of the last times we spend together. What have you got to lose?"

My self-respect, my honor, my virtue, my pride, she

thought. But aloud, she said, "I suppose it wouldn't hurt."

He chuckled. "No, it wouldn't. I'll see you at eleven on Christmas morning."

He hung up before she could change her mind. "I don't want to," she told the telephone. "This is a terrible mistake, and I'm sure that I'll regret it for the rest of my life."

After a minute, she realized that she was talking to a piece of equipment. She shook her head sadly. Coltrain was driving her out of her mind.

SHE WENT TO the store early on Christmas Eve and bought a turkey. The girl at the check-out stand was one of her patients. She grinned as she totaled the price of the turkey, the bottle of wine and the other groceries Lou had bought to cook Christmas dinner.

"Expecting company, Doctor?" she teased.

Lou flushed, aware that the woman behind her was one of Coltrain's patients. "No. No. I'm going to cook the turkey and freeze what I don't eat."

"Oh." The girl sounded disappointed.

"Going to drink all that wine alone, too?" the woman behind her asked wickedly. "And you a doctor!"

Lou handed over the amount the cashier asked for. "I'm not on duty on Christmas Day," she said irritably. "Besides, I cook with wine!"

"You won't cook with that," the cashier noted. She held up the bottle and pointed to the bottom of the label. It stated, quite clearly, Nonalcoholic Wine.

Lou had grabbed the bottle from the wrong aisle.

But it worked to her advantage. She grinned at the woman behind her, who looked embarrassed.

The clerk packaged up her purchases and Lou pushed them out to her car. At least she'd gotten around that tricky little episode.

Back home, she put the turkey on to bake and made rolls from scratch. Nonalcoholic wine wasn't necessarily a bad thing, she told herself. She could serve it at dinner without having to worry about losing her wits with Coltrain.

The weather was sunny and nice, and the same was predicted for the following day. A white Christmas was out of the question, of course, but she wondered what it would be like to have snow on the ground.

She turned on the television that night, when the cooking was done and everything was put into the refrigerator for the next day. Curled up in her favorite armchair in old jeans, a sweatshirt and in her sock feet, she was relaxing after her housecleaning and cooking when she heard a car drive up.

It was eight o'clock and she wasn't on call. She frowned as she went to the front door. A gray Jaguar was sitting in the driveway and as she looked, a tall, redheaded man in jeans and a sweatshirt and boots got out of the car carrying a big box.

"Open the door," he called as he mounted the steps.

"What's that?" she asked curiously.

"Food and presents."

She was surprised. She hadn't expected him tonight and she fumbled and faltered as she let him in and closed the door again.

He unloaded the box in the kitchen. "Salad." He

indicated a covered plastic bowl. "Dressing." He indicated a foil-covered pan. "And a chocolate pound cake. No, I didn't make it," he added when she opened her mouth. "I bought it. I can't bake a cake. Is there room in the fridge for this?"

"You could have called to ask before you brought it," she reminded him.

He grinned. "If I'd phoned, you'd have listened to the answering machine and when you knew it was me, you'd have pretended not to be home."

She flushed. He was right. It was disconcerting to have someone so perceptive second-guessing her every move. "Yes, there's room."

She opened the refrigerator door and helped him fit his food in.

He went back to the big box and pulled out two packages. "One for me to give you—" he held up one "—and one for you to give me."

She glared at him. "I got you a present," she muttered.

His eyebrows shot up. "You did?"

Her lower lip pulled down. "Just because I didn't plan to spend Christmas with you didn't mean I was low enough not to get you something."

"You didn't give it to me at the office party," he recalled.

She flushed. "You didn't give me anything at the office party, either."

He smiled. "I was saving it for tomorrow."

"So was I," she returned.

"Can I put these under the tree?"

She shrugged. "Sure."

Curious, she followed him into the living room. The tree was live and huge; it covered the whole corner and reached almost to the nine-foot ceiling. It was full of lights and decorations and under it a big metal electric train sat on its wide tracks waiting for power to move it.

"I didn't notice that when I was here before," he said, delighted by the train. He stooped to look at it more closely. "This is an American Flyer by Lionel!" he exclaimed. "You've had this for a while, haven't you?"

"It's an antique," she recalled. "My mother got it for me." She smiled. "I love trains. I have two more sets and about a mile of track in a box in the closet, but it seemed sort of pointless to set all those trains up with just me to run them."

He looked up at her with sparkling eyes. "Which closet are they in?" he asked in a conspiratorial tone.

"The hall closet." Her eyes brightened. "You like trains?"

"Do I like trains? I have HO scale, N scale, G scale and three sets of new Lionel O scale trains at home."

She gasped. "Oh, my goodness!"

"That's what I say. Come on!"

He led her to the hall closet, opened it, found the boxes and started handing them out to her.

Like two children, they sat on the floor putting tracks together with switches and accessories for the next two hours. Lou made coffee and they had it on the floor while they made connections and set up the low wooden scale buildings that Lou had bought to go with the sets.

When they finished, she turned on the power. The

wooden buildings were lit. So were the engines and the cabooses and several passenger cars.

"I love to sit and watch them run in the dark," she said breathlessly as he turned on the switch box and the trains began to move. "It's like watching over a small village with the people all snug in their houses."

"I know what you mean." He sprawled, chest down, on the floor beside her to watch the trains chug and whistle and run around the various tracks. "God, this is great! I had no idea you liked trains!"

"Same here," she said, chuckling. "I always felt guilty about having them, in a way. Somewhere out there, there must be dozens of little kids who would do anything for just one train and a small track to run it on. And here I've got all this and I never play with it."

"I know how it is. I don't even have a niece or nephew to share mine with."

"When did you get your first train?"

"When I was eight. My granddad bought it for me so he could play with it," he added with a grin. "He couldn't afford a big set, of course, but I didn't care. I never had so much fun." His face hardened at the memories. "When Dad took me to Houston, I missed the train almost as much as I missed my granddad and grandmother. It was a long time before I got back there." He shrugged. "The train still worked by then, though, and it was more fun when the threat of my father was gone."

She rolled onto her side, peering at him in the dim light from the tree and the small village. "You said that you never told Jane about your father."

"I didn't," he replied. "It was something I was deeply ashamed of for a long time."

"Children do what they're told, whether it's right or wrong," she reminded him. "You can't be held responsible for everything."

"I knew it was wrong," he agreed. "But my father was a brutal man, and when I was a young boy, I was afraid of him." His head turned. He smiled at her. "You'd understand that."

"Yes."

He rested his chin on his hands and watched the trains wistfully. "I took my medicine—juvenile hall and years of probation. But people helped me to change. I wanted to pass that on, to give back some of the care that had been given to me. That's why I went into medicine. I saw it as an opportunity to help people."

"And you have," she said. Her eyes traced the length of his fit, hard-muscled body lovingly. He was so different away from the office. She'd never known him like this, and so soon, it would all be over. She'd go away. She wouldn't see him again. Her sad eyes went back to the trains. The sound of them was like a lullaby, comforting, delightful to the ears.

"We need railroad caps and those wooden whistles that sound like old steam engines," he remarked.

She smiled. "And railroad gloves and crossing guards and flashing guard lights."

"If there was a hobby shop nearby, we could go and get them. But everything would be closed up on Christmas Eve, anyway."

"I guess so."

He pursed his lips, without looking at her. "If you

stayed, after the New Year, we could pool our layouts and have one big one. We could custom-design our own buildings and bridges, and we could go in together and buy one of those big transformer outfits that runs dozens of accessories."

She was thinking more of spending that kind of time with Coltrain than running model engines, but it sounded delightful all the same. She sighed wistfully. "I would have enjoyed that," she murmured. "But I've signed a new contract. I have to go."

"Contracts can be broken," he said. "There's always an escape clause if you look hard enough."

Her hips shifted on the rug they were lying on. "Too many people are gossiping about us already," she said. "Even at the grocery store, the clerk noticed that I bought a turkey and wine and the lady behind me said I couldn't possibly be going to drink it alone."

"You bought wine?" he mused.

"Nonalcoholic wine," she said, correcting him.

He chuckled. "On purpose?"

"Not really. I picked up the wrong bottle. But it was just as well. The lady behind me was making snide comments about it." She sighed. "It rubbed me the wrong way. She wouldn't have known that my father was an alcoholic."

"How did he manage to keep his job?"

"He had willing young assistants who covered for him. And finally, the hospital board forced him into early retirement. He *had* been a brilliant surgeon," she reminded him. "It isn't easy to destroy a career like that."

"It would have been better than letting him risk other people's lives."

"But he didn't," she replied. "Someone was always there to bail him out."

"Lucky, wasn't he, not to have been hit with a multimillion-dollar malpractice suit."

He reached out and threw the automatic switches to change the trains to another set of tracks. "Nice," he commented.

"Yes, isn't it? I love trains. If I had more leisure time, I'd do this every day. I'm glad we're not on call this weekend. How did you manage it?"

"Threats and bribery," he drawled. "We both worked last Christmas holidays, remember?"

"I guess we did. At each other's throats," she recalled demurely.

"Oh, that was necessary," he returned, rolling lazily onto his side and propping on an elbow. "If I hadn't snapped at you constantly, I'd have been laying you down on examination couches every other day."

"Wh...what?" she stammered.

He reached out and brushed back a long strand of blond hair from her face. "You backed away every time I came close to you," he said quietly. "It was all that saved you. I've wanted you for a long, long time, Dr. Blakely, and I've fought it like a madman."

"You were in love with Jane Parker," she said.

"Not for a long time," he said. He traced her cheek lightly. "The way I felt about her was a habit. It was one I broke when she married Todd Burke. Although, like you, he seems to think Jane and I were an item even after they married. He's taken a lot of convincing. So have you."

She moved uncomfortably. "Everyone talked about you and Jane, not just me."

"I know. Small communities have their good points and their bad points." His finger had reached her mouth. He was exploring it blatantly.

"Could you...not do that, please?" she asked unsteadily.

"Why? You like it. So do I." He moved closer, easing one long, hard-muscled leg over hers to stay her as he shifted so that she lay on her back, looking up at him in the dim light.

"I can feel your heart beating right through your rib cage," he remarked with his mouth poised just above hers. "I can hear your breath fluttering." His hand slid blatantly right down over her breast, pausing there to tease its tip into a hard rise. "Feel that?" he murmured, bending. "Your body likes me."

She opened her mouth, but no words escaped the sudden hard, warm pressure of his lips. She stiffened, but only for a few seconds. It was Christmas Eve and she loved him. There was no defense; none at all.

He seemed to know that, because he wasn't insistent or demanding. He lay, just kissing her, his lips tender as they moved against hers, his hand still gently caressing her body.

"We both know," he whispered, "why your body makes every response it does to the stimuli of my touch. But what no one really understands is why we both enjoy it so much."

"Cause...and effect?" she suggested, gasping when

his hand found its way under the sweatshirt and the lacy bra she was wearing to her soft flesh.

He shook his head. "I don't think so. Reach behind you and unfasten this," he added gently, tugging on the elastic band.

She did as he asked, feeling brazen.

"That's better." He traced over her slowly, his eyes on her face while he explored every inch of her above the waist. "Can you give this up?" he asked seriously.

"Wh...what?"

"Can you give it up?" he replied. "You aren't responsive to other men, or you wouldn't still be in your present pristine state. You allow me liberties that I'm certain you've never permitted any other man." He cupped her blatantly and caressed her. She arched, shivering. "You see?" he asked quietly. "You love my touch. I can give you something that you've apparently never experienced. Do you think you can find it with someone else, Lou?"

She felt his mouth cover hers. She didn't have enough breath to answer him, although the answer was certainly in the negative. She couldn't bear the thought of letting someone else be this intimate with her. She looped her arms around his neck and only sighed jerkily when he moved, easing his length against her, his legs between both of hers, so that when his hips pressed down again, she could feel every hardening line of his body.

"Jebediah," she moaned, and she wasn't certain if she was protesting or pleading.

His mouth found her closed eyelids and tasted the

helpless tears of pleasure that rained from them. His hips shifted and she jerked at the surge of pleasure.

He felt it, too, like a throbbing ache. "We're good together," he whispered. "Even like this. Can you imagine how it would feel to lie naked under me like this?"

She cried out, burying her face in his neck.

His lips traced her eyelashes, his tongue tasted them. But his body lay very still over hers, not moving, not insisting. Her nails dug into his shoulders as she felt her control slipping away.

But he still had his own control. He soothed her, every soft kiss undemanding and tender. But he didn't move away.

"A year," he whispered. "And we knew nothing about each other, nothing at all." He nibbled her lips, smiling when they trembled. "Trains and old movies, opera and cooking and horseback riding. We have more in common than I ever dreamed."

She had to force her body to lie still. She wanted to wrap her legs tight around him and kiss him until she stopped aching.

He seemed to know it, because his hips moved in a sensual caress that made her hands clench at his shoulders. "No fear of the unknown?" he whispered wickedly. "No virginal terror?"

"I'm a doctor." She choked out the words.

"So am I."

"I mean, I know...what to expect."

He chuckled. "No, you don't. You only know the mechanics of it. You don't know that you're going to crave almost more than I can give you, or that at the last minute you're going to sob like a hurt child."

She was too far gone to be embarrassed. "I don't have anything," she said miserably.

"Anything...?" He probed gently.

"To use."

"Oh. That." He chuckled and kissed her again, so tenderly that she felt cherished. "You won't need it tonight. I don't think babies should be born out of wedlock. Do you?"

She wasn't thinking. "Well, no. What does that have to do...with this?"

"Lou!"

She felt her cheeks burn. "Oh! You mean...!"

He laughed outrageously. "You've really gone off the deep end, haven't you?" he teased. "When people make love, the woman might get pregnant," he explained in a whisper. "Didn't you listen to the biology lectures?"

She hit him. "Of course I did! I wasn't thinking... Jeb!"

He was closer than he'd ever been and she was shivering, lost, helpless as she felt him in a burning, aching intimacy that only made it all worse.

He pressed her close and then rolled away, while he could. "God, we're explosive!" he said huskily, lying very still on his belly. "You're going to have to marry me soon, Lou. Very soon."

She was sitting up, holding her knees to her chest, trying to breathe. It had never been that bad. She said so, without realizing that she'd spoken aloud.

"It will get worse, too," he said heavily. "I want you. I've never wanted you so much."

"But, Jane..."

He was laughing, very softly. He wasn't angry anymore. He rolled over and sat up beside her. He turned her face up to his. "I broke it off with Jane," he said gently. "Do you want to know why, now?"

"You…you did?"

He nodded.

"You never said that you ended it."

"There was no reason to. You wouldn't let me close enough to find out if we had anything going for us, and it didn't seem to matter what I said, you wanted to believe that I was out of my mind over Jane."

"Everyone said you were," she muttered.

He lifted an eyebrow. "I'm not everyone."

"I know." She reached out hesitantly and touched him. It was earthshaking, that simple act. She touched his hair and his face and then his lean, hard mouth. A funny smile drew up her lips.

"Don't stop there," he murmured, drawing her free hand down to his sweatshirt.

Her heart jumped. She looked at him uncertainly.

"I won't let you seduce me," he mused. "Does that make you feel more confident?"

"It was pretty bad a few minutes ago," she said seriously. "I don't want… Well, to hurt you."

"This won't," he said. "Trust me."

"I suppose I must," she admitted. "Or I'd have left months ago for another job."

"That makes sense."

He guided her hand under the thick, white fabric and drew it up until her fingers settled in the thick, curling hair that covered his chest. But it wasn't enough. She wanted to look…

There was just enough light so that he could see

what she wanted in her expression. With a faint smile, he pulled the sweatshirt off and tossed it to one side.

She stared. He was beautiful like that, she thought dizzily, with broad shoulders and muscular arms. His chest was covered by a thick, wide wedge of reddish-gold hair that ran down to the buckle of his belt.

He reached for her, lifting her over him so that they were sitting face-to-face, joined where their bodies forked. She shivered at the stark intimacy, because she could feel every muscle, almost every cell of him.

"It gets better," he said softly. He reached down and found the hem of her own sweatshirt. Seconds later, that and her bra joined his sweatshirt on the floor. He looked down at her, savoring the hard peaks that rose like rubies from the whiteness of her breasts. Then he drew her to him and enveloped her against him, so that they were skin against skin. And he shivered, too, this time.

Her hands smoothed over his back, savoring his warm muscles. She searched for his mouth and for the first time, she kissed him. But even though it was sensual, and she could feel him wanting her, there was tenderness between them, not lust.

He groaned as his body surged against her, and then he laughed at the sudden heat of it.

"Jeb?" she whispered at his lips.

"It's all right," he said. "We won't go all the way. Kiss me again."

She did, clinging, and the world rocked around them.

"I love you," she murmured brokenly. "So much!"

His mouth bit into hers hungrily, his arms contracted. For a few seconds, it was as if electricity fused them together. Finally he was able to lift his lips, and his hands caught her hips to keep them still.

"Sorry," she said demurely.

"Oh, I like it," he replied ruefully. "But we're getting in a bit over our heads."

He lifted her away and stood up, pulling her with him. They looked at each other for a long moment before he handed her things to her and pulled his sweatshirt back on.

He watched the trains go around while she replaced her disheveled clothing. Then, with his hands in his pockets, he glanced down at her.

"That's why I broke up with Jane," he said matter-of-factly.

She was jealous, angry. "Because she wouldn't go all the way with you?"

He chuckled. "No. Because I didn't want her sexually."

She watched the trains and counted the times they crossed the joined tracks. Her mind must not be working. "What did you say?" she asked politely, turning to him.

"I said I was never able to want Jane sexually," he said simply. "To put it simply, she couldn't arouse me."

CHAPTER ELEVEN

"A WOMAN CAN arouse any man if she tries hard enough," she said pointedly.

"Maybe so," he said, smiling, "but Jane just never interested me like that. It was too big a part of marriage to take a chance on, so I gradually stopped seeing her. Burke came along, and before any of us knew it, she was married. But I was her security blanket after the accident, and it was hard for her to let go. You remember how she depended on me."

She nodded. Even at the time, it had hurt.

"But apparently she and her husband have more than a platonic relationship, if their forthcoming happy event is any indication," he said, chuckling. "And I'm delighted for them."

"I never dreamed that it was like that for you, with her," she said, dazed. "I mean, you and I...!"

"Yes, indeed, you and I," he agreed, nodding. "I touch you and it's like a shot of lightning in my veins. I get drunk on you."

"So do I, on you," she confessed. "But there's a difference, isn't there? I mean, you just want me."

"Do I?" he asked gently. "Do I really just want you? Could lust be as tender as this? Could simple desire explain the way we are together?"

"I love you," she said slowly.

"Yes," he said, his eyes glittering at her. "And I love you, Lou," he added quietly.

Dreams came true. She hadn't known. Her eyes were full of wonder as she looked at him and saw them in his own eyes. It was Christmas, a time of miracles, and here was one.

He didn't speak. He just looked at her. After a minute, he picked up the two parcels he'd put under the tree and handed them to her.

"But it's not Christmas," she protested.

"Yes, it is. Open them."

She only hesitated for a minute, because the curiosity was too great. She opened the smallest one and inside was a gray jeweler's box. With a quick glance at him, she opened it, to find half a key chain inside. She felt her heart race like a watch. It was half of a heart, in pure gold.

"Now the other one," he said, taking the key chain while she fumbled the paper off the second present.

Inside that box was the other half of the heart.

"Now put them together," he instructed.

She did, her eyes magnetized to the inscription. It was in French: *plus que hier, moins que demain.*

"Can you read it?" he asked softly.

"It says—" she had to stop and clear her throat "—more than yesterday, less than tomorrow."

"Which is how much I love you," he said. "I meant to ask you again tomorrow morning to marry me," he said. "But this is as good a time as any for you to say yes. I know you're afraid of marriage. But I love you and you love me. We've got enough in common to keep us together even after all the passion burns out, if it ever does. We'll work out something about your job and children. I'm not your father and you're not your mother. Take a chance, Lou. Believe me, there's very little risk that we won't make it together."

She hadn't spoken. She had both halves of the key chain in her hands and she was looking at them, amazed that he would have picked something so sentimental and romantic for a Christmas gift. He hadn't known if he could get her to stay or not, but he would have shown her his heart all the same. It touched her as a more expensive present wouldn't have.

"When did you get them?" she asked through a dry throat.

"After you left the jeweler's," he said surprisingly. "I believe in miracles," he added gently. "I see incredible things every day. I'm hoping for another one, right now."

She raised her eyes. Even in the dim light, he could see the sparkle of tears, the hope, the pleasure, the disbelief in her face.

"Yes?" he asked softly.

She couldn't manage the word. She nodded, and the next instant, she was in his arms, against him, close and safe and warm while his mouth ravished her lips.

It was a long time before he had enough to satisfy him, even momentarily. He wrapped her up tightly and rocked her in his arms, barely aware of the train chugging along at their feet. His arms were faintly unsteady and his voice, when he laughed, was husky and deep.

"My God, I thought I was going to lose you." He ground out the words. "I didn't know what to do, what to say, to keep you here."

"All you ever had to say was that you loved me," she whispered. "I would have taken any risk for it."

His arms tightened. "Didn't you know, you blind bat?"

"No, I didn't! I don't read minds, and you never said—!"

His mouth covered hers again, stopping the words. He laughed against her breath, anticipating arguments over the years that would be dealt with in exactly this way, as she gave in to him generously, headlong in her response, clinging as if she might die without his mouth on hers.

"No long engagement," he groaned against her mouth. "I can't stand it!"

"Neither can I," she admitted. "Next week?"

"Next week!" He kissed her again. "And I'm not going home tonight."

She laid her cheek against his chest, worried.

He smoothed her hair. "We won't make love," he assured her. "But you'll sleep in my arms. I can't bear to be parted from you again."

"Oh, Jeb," she whispered huskily. "That's the sweetest thing to say!"

"Don't you feel it, too?" he asked knowingly.

"Yes. I don't want to leave you, either."

He chuckled with the newness of belonging to someone. It was going to be, he decided, the best marriage of all time. He looked down into her eyes and saw years and years of happiness ahead of them. He said so. She didn't answer him. She reached up, and her lips said it for her.

THE GOING-AWAY party that Jane Burke threw for Lou became a congratulatory party, because it fell on the day after Coltrain and Lou were married.

They almost stayed at home, so wrapped up in the ecstasy of their first lovemaking that they wouldn't even get out of bed the next morning.

That morning, he lay looking at his new bride with wonder and unbounded delight. There were tears in her eyes, because it had been painful for her at first. But the love in them made him smile.

"It won't be like that again," he assured her.

"I know." She looked at him blatantly, with pride in his fit, muscular body, in his manhood. She lifted her eyes back up. "I was afraid…"

He traced her mouth, his eyes solemn. "It will be easier the next time," he said tenderly. "It will get better every time we love each other."

"I know. I'm not afraid anymore." She touched his hard mouth and smiled. "You were apprehensive, too, weren't you?"

"At first," he had to admit.

"I thought you were never going to start," she said on a sigh. "I know why you took so long, so that I'd be ready when it happened, but I wondered if you were planning on a night of torture."

He chuckled. "You weren't the only one who suffered." He kissed her tenderly. "It hurt me, to have to hurt you, did you know? I wanted to stop, but it was too late. I was in over my head before I knew it. I couldn't even slow down."

"Oh, I never noticed," she told him, delighted. "You made me crazy."

"That goes double for me."

"I thought I knew everything," she mused. "I'm a doctor, after all. But theory and practice are very different."

"Yes. Later, when you're in fine form again, I'll show you some more ways to put theory into practice," he drawled.

She laughed and pummeled him.

They were early for Jane's get-together, and the way they clung to each other would have been more than enough to prove that they were in love, without the matching Victorian wedding bands they'd chosen.

"You look like two halves of a whole," Jane said, looking from Lou's radiant face to Copper's.

"We know," he said ruefully. "They rode us high at the hospital when we made rounds earlier."

"Rounds!" Todd exclaimed. "On your honeymoon?"

"We're doctors," Lou reminded him, grinning. "It goes with the job description. I'll probably be trying to examine patients on the way into the delivery room eventually."

Jane clung to her husband's hand and sighed. "I can't wait for that to happen. Cherry's over the moon, too. She'll be such a good older sister. She works so hard at school. She's studying to be a surgeon, you know," she added.

"I wouldn't know," Copper muttered, "having already had four letters from her begging for an hour of my time to go over what she needs to study most during her last few years in school."

Jane chuckled. "That's my fault. I encouraged her to talk to you."

"It's all right," he said, cuddling Lou closer. "I'll make time for her."

"I see that everything finally worked out for you two," Todd said a little sheepishly. "Sorry about the last time we met."

"Oh, you weren't the only wild-eyed lunatic around, Mr. Burke," Lou said reminiscently. "I did my share of conclusion jumping and very nearly ruined my life because of it." She looked up at Coltrain adoringly. "I'm glad doctors are persistent."

"Yes." Coltrain chuckled. "So am I. There were times when I despaired. But Lionel saved us."

They frowned. "What?"

"Electric trains," Coltrain replied. "Don't you people know anything?"

"Not about trains. Those are kids' toys, for God's sake," Burke said.

"No, they are not," Lou said. "They're adult toys. People buy them for their children so they'll have an excuse to play with them. Not having children, we have no excuses."

"That's why we want to start a family right away," Coltrain said with a wicked glance at Lou. "So that we have excuses. You should see her layout," he added admiringly. "My God, it's bigger than mine!"

Todd and Jane tried not to look at each other, failed and burst into outrageous laughter.

Coltrain glared at them. "Obviously," he told his new wife, "some people have no class, no breeding and no respect for the institution of marriage."

"What are you two laughing at?" Drew asked curiously, having returned to town just in time for the party, if not the wedding.

Jane bit her lower lip before she spoke. "Hers is bigger than his." She choked.

"Oh, for God's sake, come and dance!" Coltrain told Lou, shaking his head as he dragged her away. The others, behind them, were still howling.

Coltrain pulled Lou close and smiled against her hair as they moved to the slow beat of the music. There was a live band. Jane had pulled out all the stops, even if it wasn't going to be a goodbye party.

"Nice band," Dana remarked from beside them. "Congratulations, by the way," she added.

"Thanks," they echoed.

"Nickie didn't come," she added, tongue-in-cheek. "I believe she's just accepted a job in a Victoria hospital as a nurse trainee."

"Good for her," Coltrain said.

Dana chuckled. "Sure. See you."

She wandered away toward one of the hospital staff.

"She's a good loser, at least," Lou said drowsily.

"I wouldn't have been," he mused.

"You've got a new partner coming," she remembered suddenly, having overlooked it in the frantic pace of the past few days.

"Actually," he replied, "I don't know any doctors from Johns Hopkins who would want to come to Jacobsville to practice in a small partnership. The minute I do, of course, I'll hire him on the...oof!"

She'd stepped on his toe, hard.

"Well, I had to say something," he replied, wincing

as he stood on his foot. "You were holding all the aces. A man has his pride."

"You could have said you loved me," she said pointedly.

"I did. I do." He smiled slowly. "In a few hours, I'll take you home and prove it and prove it and prove it."

She flushed and pressed closer into his arms. "What a delicious idea."

"I thought so, too. Dance. At least while we're dancing I can hold you in public."

"So you can!"

Drew waltzed by with a partner. "Why don't you two go home?" he asked.

They laughed. "Time enough for private celebrations."

"I hope you have enough champagne," Drew said dryly, and danced on.

As IT HAPPENED, they had a magnum of champagne between them before Coltrain coaxed his wife back into bed and made up for her first time in ways that left her gasping and trembling in the aftermath.

"That," she gasped, "wasn't in any medical book I ever read!"

"Darlin', you've been reading the wrong books," he whispered, biting her lower lip softly. "And don't go to sleep. I haven't finished yet."

"What?"

He laughed at her expression. "Did you think that was *all?*"

Her eyes widened as he moved over her and slid between her long legs. "But, it hasn't been five minutes, you can't, you *can't...!*"

He not only could. He did.

TWO MONTHS LATER, on Valentine's Day, Copper Coltrain gave his bride of six weeks a ruby necklace in the shape of a heart. She gave him the results of the test she'd had the day before. He told her later that the "valentine" she'd given him was the best one he'd ever had.

Nine months later, Lou's little valentine was delivered in Jacobsville's hospital; and he was christened Joshua Jebediah Coltrain.

* * * * *

KINGMAN

For Matt and Elisha

CHAPTER ONE

TIFFANY SAW HIM in the distance, riding the big black stallion that had already killed one man. She hated the horse, even as she admitted silently how regal it looked with the tall, taciturn man on its back. A killer horse it might be, but it respected Kingman Marshall. Most people around Jacobsville, Texas, did. His family had lived on the Guadalupe River there since the Civil War, on a ranch called Lariat.

It was spring, and that meant roundup. It was nothing unusual to see the owner of Lariat in the saddle at dawn lending a hand to rope a stray calf or help work the branding. King kept fit with ranch work, and despite the fact that he shared an office and a business partnership with her father in land and cattle, his staff didn't see a lot of him.

This year, they were using helicopters to mass the far-flung cattle, and they had a corral set up on a wide flat stretch of land where they could dip the cattle, check them, cut out the calves for branding and separate them from their mothers. It was physically demanding work, and no job for a tenderfoot. King wouldn't let Tiffany near it, but it wasn't a front-row seat at the corral that she wanted. If she could just get his attention away from the milling cattle on the wide, rolling plain that led to the Guadalupe River, if he'd just look her way...

She stood up on a rickety lower rung of the gray wood fence, avoiding the sticky barbed wire, and waved her creamy Stetson at him. She was a picture of young elegance in her tan jodhpurs and sexy pink silk blouse and high black boots. She was a debutante. Her father, Harrison Blair, was King's business partner and friend, and if she chased King, her father encouraged her. It would be a marriage made in heaven. That is, if she could find some way to convince King of it. He was elusive and quite abrasively masculine. It might take more than a young lady of almost twenty-one with a sheltered, monied background to land him. But, then, Tiffany had confidence in herself; she was beautiful and intelligent.

Her long black hair hung to her waist in back, and she refused to have it cut. It suited her tall, slender figure and made an elegant frame for her soft oval face and wide green eyes and creamy complexion. She had a sunny smile, and it never faded. Tiffany was always full of fire, burning with a love of life that her father often said had been reflected in her long-dead mother.

"King!" she called, her voice clear, and it carried in the early-morning air.

He looked toward her. Even at the distance, she could see that cold expression in his pale blue eyes, on his lean, hard face with its finely chiseled features. He was a rich man. He worked hard, and he played hard. He had women, Tiffany knew he did, but he was nothing if not discreet. He was a man's man, and he lived like one. There was no playful boy in that tall, fit body. He'd grown up years ago, the boyishness burned out of him by a rich, alcoholic father who demanded blind obedience from the only child of his shallow, runaway wife.

She watched him ride toward her, easy elegance in the saddle. He reined in at the fence, smiling down at her with faint arrogance. He was powerfully built, with long legs and slim hips and broad shoulders. There wasn't an ounce of fat on him, and with his checked red shirt open at the throat, she got fascinating glimpses of bronzed muscle and thick black hair on the expanse of his sexy chest. Jeans emphasized the powerful muscles of his legs, and he had big, elegant hands that hers longed to feel in passion. Not that she was likely to. He treated her like a child most of the time, or at best, a minor irritation.

"You're out early, tidbit," he remarked in a deep, velvety voice with just a hint of Texas drawl. His eyes, under the shade of his wide-brimmed hat, were a pale, grayish blue and piercing as only blue eyes could be.

"I'm going to be twenty-one tomorrow," she said pertly. "I'm having a big bash to celebrate, and you have to come. Black tie, and don't you dare bring anyone. You're mine, for the whole evening. It's my birthday and on my birthday I want presents—and you're it. My big present."

His dark brows lifted with amused indulgence. "You might have told me sooner that I was going to be a birthday present," he said. "I have to be in Omaha early Saturday."

"You have your own plane," she reminded him. "You can fly."

"I have to sleep sometimes," he murmured.

"I wouldn't touch that line with a ten-foot pole," she drawled, peeking at him behind her long lashes. "Will you come? If you don't, I'll stuff a pillow up my dress and accuse you of being the culprit. And your reputation will be ruined, you'll be driven out of town on a rail, they'll tar and feather you…"

He chuckled softly at the vivid sparkle in her eyes, the radiant smile. "You witch," he accused. "They'd probably give me a medal for getting through your defenses."

She wondered how he knew that, and reasoned that her proud parent had probably told him all about her reputation for coolness with men.

He lit a cigarette, took a long draw from and blew it out with faint impatience. "Little girls and their little whims," he mused. "All right, I'll whirl you around the floor and toast your coming-of-age, but I won't stay. I can't spare the time."

"You'll work yourself to death," she complained, and she was solemn now. "You're only thirty-four and you look forty."

"Times are hard, honey," he mused, smiling at the intensity in that glowering young face. "We've had low prices and drought. It's all I can do to keep my financial head above water."

"You could take the occasional break," she advised. "And I don't mean a night on the town. You could get away from it all and just rest."

"They're full up at the Home," he murmured, grinning at her exasperated look. "Honey, I can't afford vacations, not with times so hard. What are you wearing for this coming-of-age party?" he asked to divert her.

"A dream of a dress. White silk, very low in front, with diamanté straps and a white gardenia in my hair." She laughed.

He pursed his lips. He might as well humor her. "That sounds dangerous," he said softly.

"It will be," she promised, teasing him with her eyes. "You might even notice that I've grown up."

He frowned a little. That flirting wasn't new, but it was disturbing lately. He found himself avoiding little Miss Blair, without really understanding why. His body stirred even as he looked at her, and he moved restlessly in the saddle. She was years too young for him, and a virgin to boot, according to her doting, sheltering father. All those years of obsessive parental protection had led to a very immature and unavailable girl. It wouldn't do to let her too close. Not that anyone ever got close to Kingman Marshall, not even his infrequent lovers. He had good reason to keep women at a distance. His upbringing had taught him too well that women were untrustworthy and treacherous.

"What time?" he asked on a resigned note.

"About seven?"

He paused thoughtfully for a minute. "Okay." He tilted his wide-brimmed hat over his eyes. "But only for an hour or so."

"Great!"

He didn't say goodbye. Of course, he never had. He wheeled the stallion and rode off, man and horse so damned arrogant that she felt like flinging something at his tall head. He was delicious, she thought, and her body felt hot all over just looking at him. On the ground he towered over her, lean and hard-muscled and sexy as all hell. She loved watching him.

With a long, unsteady sigh, she finally turned away and remounted her mare. She wondered sometimes why she bothered hero-worshiping such a man. One of these days he'd get married and she'd just die. God forbid that he'd marry anybody but her!

That was when the first shock of reality hit her squarely between the eyes. Why, she had to ask herself, would a man like that, a mature man with all the worldly advantages, want a young and inexperienced woman like her at his side? The question worried her so badly that she almost lost control of her mount. She'd never questioned her chances with King before. She'd never dared. The truth of her situation was unpalatable and a little frightening. She'd never even considered a life without him. What if she had to?

As she rode back toward her own house, on the property that joined King's massive holdings, she noticed the color of the grass. It was like barbed wire in places, very dry and scant. That boded ill for the cattle, and if rain didn't come soon, all that new grass was going to burn up under a hot Texas sun. She knew a lot about the cattle business. After all, her father had owned feedlots since her youth, and she was an only child who worked hard to share his interests. She knew that if there wasn't enough hay by the end of summer, King was going to have to import feed to get his cattle through the winter. The cost of that was prohibitive. It had something to do with black figures going red in the last column, and that could mean disaster for someone with a cow-calf operation the size of King's.

Ah, well, she mused, if King went bust, she supposed that she could get a job and support him. Just the thought of it doubled her over with silvery laughter. King's pride would never permit that sort of help.

Even the Guadalupe was down. She sat on a small rise in the trees, looking at its watery width. The river, like this part of Texas, had a lot of history in it. Archaeologists had found Indian camps on the Guadalupe that dated back seven thousand years, and because of that, part of it had been designated a National Historic Shrine.

In more recent history, freight handlers on their way to San Antonio had crossed the river in DeWitt County on a ferryboat. In Cuero, a nice drive from Lariat, was the beginning of the Chisolm Trail. In nearby Goliad County was the small town of Goliad, where Texas patriots were slaughtered by the Mexican army back in 1836, just days after the bloodbath at the Alamo. Looking at the landscape, it was easy to imagine the first Spanish settlers, the robed priests founding missions, the Mexican Army with proud, arrogant Santa Anna at its fore, the Texas patriots fighting to the last breath, the pioneers and the settlers, the Indians and the immigrants, the cowboys and cattle barons and desperadoes. Tiffany sighed, trying to imagine it all.

King, she thought, would have fitted in very well with the past. Except that he had a blasé attitude toward life and women, probably a result of having too much money and time on his hands. Despite his hard work at roundup, he spent a lot of time in his office, and on the phone, and also on the road. He was so geared to making money that he seemed to have forgotten how to enjoy it. She rode home slowly, a little depressed because she'd had to work so hard just to get King to agree to come to her party. And still haunting her was that unpleasant speculation about a future without King.

Her father was just on his way out the door when she walked up from the stables. The house was stucco, a big sprawling yellow ranch house. It had a small formal garden off the patio, a swimming pool behind, a garage where Tiffany's red Jaguar convertible and her father's gray Mercedes-Benz dwelled, and towering live oak and pecan trees all around. The Guadalupe River was close, but not too close, and Texas stretched like a yellow-green bolt of cloth in all directions to an open, spacious horizon.

"There you are," Harrison Blair muttered. He was tall and gray-headed and green-eyed. Very elegant, despite his slight paunch and his habit of stooping because of a bad back. "I'm late for a board meeting. The caterer called about your party…something about the cheese straws not doing."

"I'll give Lettie a ring. She'll do them for her if I ask her nicely," she promised, grinning as she thought of the elderly lady who was her godmother. "King's coming to my party. I ran him to ground at the river."

He looked over his glasses at her, his heavily lined face vaguely reminiscent of an anorexic bassett hound; not that she'd ever have said anything hurtful to her parent. She adored him. "You make him sound like a fox," he remarked. "Careful, girl, or you'll chase him into a hollow stump and lose him."

"Not me," she laughed, her whole face bright with young certainty. "You just wait. I'll be dangling a diamond one of these days. He can't resist me. He just doesn't know it yet."

He only shook his head. She was so young. She hadn't learned yet that life had a way of giving with one hand, only to take back with the other. Oh, well, she had plenty of years to learn those hard lessons. Let her enjoy it while she could. He knew that King would never settle for a child-woman like his beautiful daughter, but it was something she was going to have to accept one of these days.

"I hope to be back by four," he said, reaching down to peck her affectionately on one cheek. "Are we having champagne? If we are, I hope you told the caterer. I'm not breaking out my private stock until you get married."

"Yes, we are, and yes, I told them," she assured him. "After all, I don't become twenty-one every day."

He studied her with quiet pride. "You look like your mother," he said. "She'd be as proud of you as I am."

She smiled faintly. "Yes." Her mother had been dead a long time, but the memories were bittersweet. The late Mrs. Blair had been vivacious and sparkling, a sapphire in a diamond setting. Her father had never remarried, and seemed not to be inclined toward the company of other women. He'd told Tiffany once that true love was a pretty rare commodity. He and her mother had been so blessed. He was content enough with his memories.

"How many people are we expecting, by the way?" he asked as he put on his Stetson.

"About forty," she said. "Not an overwhelming number. Just some of my friends and some of King's." She grinned. "I'm making sure they're compatible before I railroad him to the altar."

He burst out laughing. She was incorrigible and definitely his child, with her keen business sense, he told himself.

"Do you reckon they'll have a lot in common?"

She pursed her pretty lips. "Money and cattle," she reminded him, "are always a good mix. Besides, King's friends are almost all politicians. They pride themselves on finding things in common with potential voters."

He winked. "Good thought."

She waved and went to call Lettie about doing the cheese straws and the caterers to finalize the arrangements. She was a good hostess, and she enjoyed parties. It was a challenge to find compatible people and put them together in a hospitable atmosphere. So far, she'd done well. Now it was time to show King how organized she was.

The flowers and the caterer had just arrived when she went down the long hall to her room to dress. She was nibbling at a chicken wing on the way up, hoping that she wouldn't starve. There was going to be an hors d'oeuvres table and a drinks bar, but no sit-down dinner. She'd decided that she'd rather dance than eat, and she'd hired a competent local band to play. They were in the ballroom now, tuning up, while Cass, the housekeeper, was watching some of the ranch's lean, faintly disgusted cowboys set up chairs and clear back the furniture. They hated being used as inside labor and their accusing glances let her know it. But she grinned and they melted. Most of them were older hands who'd been with her father since she was a little girl. Like her father, they'd spoiled her, too.

She darted up the staircase, wild with excitement about the evening ahead. King didn't come to the house often, only when her father wanted to talk business away from work, or occasionally for drinks with some of her father's acquaintances. To have him come to a party was new and stimulating. Especially if it ended the way she planned. She had her sights well and truly set on the big rancher. Now she had to take aim.

CHAPTER TWO

TIFFANY'S EVENING GOWN was created by a San Antonio designer, who also happened to own a boutique in one of the larger malls there. Since Jacobsville was halfway between San Antonio and Victoria, it wasn't too long a drive. Tiffany had fallen in love with the gown at first sight. The fact that it had cost every penny of her allowance hadn't even slowed her down. It was simple, sophisticated, and just the thing to make King realize she was a woman. The low-cut bodice left the curve of her full breasts seductively bare and the diamanté straps were hardly any support at all. They looked as if they might give way any second, and that was the charm of the dress. Its silky white length fell softly to just the top of her oyster satin pumps with their rhinestone clips. She put her long hair in an elaborate hairdo, and pinned it with diamond hairpins. The small silk gardenia in a soft wave was a last-minute addition, and the effect was dynamite. She looked innocently seductive. Just right.

She was a little nervous as she made her way down the curve of the elegant, gray-carpeted staircase. Guests were already arriving, and most of these early ones were around King's age. They were successful businessmen, politicians mostly, with exquisitely dressed wives and girlfriends on their arms. For just an instant, Tiffany felt young and uneasy. And then she pinned on her finishing-school smile and threw herself into the job of hostessing.

She pretended beautifully. No one knew that her slender legs were unsteady. In fact, a friend of one of the younger politicians, a bachelor clerk named Wyatt Corbin, took the smile for an invitation and stuck to her like glue. He was good-looking in a tall, gangly redheaded way, but he wasn't very sophisticated. Even if he had been, Tiffany had her heart set on King, and she darted from group to group, trying to shake her admirer.

Unfortunately he was stubborn. He led her onto the dance floor and into a gay waltz, just as King came into the room.

Tiffany felt like screaming. King looked incredibly handsome in his dark evening clothes. His tuxedo emphasized his dark good looks, and the white of his silk shirt brought out his dark eyes and hair. He spared Tiffany an amused glance and turned to meet the onslaught of two unattached, beautiful older women. His secretary, Carla Stark, hadn't been invited—Tiffany had been resolute about that. There was enough gossip about those two already, and Carla was unfair competition.

It was the unkindest cut of all, and thanks to this redheaded clown dancing with her, she'd lost her chance. She smiled sweetly at him and suddenly brought down her foot on his toe with perfect accuracy.

"Ouch!" he moaned, sucking in his breath.

"I'm so sorry, Wyatt," Tiffany murmured, batting her eyelashes at him. "Did I step on your poor foot?"

"My fault, I moved the wrong way," he drawled, forcing a smile. "You dance beautifully, Miss Blair."

What a charming liar, she thought. She glanced at King, but he wasn't even looking at her. He was talking and smiling at a devastating blonde, probably a politician's daughter, who looked as if she'd just discovered the best present of all under a Christmas tree. *No thanks to me*, Tiffany thought miserably.

Well, two could play at ignoring, she thought, and turned the full effect of her green eyes on Wyatt. Well, happy birthday to me, she thought silently, and asked him about his job. It was assistant city clerk or some such thing, and he held forth about his duties for the rest of the waltz, and the one that followed.

King had moved to the sofa with the vivacious little blonde, where he looked as if he might set up housekeeping. Tiffany wanted to throw back her head and scream with outrage. Whose party was this, anyway, and which politician was that little blonde with? She began scanning the room for unattached older men.

"I guess I ought to dance with Becky, at least once," Wyatt sighed after a minute. "She's my cousin. I didn't have anyone else to bring. Excuse me a second, will you?"

He left her and went straight toward the blonde who was dominating King. But if he expected the blonde to sacrifice that prize, he was sadly mistaken. They spoke in whispers, while King glanced past Wyatt at Tiffany with a mocking, worldly look. She turned her back and went to the punch bowl.

Wyatt was back in a minute. "She doesn't mind being deserted," he chuckled. "She's found a cattle baron to try her wiles on. That's Kingman Marshall over there, you know."

Tiffany looked at him blankly. "Oh, is it?" she asked innocently, and tried not to show how furious she really was. Between Wyatt and his cousin, they'd ruined her birthday party.

"I wonder why he's here?" he frowned.

She caught his hand. "Let's dance," she muttered, and dragged him back onto the dance floor.

For the rest of the evening, she monopolized Wyatt, ignoring King as pointedly as if she'd never seen him before and never cared to again. Let him flirt with other women at her party. Let him break her heart. He was never going to know it. She'd hold her chin up if it killed her. She smiled at Wyatt and flirted outrageously, the very life and soul of her party, right up to the minute when she cut the cake and asked Wyatt to help her serve it. King didn't seem to notice or care that she ignored him. But her father was puzzled, staring at her incomprehensibly.

"This party is so boring," Tiffany said an hour later, when she felt she couldn't take another single minute of the blonde clinging to King on the dance floor. "Let's go for a ride."

Wyatt looked uncomfortable. "Well... I came in a truck," he began.

"We'll take my Jag."

"You've got a Jaguar?"

She didn't need to say another word. Without even a glance in King's direction, she waved at her father and blew him a kiss, dragging Wyatt along behind her toward the front door. Not that he needed much coaxing. He seemed overwhelmed when she tossed him the keys and climbed into the passenger seat of the sleek red car.

"You mean, I can drive this?" he burst out.

"Sure. Go ahead. It's insured. But I like to go fast, Wyatt," she said. And for tonight, that was true. She was sick of the party, sick of King, sick of her life. She hurt in ways she'd never realized she could. She only wanted to get away, to escape.

He started the car and stood down on the accelerator. Tiffany had her window down, letting the breeze whip through her hair. She deliberately pulled out the diamond hairpins and tucked them into her purse, letting her long, black hair free and fly on the wind. The champagne she'd had to drink was beginning to take effect and was making her feel very good indeed. The speed of the elegant little car added to her false euphoria. Why, she didn't care about King's indifference. She didn't care at all!

"What a car!" Wyatt breathed, wheeling it out onto the main road.

"Isn't it, though?" she laughed. She leaned back and closed her eyes. She wouldn't think about King. "Go faster, Wyatt, we're positively crawling! I love speed, don't you?"

Of course he did. And he didn't need a second prompting. He put the accelerator peddle to the floor, and twelve cylinders jumped into play as the elegant vehicle shot forward like its sleek and dangerous namesake.

She laughed, silvery bells in the darkness, enjoying

the unbridled speed, the fury of motion. Yes, this would blow away all the cobwebs, all the hurt, this would...!

The sound of sirens behind them brought her to her senses. She glanced over the seat and saw blue bubbles spinning around, atop a police car.

"Oh, for heaven's sake, where did he come from!" she gasped. "I never saw the car. They must parachute down from treetops," she muttered, and then giggled at her own remark.

Wyatt slowed the car and pulled onto the shoulder, his face rapidly becoming the color of his hair. He glanced at Tiffany. "Gosh, I'm sorry. And on your birthday, too!"

"I don't care. I told you to do it," she reminded him.

A tall policeman came to the side of the car and watched Wyatt fumble to power the window down.

"Good God. *Wyatt?*" the officer gasped.

"That's right, Bill," Wyatt sighed, producing his driver's license. "Tiffany Blair, this is Bill Harris. He's one of our newest local policemen and a cousin of mine."

"Nice to meet you, Officer—although I wish it was under better circumstances," Tiffany said with a weak smile. "I should get the ticket, not Wyatt. It's my car, and I asked him to go faster."

"I clocked you at eighty-five, you know," he told Wyatt gently. "I sure do hate to do this, Wyatt. Mr. Clark is going to be pretty sore at you. He just had a mouthful to say about speeders."

"The mayor hates me anyway," Wyatt groaned.

"I won't tell him you got a ticket if you don't." Bill grinned.

"Want to bet he'll find out anyway? Just wait."

"It's all my fault," Tiffany muttered. "And it's my birthday...!"

A sleek, new black European sports car slid in behind the police car and came to a smooth, instant stop. A minute later, King got out and came along to join the small group.

"What's the trouble, Bill?" he asked the policeman.

"They were speeding, Mr. Marshall," the officer said. "I'll have to give him a ticket. He was mortally flying."

"I can guess why," King mused, staring past Wyatt at a pale Tiffany.

"Nobody held a gun on me," Wyatt said gently. "It's my own fault. I could have refused."

"The first lesson of responsibility," King agreed. "Learning to say no. Come on, Tiffany. You've caused enough trouble for one night. I'll drop you off on my way out."

"I won't go one step with you, King...!" she began furiously.

He went around to the passenger side of the Jag, opened the door, and tugged her out. His lean, steely fingers on her bare arm raised chills of excitement where they touched. "I don't have time to argue. You've managed to get Wyatt in enough trouble." He turned to Wyatt. "If you'll bring the Jag back, I think your cousin is ready to leave. Sorry to spoil your evening."

"It wasn't spoiled at all, Mr. Marshall," Wyatt said with a smile at Tiffany. "Except for the speeding ticket, I enjoyed every minute of it!"

"I did, too, Wyatt," Tiffany said. "I... King, will you stop dragging me?"

"No. Good night, Wyatt. Bill."

A chorus of good-nights broke the silence as King led an unwilling, sullen Tiffany back to his own leather-trimmed sports car. He helped her inside, got in under the wheel and started the powerful engine.

"I hate you, King," she ground out as he pulled onto the highway.

"Which is no reason at all for making a criminal of Wyatt."

She glared at him hotly through the darkness. "I did not make him a criminal! I only offered to let him drive the Jaguar."

"And told him how fast to go?"

"He wasn't complaining!"

He glanced sideways at her. Despite the rigid set of her body, and the temper on that lovely face, she excited him. One diamanté strap was halfway down a silky smooth arm, revealing more than a little of a tip-tilted breast. The silk fabric outlined every curve of her body, and he could smell the floral perfume that wafted around her like a seductive cloud. She put his teeth on edge, and it irritated him beyond all reason.

He lit a cigarette that he didn't even want, and abruptly put it out, remembering belatedly that he'd quit smoking just last week. And he was driving faster than he normally did. "I don't know why in hell you invited me over here," he said curtly, "if you planned to spend the whole evening with the damned city clerk."

"Assistant city clerk," she mumbled. She darted a glance at him and pressed a strand of long hair away from her mouth. He looked irritated. His face was harder than usual, and he was driving just as fast as Wyatt had been.

"Whatever the hell he is."

"I didn't realize you'd even noticed what I was doing, King," she replied sweetly, "what with Wyatt's pretty little cousin wrapped around you like a ribbon."

His eyebrows arched. "Wrapped around me?"

"Wasn't she?" she asked, averting her face. "Sorry. It seemed like it to me."

He pulled the car onto the side of the road and turned toward her, letting the engine idle. The hand holding the steering wheel clenched, but his dark eyes were steady on hers; she could see them in the light from the instrument panel.

"Were you jealous, honey?" he taunted, in a tone she'd never heard him use. It was deep and smooth and low-pitched. It made her young body tingle in the oddest way.

"I thought you were supposed to be my guest, that's all," she faltered.

"That's what I thought, too, until you started vamping Wyatt what's-his-name."

His finger toyed with the diamanté strap that had fallen onto her arm. She reached to tug it up, but his lean, hard fingers were suddenly there, preventing her.

Her eyes levered up to meet his quizzically, and in the silence of the car, she could hear her own heartbeat, like a faint drum.

The lean forefinger traced the strap from back to front, softly brushing skin that had never known a man's touch before. She stiffened a little, to feel it so lightly tracing the slope of her breast.

"They...they'll miss us," she said in a voice that sounded wildly high-pitched and frightened.

"Think so?"

He smiled slowly, because he was exciting her, and he liked it. He could see her breasts rising and falling with quick, jerky breaths. He could see her nipples peaking under that silky soft fabric. The pulse in her throat was quick, too, throbbing. She was coming-of-age tonight, in more ways than one.

He reached beside him and slowly, blatantly, turned off the engine before he turned back to Tiffany. There was a full moon, and the light of it and the subdued light of the instrument panel gave him all the illumination he needed.

"King," she whispered shakily.

"Don't panic," he said quietly. "It's going to be delicious."

She watched his hand move, as if she were paralyzed. It drew the strap even further off her arm, slowly, relentlessly, tugging until that side of her silky bodice fell to the hard tip of her nipple. And then he gave it a whisper of a push and it fell completely away, baring her pretty pink breast to eyes that had seen more than their share of women. But this was different. This was Tiffany, who was virginal and young and completely without experience.

That knowledge hardened his body. His lean fingers traced her collarbone, his eyes lifted to search her quiet, faintly shocked face. Her eyes were enormous. Probably this was all new to her, and perhaps a little frightening as well.

"You're of age, now. It has to happen with some-one," he said.

"Then... I want it to happen...with you," she whis-pered, her voice trembling, like her body.

His pulse jumped. His eyes darkened, glittered. "Do you? I wonder if you realize what you're getting into," he murmured. He bent toward her, noticing her sudden tension, her wide-eyed apprehension. He checked the slow movement, for an instant; long enough to whis-per, "I won't hurt you."

She leaned back against the leather seat as he turned toward her, her body tautening, trembling a little. But it wasn't fear that motivated her. As she met his smol-dering eyes, she slowly arched her back, to let the rest of the bodice fall, and saw the male desire in his dark eyes as they looked down at what the movement had uncovered.

"Your breasts are exquisite," he said absently, that tracing hand moving slowly, tenderly, down one tip-tilted slope, making her shudder. "Perfect."

"They ache," she whispered on a sob, her eyes half closed, in thrall to some physical paralysis that made her throb all over with exquisite sensations.

"I can do something about that," he mused with a brief smile.

His forefinger found the very tip of one small breast and traced around it gently, watching it go even harder, feeling it shudder with the tiny consummation. He heard the faint gasp break from her lips and looked up at her face, at her wide, misty eyes.

"Yes," he said, as if her expression told him everything. And it did. She wanted him. She'd let him do anything he wanted to do, and he felt hot all over.

She moved against the seat, her body in helpless control now, begging for something, for more than this. Her head went back, her full lips parting, hungry.

He slid his arm under her neck, bringing her body closer to his, his mouth poised just above hers. He watched her as his hand moved, and his lean fingers slowly closed over her breast, taking its soft weight and teasing the nipple with his thumb.

She cried softly at the unexpected pleasure, and bit her lower lip in helpless agony.

"Don't do that," he whispered, bending. "Let me…"

His hard lips touched hers, biting softly at them, tracing them warmly from one side to the other. His nose nuzzled against hers, relaxing her, gentling her, while his hand toyed softly with her breast. "Open your mouth, baby," he breathed as his head lowered again, and he met her open mouth with his.

She moaned harshly at the wild excitement he was arousing in her. She'd never dreamed that a kiss could be so intimate, so sweetly exciting. His tongue pushed past her startled lips, into the soft darkness of her mouth, teasing hers in a silence broken only by the sounds of breathing, and cloth against cloth.

"King," she breathed under his lips. Her hands bit into his hair, his nape, tugging. "Hard, King," she whispered shakily, "hard, hard…!"

He hadn't expected that flash of ardor. It caused him to be far rougher than he meant to. He crushed her mouth under his, the force of it bending her head back against his shoulder. His searching hand found first

one breast, then the other, savoring the warm silk of
their contours, the hard tips that told him how aroused
she was.

He forgot her age and the time and the place, and
suddenly jerked her across him, his hands easing her
into the crook of his arm as he bent his head to her
body.

"Sweet," he whispered harshly, opening his mouth
on her breast. "God, you're sweet…!"

She cried out from the shock of pleasure his mouth
gave her, a piercing little sound that excited him even
more, and her body arched up toward him like a silky
pink sacrifice. Her hands tangled in his thick black
hair, holding him there, tears of mingled frustration
and sweet anguish trailing down her hot cheeks as the
newness of passion racked her.

"Don't…stop," she whimpered, her hands contract-
ing at his nape, pulling him back to her. "Please!"

"I wonder if I could," he murmured with faint self-
contempt as he gave in to the exquisite pleasure of tasting her soft skin. "You taste of gardenia petals, except
right…here," he whispered as his lips suddenly tugged
at a hard nipple, working down until he took her silky
breast into his mouth in a warm, soft suction that made
her moan endlessly.

His steely fingers bit into her side as he moved the
dress further down and shifted her, letting his mouth
press warmly against soft skin, tracing her stomach
into the soft elastic of her briefs, tracing the briefs to
her hips and waist and then back up to the trembling
softness of her breasts.

She found the buttons of his jacket, his silk shirt,

and fumbled at them, whimpering as she struggled to make them come apart. She wanted to touch him, experience him as he was experiencing her. Without a clue as to what he might want, she tugged at the edges until he moved her hand aside and moved the fabric away for her. She flattened her palm against thick hair and pure man, caressing him with aching pleasure.

"Here," he whispered roughly, moving her so that her soft breasts were crushed against the abrasive warmth of his chest.

He wrapped her up tight, then, moving her against his hair-roughened skin in a delirium of passion, savoring the feel of her breasts, the silkiness of her skin against him. His body was demanding satisfaction, now, hard with urgent need. His hand slid down her back to her spine and he turned her just a little so that he could press her soft hips into his, and let her know how desperately he wanted her.

She gasped as she felt him in passion, felt and understood the changed contours of his body. Her face buried itself in his hot throat and she trembled all over.

"Are you shocked, Tiffany?" he whispered at her ear, his voice a little rough as if he weren't quite in control. "Didn't you know that a man's body grows hard with desire?"

She shivered a little as he moved her blatantly against him, but it didn't shock her. It delighted her. "It's wicked, isn't it, to do this together?" she whispered shakily. Her eyes closed. "But no, I'm not shocked. I want you, too. I want…to be with you. I want to know how it feels to have you…"

He heard the words with mingled joy and shock. His

whirling mind began to function again. *Want. Desire. Sex.* His eyes flew open. She was only twenty-one, for God's sake! And a virgin. His business partner's daughter. What the hell was he doing?

He jerked away from her, his eyes going helplessly to her swollen, taut breasts before he managed to pull her arms from around his neck and push her back in her seat. He struggled to get out of the car, his own aching body fighting him as he tried to remove himself from unbearable temptation in time.

He stood by the front fender, his shirt open, his chest damp and throbbing, his body hurting. He bent over a little, letting the wind get to his hot skin. He must be out of his mind!

Tiffany, just coming to her own senses, watched him with eyes that didn't quite register what was going on. And then she knew. It had almost gone too far. He'd started to make love to her, and then he'd remembered who they were and he'd stopped. He must be hurting like the very devil.

She wanted to get out of the car and go to him, but that would probably make things even worse. She looked down and realized that she was nude to the hips. And he'd seen her like that, touched her...

She tugged her dress back up in a sudden flurry of embarrassment. It had seemed so natural at the time, but now it was shameful. She felt for the straps and pulled the bodice up, keeping her eyes away from her hard, swollen nipples. King had suckled them...

She shuddered with the memory, with new knowledge of him. He'd hate her now, she thought miserably. He'd hate her for letting him go so far, for teasing him. There were names for girls who did that. But she hadn't pulled away, or said no, she recalled. He'd been the one to call a halt, because she couldn't.

Her face went scarlet. She smoothed back her disheveled hair with hands that trembled. How could she face her guests now, like this? Everyone would know what had happened. And what if Wyatt should come along in the Jaguar…?

She looked behind them, but there was no car in sight. And then she realized that they were on King's property, not hers. Had he planned this?

After another minute, she saw him straighten and run a hand through his sweaty hair. He rebuttoned his shirt and tucked it back into his trousers. He did the same with his evening jacket and straightened his tie.

When he finally turned back to get into the car, he looked pale and unapproachable. Tiffany glanced at him as he climbed back in and closed the door, wondering what to say.

"I'll drive you home," he said tersely. "Fasten your seat belt," he added, because she didn't seem to have enough presence of mind to think of it herself.

He started the car without looking at her and turned it around. Minutes later, they were well on the way to her father's house.

It was ablaze with lights, although most of the cars had gone. She looked and saw the Jaguar sitting near the front door. So Wyatt was back. She didn't know what kind of car he was driving, so she couldn't tell if he'd gone or not. She hoped he had, and his cousin with him. She didn't want to see them again.

King pulled up at the front door and stopped, but he didn't cut the engine.

She reached for the door handle and then looked back at him, her face stiff and nervous.

"Are you angry?" she asked softly.

He stared straight ahead. "I don't know."

She nibbled her lower lip, and tasted him there. "I'm not sorry," she said doggedly, her face suddenly full of bravado.

He turned then, his eyes faintly amused. "No. I'm not sorry, either."

She managed a faint smile, despite her embarrassment. "You said it had to happen eventually."

"And you wanted it to happen with me. So you said."

"I meant it," she replied quietly. Her eyes searched his, but she didn't find any secrets there. "I'm not ashamed."

His dark eyes trailed down her body. "You're exquisite, little Tiffany," he said. "But years too young for an affair, and despite tonight's showing, I don't seduce virgins."

"Is an affair all you have to offer?" she asked with new maturity.

He pursed his lips, considering that. "Yes, I think it is. I'm thirty-four. I like my freedom. I don't want the commitment of a wife. Not yet, at least. And you're not old enough for that kind of responsibility. You need a few years to grow up."

She was grown up, but she wasn't going to argue the point with him. Her green eyes twinkled. "Not in bed, I don't."

He took a deep breath. "Tiffany, there's more to a

relationship than sex. About which," he added shortly, "you know precious little."

"I can learn," she murmured.

"Damned fast, judging by tonight," he agreed with a wicked smile. "But physical pleasure gets old quickly."

"Between you and me?" she asked, her eyes adoring him. "I don't really think it ever would. I can imagine seducing you in all sorts of unlikely places."

His heart jumped. He shouldn't ask. He shouldn't... "Such as?" he asked in spite of himself.

"Sitting up," she breathed daringly. "In the front seat of a really elegant European sports car parked right in front of my house..."

His blood was beating in his temple. She made him go hot all over with those sultry eyes, that expression...

"You'd better go inside," he said tersely.

"Yes, I suppose I had," she murmured dryly. "It really wouldn't do, would it, what with the risk of someone coming along and seeing us."

It got worse by the second. He was beginning to hurt. "Tiffany..."

She opened the door and glanced back at his hard, set face. He was very dark, and she loved the way he looked in evening clothes. Although now, she'd remember him with his shirt undone and her hands against that sexy, muscular chest.

"Run while you can, cattle baron," she said softly. "I'll be two steps behind."

"I'm an old fox, honey," he returned. "And not easy game."

"We'll see about that," she said, smiling at him. "Good night, lover."

He caught his breath, watching her close the door and blow him a kiss. He had to get away, to think. The last thing he wanted was to find himself on the receiving end of a shotgun wedding. Tiffany was all too tempting, and the best way to handle this was to get away from her for a few weeks, until they both cooled off. A man had to keep a level head, in business and in personal relationships.

He put the car in gear and drove off. Yes, that was what he should do. He'd find himself a nice business trip. Tiffany would get over him. And he'd certainly get over her. He'd had women. He'd known this raging hunger before. But he couldn't satisfy it with a virgin.

He thought about her, the way she'd let him see her, and the aching started all over again. His face hardened as he stepped down on the accelerator. Maybe a long trip would erase that image. Something had to!

Tiffany went back into the house, breathless and worried that her new experiences would show. But they didn't seem to. Wyatt came and asked where she and King had been and she made some light, outrageous reply.

For the rest of the evening, she was the belle of her own ball. But deep inside she was worried about the future. King wasn't going to give in without a fight. She hoped she had what it took to land that big Texas fish. She wanted him more than anything in the whole world. And she wasn't a girl who was used to disappointments.

CHAPTER THREE

"WELL, KING'S LEFT the country," Harrison Blair murmured dryly three days after Tiffany's party. "You don't seem a bit surprised."

"He's running scared," she said pertly, grinning up at her father from the neat crochet stitches she was using to make an afghan for her room. "I don't blame him. If I were a man being pursued by some persistent woman, I'm sure that I'd run, too."

He shook his head. "I'm afraid he isn't running from you," he mused. "He took his secretary with him."

Her heart jumped, but she didn't miss a stitch. "Did he? I hope Carla enjoys the trip. Where did they go?"

"To Nassau. King's talking beef exports with the minister of trade. But I'm sure Carla took a bathing suit along."

She put in three more stitches. Carla Stark was a redhead, very pretty and very eligible and certainly no virgin. She wanted to throw her head back and scream, but that would be juvenile. It was a temporary setback, that was all.

"Nothing to say?" her father asked.

She shrugged. "Nothing to say."

He hesitated. "I don't want to be cruel," he began. "I know you've set your heart on King. But he's thirty-four, sweetheart. You're a very young twenty-one. Maturity takes time. And I've been just a tad over-protective about you. Maybe I was wrong to be so strict about young men."

"It wouldn't really have mattered," she replied rue-fully. "It was King from the time I was fourteen. I couldn't even get interested in boys my own age."

"I see."

She put the crochet hook through the ball of yarn and moved it, along with the partially finished afghan, to her work basket. She stood up, pausing long enough to kiss her father's tanned cheek. "Don't worry about me. You might not think so, but I'm tough."

"I don't want you to wear your heart out on King."

She smiled at him. "I won't!"

"Tiff, he's not a marrying man," he said flatly. "And modern attitudes or no, if he seduces you, he's history. He's not playing fast and loose with you."

"He already told me that himself," she assured him. "He doesn't have any illusions about me, and he said that he's not having an affair with me."

He was taken aback. "He did?"

She nodded. "Of course, he also said he didn't want a wife. But all relationships have these little minor set-backs. And no man really wants to get married, right?"

His face went dark. "Now listen here, you can't se-duce him, either!"

"I can if I want to," she replied. "But I won't, so stop looking like a thundercloud. I want a home of my own and children, not a few months of happiness fol-lowed by a diamond bracelet and a bouquet of roses."

"Have I missed something here?"

"Lettie said that's how King kisses off his women," she explained. "With a diamond bracelet and a bouquet of roses. Not that any of them last longer than a couple of months," she added with a rueful smile. "Kind of them, isn't it, to let him practice on them until he's ready to marry me?"

His eyes bulged. "What ever happened to the double standard?"

"I told you, I don't want anybody else. I couldn't really expect him to live a life of total abstinence when he didn't know he was going to marry me one day. I mean, he was looking for the perfect woman all this time, and here I was right under his nose. Now that he's aware of me, I'm sure there won't be anybody else. Not even Carla."

Harrison cleared his throat. "Now, Tiffany…"

She grinned. "I hope you want lots of grandchildren. I think kids are just the greatest things in the world!"

"Tiffany…"

"I want a nice cup of tea. How about you?"

"Oolong?"

She grimaced. "Green. I ran out of oolong and forgot to ask Mary to put it on the grocery list this week."

"Green's fine, then, I guess."

"Better than coffee," she teased, and made a face. "I won't be a minute."

He watched her dart off to the kitchen, a pretty picture in jeans and a blue T-shirt, with her long hair in a neat ponytail. She didn't look old enough to date, much less marry.

She was starry-eyed, thinking of a home and children and hardly considering the reality of life with a

man like King. He wouldn't want children straight off
the bat, even if she thought she did. She was far too
young for instant responsibility. Besides that, King
wouldn't be happy with an impulsive child who wasn't
mature enough to handle business luncheons and the
loneliness of a home where King spent time only infrequently. Tiffany would expect constant love and
attention, and King couldn't give her that. He sighed,
thinking that he was going to go gray-headed worrying
about his only child's upcoming broken heart. There
seemed no way to avoid it, no way at all.

TIFFANY WASN'T THINKING about business lunches or
having King home only once in a blue moon. She was
weaving dreams of little boys and girls playing around
her skirts on summer days, and King holding hands
with her while they watched television at night. Over
and above that, she was plotting how to bring about
his downfall. First things first, she considered, and
now that she'd caught his eye, she had to keep it focused on herself.

She phoned his office to find out when he was coming back, and wrangled the information that he had a
meeting with her father the following Monday just before lunch about a stock transfer.

She spent the weekend planning every move of her
campaign. She was going to land that sexy fighting fish,
one way or another.

SHE FOUND AN excuse to go into Jacobsville on Monday
morning, having spent her entire allowance on a new
sultry jade silk dress that clung to her slender curves

as if it were a second skin. Her hair was put up neatly in an intricate hairdo, with a jade clip holding a wave in place. With black high heels and a matching bag, she looked elegant and expensive and frankly seductive as she walked into her father's office just as he and King were coming out the door on their way to lunch.

"Tiffany," her father exclaimed, his eyes widening at the sight of her. He'd never seen her appear quite so poised and elegant.

King was doing his share of looking, as well. His dark eyebrows dove together over glittering pale eyes and his head moved just a fraction to the side as his gaze went over her like seeking hands.

"I don't have a penny left for lunch," she told her father on a pitiful breath. "I spent everything in my purse on this new dress. Do you like it?" She turned around, her body exquisitely posed for King's benefit. His jaw clenched and she had to repress a wicked smile.

"It's very nice, sweetheart," Harrison agreed. "But why can't you use your credit card for lunch?"

"Because I'm going to get some things for an impromptu picnic," she replied. Her eyes lowered demurely.

"You could come to lunch with us," Harrison began.

King looked hunted.

Tiffany saw his expression and smiled gently. "That's sweet of you, Dad, but I really haven't time. Actually, I'm meeting someone. I hope he likes the dress," she added, lowering her head demurely. She was lying her head off, but they didn't know it. "Can I have a ten-dollar bill, please?"

Harrison swept out his wallet. "Take two," he said,

handing them to her. He glared at her. "It isn't Wyatt,
I hope," he muttered. "He's too easily led."

"No. It's not Wyatt. Thanks, Dad. See you, King."

"Who is it?"

King's deep, half-angry voice stopped her at the
doorway. She turned, her eyebrows lifted as if he'd
shocked her with the question. "Nobody you know,"
she said honestly. "I'll be in by bedtime, Dad."

"How can you go on a picnic in that dress?" King
asked shortly.

She smoothed her hand down one shapely hip. "It's
not *that* sort of picnic," she murmured demurely. "We're
going to have it on the carpet in his living room. He has
gas logs in his fireplace. It's going to be so romantic!"

"It's May," King ground out. "Too hot for fires in
the fireplace."

"We won't sit too close to it," she said. "Ta, ta."

She went out the door and dived into the elevator,
barely able to contain her glee. She'd shaken King. Let
him stew over that lie for the rest of the day, she told
herself, and maybe he'd feel as uncomfortable as she'd
felt when he took his secretary to Nassau!

OF COURSE THERE was no picnic, because she wasn't
meeting anyone. She stopped by a fish and chips place
and got a small order and took it home with her. An
hour later, she was sprawled in front of her own fireplace, unlit, with a trendy fashion magazine. Lying on
her belly on the thick beige carpet, in tight-fitting designer jeans and a low-cut tank top, barefoot and with
her long hair loose, she looked the picture of youth.

King's sudden appearance in the doorway shocked

her. She hadn't expected to be found out, certainly not so quickly.

"Where is he?" he asked, his hands in his slacks' pockets. He glanced around the spacious room. "Hiding under the sofa? Behind a chair?"

She was frozen in position with a small piece of fish in her hand as she gaped at him.

"What a tangled web we weave," he mused.

"I wasn't deceiving you. Well, maybe a little," she acknowledged. Her eyes glared up at him. "You took Carla to Nassau, didn't you? I hope you had fun."

"Like hell you do."

He closed the door behind him abruptly and moved toward her, resplendent in a gray suit, his black hair catching the light from the ceiling and glowing with faint blue lights.

She rolled over and started to get up, but before she could move another inch, he straddled her prone figure and with a movement so smooth that it disconcerted her, he was suddenly full-length over her body on the carpet, balancing only on his forearms.

"I suppose you'll taste of fish," he muttered as he bent and his hard mouth fastened roughly on her lips.

She gasped. His hips shifted violently, his long legs insistent as they parted her thighs and moved quickly between them. His hands trapped her wrists, stilling her faint instinctive protest at the shocking intimacy of his position.

He lifted his mouth a breath away and looked straight into her eyes. One lean leg moved, just briefly, and he pushed forward against her, his body suddenly rigid. He let her feel him swell with desire, and something wickedly masculine flared in his pale, glittering eyes as new sensations registered on her flushed face.

"Now you know how it happens," he murmured, dropping his gaze to her soft, swollen mouth. "And how it feels when it happens. Draw your legs up a little. I want you to feel me completely against you there."

"King!"

He shifted insistently, making her obey him. She felt the intimacy of his hold and gasped, shivering a little at the power and strength of him against her so intimately.

"Pity, that you don't have anybody to compare me with," he mused deeply as his head bent. "But that might be a good thing. I wouldn't want to frighten you…"

His mouth twisted, parting her lips. It was so different from the night of her party. Then, she'd been the aggressor, teasing and tempting him. He was aroused and insistent and she felt young and uncertain, especially when he began to move in a very seductive way that made her whole body tingle and clench with sensual pleasure.

He heard the little gasp that escaped the lips under his hard mouth, and his head lifted.

He searched her eyes, reading very accurately her response to him. "Didn't you know that pleasure comes of such intimacy?" he whispered.

"Only from…books," she confessed breathlessly. She shivered as he moved again, just enough to make her totally aware of her body's feverish response to that intimate pressure.

"Isn't this more exciting than reading about it?" he

teased. His mouth nibbled at her lips. "Open them," he whispered. "Deep kisses are part of the process."

"King, I'm not...not...sure..."

"You're sure," he whispered into her mouth. "You're just apprehensive, and that's natural. They told you it was going to hurt, didn't they?"

She swallowed, aware of dizziness that seemed to possess her.

His teeth nibbled sensually at her lower lip. "I'll give you all the time you need, when it happens," he murmured lazily. "If I can arouse you enough, you won't mind if I hurt you a little. It might even intensify the pleasure."

"I don't understand."

His open mouth brushed over hers. "I know," he murmured. "That's what excites me so. Slide your hands up the back of my thighs and hold me against you."

"Wh...what?"

His mouth began to move between her lips. "You wore that dress to excite me. All right. I'm excited. Now satisfy me."

"I...but I...can't..." she gasped. "King!"

His hands were under her, intimate, touching her in shocking ways.

"Isn't this what you wanted? It's what you implied when you struck that seductive pose and invited me to ravish you right there on the floor of your father's office."

"I did not!"

His thumbs pressed against her in a viciously arousing way, so that when he pushed down with his hips, she lifted to meet them, groaning harshly at the shock

of delight that was only the tip of some mysterious
iceberg of ecstasy.

"Tell me that again," he challenged.

She couldn't. She was burning up, dying, in anguish.
A stranger's hands fought her tank top and the tiny bra
under it, pushing them out of the way only seconds before those same hands tugged at his shirt and managed
to get under it, against warm muscle and hair.

While he kissed her, she writhed under him, shivering when she felt his skin against her own. Deliri-
ous with fevered need, she slid her hands down his flat
belly and even as he dragged his mouth from hers to
protest, they pressed, trembling, against the swollen
length of him through the soft fabric.

He moaned something, shuddered. He rolled abruptly
onto his side and drew her hand back to him, moving
it softly on his body, teaching her the sensual rhythm
he needed.

"Dear God," he whispered, kissing her hungrily.
"No, baby, don't stop," he groaned when her movements
slowed. "Touch me. Yes. Yes. Oh, God, yes!"

It was fascinating to see how he reacted to her. Encouraged, she moved closer and her mouth pressed
softly, sensually, against the thick hair that covered
his chest. He was shaking now. His body was strangely
vulnerable, and the knowledge inhibited her.

He rolled onto his back, the very action betraying
his need to feel her touch on him. He lay there, still
shivering, his eyes closed, his body yielding to her
soft, curious hands.

She laid her cheek against his hot skin, awash in new

sensations, touches that had been taboo all her life. She
was learning his body as a lover would.

"Tell me what to do," she whispered as she drew
her cheek against his breastbone. "I'll do anything for
you. Anything!"

His hand held hers to him for one long, aching minute. Then he drew it up to his chest and held it there
while he struggled to breathe.

Her breasts felt cool as they pressed nakedly into
his rib cage where his shirt was pulled away. Her eyes
closed and she lay there, close to him, closer to him
than she'd ever been.

"Heavens, that was exciting," she choked. "I never
dreamed I could touch you like that, and in broad day-
light, too!"

That raw innocence caught him off guard. Laughter bubbled up into his chest, into his throat. He began
to laugh softly.

"Do hush!" she chided. "What if Mary should hear
you and walk in?"

He lifted himself on an elbow and looked down at
her bare breasts. "She'd get an eyeful, wouldn't she?"
He traced a taut nipple, arrogantly pleased that she
didn't object at all.

"I'm small," she whispered.

He smiled. "No, you're not."

She looked down to where his fingers rested against
her pale skin. "Your skin is so dark compared to mine…"

"Especially here, where you're so pale," he breathed.
His lips bent to the soft skin he was touching, and he
took her inside his mouth, gently suckling her.

She arched up, moaning harshly, her fists clenched

beside her head as she tried to deal with the mounting delight of sensation.

He heard that harsh sound and reacted to it immediately. His mouth grew insistent, hot and hungry as it suckled hard at her breast. Her body clenched and suddenly went into a shocking spasm that she couldn't control at all. It never seemed to end, the hot, shameful pleasure he gave her with that intimate caress.

She clutched him, breathless, burying her hot face in his neck while she fought to still her shaking limbs, the faint little gasps that he must certainly be able to hear.

His mouth was tender now, calming rather than stirring. He pressed tender, brief kisses all over her skin, ending only reluctantly at her trembling lips.

Her shamed eyes lifted to his, full of tears that reflected her overwhelmed emotions.

He shook his head, dabbing at them with a handkerchief he drew from his slacks' pocket. "Don't cry," he whispered gently. "Your breasts are very, very sensitive. I love the way you react to my mouth on them." He smiled. "It's nothing to worry about."

"It's…natural?" she asked.

His hand smoothed her dark hair. "For a few women, I suppose," he said. He searched her curious eyes. "I've never experienced it like this. I'm glad. There should be at least one or two firsts for me, as well as for you."

"I wish I knew more," she said worriedly.

"You'll learn." His fingers traced her nose, her softly swollen lips. "I missed you."

Her heart felt as if it could fly. She smiled. "Did you, really?"

He nodded. "Not that I wanted to," he added with such disgust that she giggled.

He propped himself on an elbow and stared down at her for a long time, his brows drawn together in deep thought.

She could feel the indecision in him, along with a tension that was new to her. Her soft eyes swept over his dark, lean face and back up to meet his curious gaze.

"You're binding me with velvet ropes," he murmured quietly. "I've never felt like this. I don't know how to handle it."

"Neither do I," she said honestly. She drew a slow breath, aware suddenly of her shameless nudity and the coolness of the air on her skin.

He saw that discomfort and deftly helped her back into her clothes with an economy of movement that was somehow disturbing.

"You make me feel painfully young," she confessed.

"You are," he said without hesitation. His pale eyes narrowed. "This is getting dangerous. I can't keep my hands off you lately. And the last thing on earth I'll ever do is seduce my business partner's only daughter."

"I know that, King," she said with an odd sort of dignity. He got to his feet and she laid down again, watching him rearrange his own shirt and vest and jacket and tie. It was strangely intimate.

He knew that. His eyes smiled, even if his lips didn't.

"What are we going to do?" she added.

He stared down at her with an unnerving intensity. "I wish to God I knew."

He pulled her up beside him. His big hands rested

warmly on her shoulders. "Wouldn't you like to go to Europe?" he asked.

Her eyebrows lifted. "What for?"

"You could go to college. Or have a holiday. Lettie could go with you," he suggested, naming her godmother. "She'd spoil you rotten and you'd come back with a hefty knowledge of history."

"I don't want to go to Europe, and I'm not all that enthralled with history."

He sighed. "Tiffany, I'm not going to sleep with you."

Her full, swollen lips pouted up at him. "I haven't asked you to." She lowered her eyes. "But I'm not going to sleep with anyone else. I haven't even thought about anyone else since I was fourteen."

He felt his mind whirling at the confession. He scowled deeply. He was getting in over his head and he didn't know how to stop. She was too young; years too young. She didn't have the maturity, the poise, the sophistication to survive in his world. He could have told her that, but she wouldn't have listened. She was living in dreams. He couldn't afford to.

He didn't answer her. His hands were deep in his pockets and he was watching her worriedly, amazed at his own headlong fall into ruin. No woman in his experience had ever wound him up to such a fever pitch of desire by just parading around in a silk dress. He'd accused her of tempting him, but it wasn't the whole truth. Ever since the night of her birthday party, he hadn't been able to get her soft body out of his mind. He wanted her. He just didn't know what to do about it. Marriage was out of the question, even more so was an affair. Whatever else she was, she was still his business partner's daughter.

"You're brooding," she murmured.

He shrugged. "I can't think of anything better to do," he said honestly. "I'm going away for a while," he added abruptly. "Perhaps this will pass if we ignore it."

So he was still going to fight. She hadn't expected anything else, but she was vaguely disappointed, just the same.

"I can learn," she said.

His eyebrow went up.

"I know how to be a hostess," she continued, as if he'd challenged her. "I already know most of the people in your circle, and in Dad's. I'm not fifteen."

His eyes narrowed. "Tiffany, you may know how to be a hostess, but you haven't any idea in hell how to be a wife," he said bluntly.

Her heart jumped wildly in her chest. "I could learn how to be one."

His face hardened. "Not with me. I don't want to get married. And before you say it," he added, holding up a hand, "yes, I want you. But desire isn't enough. It isn't even a beginning. I may be the first man you've ever wanted, Tiffany, but you aren't the first woman I've wanted."

CHAPTER FOUR

THE MOCKING SMILE on his face made Tiffany livid with jealous rage. She scrambled to her feet, her face red and taut.

"That wasn't necessary!" she flung at him.

"Yes, it was," he replied calmly. "You want to play house. I don't."

Totally at a loss, she knotted her hands at her sides and just stared at him. This sort of thing was totally out of her experience. Her body was all that interested him, and it wasn't enough. She had nothing else to bargain with. She'd lost.

It was a new feeling. She'd always had everything she wanted. Her father had spoiled her rotten. King had been another impossible item on her list of luxuries, but he was telling her that she couldn't have him. Her father couldn't buy him for her. And she couldn't flirt and tease and get him for herself. Defeat was strangely cold. It sat in the pit of her stomach like a black emptiness. She didn't know how to handle it.

And he knew. It was in his pale, glittering eyes, in that faint, arrogant smile on his hard mouth.

She wanted to rant and rave, but it wasn't the sort of behavior that would save the day. She relaxed her hands, and her body, and simply looked at him, full of inadequacies and insecurities that she'd never felt before.

"Perhaps when I'm Carla's age, I'll try again," she said with torn pride and the vestiges of a smile.

He nodded with admiration. "That's the spirit," he said gently.

She didn't want gentleness, or pity. She stuck her hands into her jeans pockets. "You don't have to leave town to avoid me," she said. "Lettie's taking me to New York next week," she lied, having arranged the trip mentally in the past few minutes. Lettie would do anything her godchild asked, and she had the means to travel wherever she liked. Besides, she loved New York.

King's eyes narrowed suspiciously. "Does Lettie know she's going traveling?"

"Of course," she said, playing her part to the hilt.

"Of course." He drew in a heavy breath and slowly let it out. His body was still giving him hell, but he wasn't going to let her know it. Ultimately she was better off out of his life.

"See you," she said lightly.

He nodded. "See you."

And he left.

LATE THAT AUTUMN, Tiffany was walking down a runway in New York wearing the latest creation of one David Marron, a young designer whose Spanish-inspired fashions were a sensation among buyers. The two had met through a mutual friend of Lettie's and David had seen incredible possibilities in Tiffany's long black hair and elegance. He dressed her in a gown that was reminiscent of lacy Spanish noblewomen of days long past, and she brought the house down at his first showing of his new spring line. She made the cover of a major fashion magazine and jumped from an unknown to a familiar face in less than six months.

Lettie, with her delicately tinted red hair and twinkling brown eyes, was elated at her accomplishment. It had hurt her deeply to see Tiffany in such an agony of pain when she'd approached her godmother and all but begged to be taken out of Texas. Lettie doted on the younger woman and whisked her away with a minimum of fuss.

They shared a luxurious Park Avenue apartment and were seen in all the most fashionable places. In those few months, Tiffany had grown more sophisticated, more mature—and incredibly more withdrawn. She was ice-cold with men, despite the enhancement of her beauty and her elegant figure. Learning to forget King was a full-time job. She was still working on it.

Just when she was aching to go home to her father where her chances of seeing King every week were excellent, a lingerie company offered her a lucrative contract and a two-week holiday filming commercials in Jamaica.

"I couldn't turn it down," she told Lettie with a groan. "What's Dad going to say? I was going to help him with his Christmas party. I won't get home until Christmas Eve. After we get back from Jamaica, I have to do a photo layout for a magazine ad campaign due to hit the stands next spring."

"You did the right thing," Lettie assured her. "My dear, at your age, you should be having fun, meeting people, learning to stand alone." She sighed gently.

"Marriage and children are for later, when you're established in a career."

Tiffany turned and stared at the older woman. "You never married."

Lettie smiled sadly. "No. I lost my fiancé in Vietnam. I wasn't able to want anyone else in that way."

"Lettie, that's so sad!"

"One learns to live with the unbearable, eventually. I had my charities to keep me busy. And, of course, I had you," she added, giving her goddaughter a quick hug. "I haven't had a bad life."

"Someday you have to tell me about him."

"Someday, I will. But for now, you go ahead to Jamaica and have a wonderful time filming your commercial."

"You'll come with me?" she asked quickly, faintly worried at the thought of being so far away without any familiar faces.

Lettie patted her hand. "Of course I will. I love Jamaica!"

"I have to call Dad and tell him."

"That might be a good idea. He was complaining earlier in the week that your letters were very far apart."

"I'll do it right now."

She picked up the receiver and dialed her father's office number, twisting the cord nervously while she waited to be put through.

"Hi, Dad!" she said.

"Don't tell me," he muttered. "You've met some dethroned prince and you're getting married in the morning."

She chuckled. "No. I've just signed a contract to do

lingerie commercials and we're flying to Jamaica to start shooting."

There was a strange hesitation. "When?"

"Tomorrow morning."

"Well, when will you be back?" he asked.

"In two weeks. But I've got modeling assignments in New York until Christmas Eve," she said in a subdued tone.

"What about my Christmas party?" He sounded resigned and depressed. "I was counting on you to arrange it for me."

"You can have a New Year's Eve party for your clients," she improvised with laughter in her voice. "I'll have plenty of time to put that together before I have to start my next assignment. In fact," she added, "I'm not sure when it will be. The lingerie contract was only for the spring line. They're doing different models for different seasons. I was spring."

"I can see why," he murmured dryly. "My daughter, the model." He sighed again. "I should never have let you get on the plane with Lettie. It's her fault. I know she's at the back of it."

"Now, Dad…"

"I'm having her stuffed and hung on my wall when she comes back. You tell her that!"

"You know you're fond of Lettie," she chided, with a wink at her blatantly eavesdropping godmother.

"I'll have her shot!"

She grimaced and Lettie, reading her expression, chuckled, unabashed by Harrison Blair's fury.

"She's laughing," she told him.

"Tell her to laugh while she can." He hesitated and

spoke to someone nearby. "King said to tell you he misses you."

Her heart jumped, but she wasn't leaving herself open to any further humiliation at his hands. "Tell him to pull the other one," she chuckled. "Listen, Dad, I have to go. I'll phone you when we're back from Jamaica."

"Wait a minute. Where in Jamaica, and is Lettie going along?"

"Of course she is! We'll have a ball. Take care, Dad. Bye!"

He was still trying to find out where she was going when she hung up on him. He glanced at King with a grimace.

The younger man had an odd expression on his face. It was one Harrison couldn't remember ever seeing there before.

"She's signed a contract," Harrison said, shoving his hands into his pockets as he glared at the telephone, as if the whole thing had been its fault.

"For what?" King asked.

"Lingerie commercials," his partner said heavily. "Just think, my sheltered daughter will be parading around in sheer nighties for the whole damned world to see!"

"Like hell she will. Where is she?" King demanded.

"On her way to Jamaica first thing in the morning. King," he added when the other man started to leave. "She's of age," he said gently. "She's a woman. I don't have the right to tell her how to live her own life. And neither do you."

"I don't want other men ogling her!"

Harrison just nodded. "I know. I don't, either. But it's her decision."

"I won't let her do it," King said doggedly.

"How do you propose to stop her? You can't do it legally. I don't think you can do it any other way, either."

"Did you tell her what I said?"

Harrison nodded again. "She said to pull the other one."

Pale blue eyes widened with sheer shock. It had never occured to him that he could lose Tiffany, that she wouldn't always be in Harrison's house waiting for him to be ready to settle down. Now she'd flown the coop and the shoe was on the other foot. She'd discovered the pleasure of personal freedom and she didn't want to settle down.

He glanced at Harrison. "Is she serious about this job? Or is it just another ploy to get my attention?"

The other man chuckled. "I have no idea. But you have to admit, she's a pretty thing. It isn't surprising that she's attracted a modeling agency."

King stared out the window with narrowed, thoughtful eyes. "Then she's thinking about making a career of it."

Harrison didn't tell him that her modeling contract might not last very long. He averted his eyes. "She might as well have a career. If nothing else, it will help her mature."

The other man didn't look at him. "She hasn't grown up yet."

"I know that. It isn't her fault. I've sheltered her from life—perhaps too much. But now she wants to try her wings. This is the best time, before she has a reason to fold them away. She's young and she thinks she has the world at her feet. Let her enjoy it while she can."

King stared down at the carpet. "I suppose that's the wise choice."

"It's the only choice," came the reply. "She'll come home when she's ready."

King didn't say another word about it. He changed the subject to business and pursued it solemnly.

MEANWHILE, TIFFANY WENT to Jamaica and had a grand time. Modeling, she discovered, was hard work. It wasn't just a matter of standing in front of a camera and smiling. It involved wardrobe changes, pauses for the proper lighting and equipment setup, minor irritations like an unexpected burst of wind and artistic temperament on the part of the cameraman.

Lettie watched from a distance, enjoying Tiffany's enthusiasm for the shoot. The two weeks passed all too quickly, with very little time for sightseeing.

"Just my luck," Tiffany groaned when they were back in New York, "I saw the beach and the hotel and the airport. I didn't realize that every free minute was going to be spent working or resting up for the next day's shoot!"

"Welcome to the world of modeling." Lettie chuckled. "Here, darling, have another celery stick."

Tiffany grimaced, but she ate the veggie platter she was offered without protest.

At night, she lay awake and thought about King. She hadn't believed his teasing assertion that he'd missed her. King didn't miss people. He was entirely self-sufficient. But how wonderful if it had been true.

That daydream only lasted until she saw a tabloid at the drugstore where she was buying hair-care products. There was a glorious color photo of King and Carla right on the front page of one, with the legend, "Do wedding bells figure in future for tycoon and secretary?"

She didn't even pick it up, to her credit. She passed over it as if she hadn't seen it. But she went to bed that evening, she cried all night, almost ruining her face for the next day's modeling session.

UNREQUITED LOVE TOOK its toll on her in the weeks that followed. The one good thing about misery was that it attracted other miserable people. She annexed one Mark Allenby, a male model who'd just broken up with his long-time girlfriend and wanted a shoulder to cry on. He was incredibly handsome and sensitive, and just what Tiffany needed for her shattered ego.

The fact that he was a wild man was certainly a bonus.

He was the sort of person who'd phone her on the spur of the moment and suggest an evening at a retro beatnik coffeehouse where the patrons read bad poetry. He loved practical jokes, like putting whoopee cushions under a couple posing for a romantic ad.

"I can see why you're single," Tiffany suggested breathlessly when she'd helped him outrun the furious photographer. "And I'll bet you never get to work for *him* again." She indicated the heavyset madman chasing them.

"Yes, I will." He chuckled. "When you make it to my income bracket, you don't have to call photographers to get work. They call you." Mark turned and blew the man a kiss, grabbed Tiffany's hand, and pulled her along to the subway entrance nearby.

"You need a makeover," he remarked on their way back to her apartment.

She stopped and looked up at him. "Why?"

"You look too girlish," he said simply, and smiled. "You need a more haute couture image if you want to grow into modeling."

She grimaced. "I'm not sure I really do, though. I like it all right. But I don't need the money."

"Darling, of course you need the money!"

"Not really. Money isn't worth much when you can't buy what you want with it," she said pointedly.

He pushed back his curly black hair and gave her his famous inscrutable he-man stare. "What do you want that you can't buy?"

"King."

"Of which country?"

She grinned. "Not royalty. That's his name. Kingman. Kingman Marshall."

"The tycoon of the tabloids?" he asked, pursing his chiseled lips. "Well, well, you do aim high, don't you? Mr. Marshall has all the women he wants, thank you. And if you have anything more serious in mind, forget it. His father taught him that marriage is only for fools. Rumor has it that his mother took his old man for every cent he had when she divorced him, and that it drove his father to suicide."

"Yes, I know," she said dully.

"Not that Marshall didn't get even. You probably heard about that, too."

"Often," she replied. "He actually took his mother to court and charged her with culpability in his father's suicide in a civil case. He won." She shivered, remembering how King had looked after the verdict—and, more importantly, how his mother had looked. She lost two-thirds of her assets and the handsome gigolo that she'd been living with. It was no wonder that King had such a low opinion of marriage, and women.

"Whatever became of the ex-Mrs. Marshall?" he asked aloud.

"She overdosed on drugs and died four years ago," she said.

"A sad end."

"Indeed it was."

"You can't blame Marshall for treating women like individually wrapped candies," he expounded. "I don't imagine he trusts anything in skirts."

"You were talking about a makeover?" she interrupted, anxious to get him off the subject of King before she started screaming.

"I was. I'll take you to my hairdresser. He'll make a new woman of you. Then we'll go shopping for a proper wardrobe."

Her pale eyes glittered with excitement. "This sounds like fun."

"Believe me, it will be," he said with a wicked grin. "Come along, darling."

They spent the rest of the day remaking Tiffany. When he took her out that night to one of the more fashionable nightspots, one of the models she'd worked with didn't even recognize her. It was a compliment of the highest order.

Lettie was stunned speechless.

"It's me," Tiffany murmured impishly, whirling in her black cocktail dress with diamond earrings dripping from her lobes. Her hair was cut very short and feathered toward her gamine face. She had just a hint of makeup, just enough to enhance her high cheekbones and perfect bone structure. She looked expensive, elegant, and six years older than she was.

"I'm absolutely shocked," Lettie said after a minute. "My dear, you are the image of your mother."

Tiffany's face softened. "Am I, really?"

Lettie nodded. "She was so beautiful. I always envied her."

"I wish I'd known her," she replied. "All I have are photographs and vague memories of her singing to me at night."

"You were very young when she died. Harrison never stopped mourning her." Her eyes were sad. "I don't think he ever will."

"You never know about Dad," Tiffany remarked, because she knew how Lettie felt about Harrison. Not that she was gauche enough to mention it. "Why don't you go out with us tonight?"

"Three's a crowd, dear. Mark will want you to himself."

"It isn't like that at all," Tiffany said gently. "He's mourning his girlfriend and I'm mourning King. We have broken hearts and our work in common, but not much else. He's a friend—and I mean that quite sincerely."

Lettie smiled. "I'm rather glad. He's very nice. But he'll end up in Europe one day in a villa, and that wouldn't suit you at all."

"Are you sure?"

Lettie nodded. "And so are you, in your heart."

Tiffany glanced at herself in the mirror with a quiet sigh. "Fine feathers make fine birds, but King isn't the sort to be impressed by sophistication or beauty. Besides, the tabloids are already predicting that he's going to marry Carla."

"I noticed. Surely you don't believe it?"

"I don't believe he'll ever marry anyone unless he's trapped into it," Tiffany said honestly, and her eyes were suddenly very old. "He's seen nothing of marriage but the worst side."

"It's a pity about that. It's warped his outlook."

"Nothing will ever change it." She smiled at Lettie. "Sure you won't come with us? You won't be a crowd."

"I won't come tonight. But ask me again."

"You can count on it."

MARK WAS BROODY as he picked at his mint ice cream.

"You're worried," Tiffany murmured.

He glanced at her wryly. "No. I'm distraught. My girl is being seen around town with a minor movie star. She seems smitten."

"She may be doing the same thing you're doing," she chided. "Seeing someone just to numb the ache."

He chuckled. "Is that what I'm doing?"

"It's what we're both doing."

He reached his hand across the table and held hers. "I'm sorry we didn't meet three years ago, while I was still heart-whole. You're unique. I enjoy having you around."

"Same here. But friendship is all it can ever be."

"Believe it or not, I know that." He put down his spoon. "What are you doing for Christmas?"

"I'll be trying to get back from a location shoot and praying that none of the airline pilots go on strike," she murmured facetiously.

"New Year's?"

"I have to go home and arrange a business party for my father." She glanced at him and her eyes began to sparkle. "I've had an idea. How would you like to visit Texas?"

His eyebrows arched. "Do I have to ride a horse?"

"Not everyone in Texas rides. We live in Jacobsville. It's not too far from San Antonio. Dad's in business there."

"Jacobsville." He fingered his wineglass with elegant dark fingers that looked very sexy in the ads he modeled for. "Why not? It's a long way from Manhattan."

"Yes, it is, and I can't bear to go home alone."

"May I ask why?"

"Of course. My own heartbreaker lives there. I told you about him. I ran away from home so that I could stop eating my heart out over him. But memories and heartache seem to be portable," she added heavily.

"I could attest to that myself." He looked up at her with wickedly twinkling black eyes. "And what am I going to be? The competition?"

"Would you mind?" she asked. "I'll gladly do the same for you anytime you like. I need your moral support."

He paused thoughtfully and then he smiled. "You know, this might be the perfect answer to both our headaches. All right. I'll do it." He finished his wine.

"I've been asked to fill a lot of roles. That's a new one." He lifted his glass and took a sip. "What the hell. I'll tangle with Kingman Marshall. I don't want to live forever. I'm yours, darling. At least, for the duration of the party," he added with a grin.

She lifted her own glass. "Here's to pride."

He answered the toast. As she drank it, she wondered how she was going to bear seeing King with Carla. At least she'd have company and camouflage. King would never know that her heart was breaking.

CHAPTER FIVE

TIFFANY AND MARK boarded the plane with Lettie the day before New Year's Eve. Tiffany looked sleek and expensive in a black figure-hugging suit with silver accessories and a black-and-white-striped scarf draped over one shoulder. Mark, in a dark suit, was the picture of male elegance. Women literally sighed when he walked past. It was odd to see a man that handsome in person, and Tiffany enjoyed watching people react to him.

Lettie sat behind them and read magazines while Mark and Tiffany discussed their respective assignments and where they might go next.

It wasn't as long a flight as she'd expected it to be. They walked onto the concourse at the San Antonio airport just in time for lunch.

Tiffany had expected her father to meet them, and sure enough, he was waiting near the gate. Tiffany ran to him to be hugged and kissed warmly before she introduced Mark.

Harrison scowled as he shook hands with the young man, but he gathered his composure quickly and the worried look vanished from his features. He greeted Lettie warmly, too, and led the three of them to the limousine near the front entrance.

"Mark's staying with us, Dad," Tiffany said. "We're both working for the same agency in Manhattan and our holidays coincided."

"We'll be glad to have you, Mark," Harrison said with a forced warmth that only Tiffany seemed to notice.

"How is King?" Lettie asked.

Harrison hesitated with a lightning glance at Tiffany. "He's fine. Shall we go?"

Tiffany wondered why her father was acting so peculiarly, but she pretended not to be interested in King or his feelings. Only with Mark.

"Did you manage to get the arrangements finalized?" Harrison asked his daughter.

She grinned. "Of course. Long distance isn't so long anymore, and it wasn't that hard. I've dealt with the same people for years arranging these 'dos' for you. The caterer, the flowers, the band, even the invitations are all set."

"You're sure?" Harrison murmured.

She nodded. "I'm sure."

"You didn't forget to send an invitation to King and Carla?" her father added.

"Of course not! Theirs were the first to go out," she said with magnificent carelessness. "I wouldn't forget your business partner."

Harrison seemed to relax just a little.

"What's wrong?" she asked, sensing some problem.

"He's out of town," he said reluctantly. "Rather, they're out of town, and not expected back until sometime next week. Or so King's office manager said. I hadn't heard from him, and I wondered why he was

willing to forgo the party. He never misses the holiday
bash. Or, at least, he never has before."

Tiffany didn't betray her feelings by so much as the
batting of an eyelash how much that statement hurt.
She only smiled. "I suppose he had other plans and
wasn't willing to change them."

"Perhaps so," he said, but he didn't look convinced.

Mark reached beside him and caught Tiffany's hand
in his, pressing it reassuringly. He seemed to sense, as
her father did, how miserable she felt at King's defec-
tion. But Mark asked Harrison a question about a land-
mark he noticed as they drove down the long highway
that would carry them to Jacobsville, and got him off
on a subject dear to his heart. By the time they reached
the towering brick family home less than an hour later,
Mark knew more about the siege at the Alamo than
he'd ever gleaned from books.

Tiffany was too busy with her arrangements to keep
Mark company that day or the next, so he borrowed
a sedan from the garage and set about learning the
area. He came back full of tidbits about the history
of the countryside, which he seemed to actually find
fascinating.

He watched Tiffany directing the traffic of imported
people helping with the party with amused indulgence.

"You're actually pretty good at this," he murmured.
"Where did you learn how to do it?"

She looked surprised. "I didn't. It just seemed to
come naturally. I love parties."

"I don't," he mused. "I usually become a decoration."

She knew what he meant. She learned quickly that

very few of the parties models attended were anything
but an opportunity for designers to show off their fashions in a relaxed setting. The more wealthy clients who
were present, the better the opportunity to sell clothes.
But some of the clients found the models more interesting than their regalia. Tiffany had gravitated toward
Mark for mutual protection at first. Afterward, they'd
become fast friends.

"You won't be a decoration here," she promised him
with a smile. "What do you think?"

She swept her hand toward the ballroom, which was
polished and packed with flowers and long tables with
embroidered linen tablecloths, crystal and china and
candelabras. Buffets would be set up there for snacks,
because it wasn't a sit-down dinner. There would be
dancing on the highly polished floor to music provided
by a live band, and mixed drinks would be served at
the bar.

"It's all very elegant," Mark pronounced.

She nodded absently, remembering other parties
when she'd danced and danced, when King had been
close at hand to smile at her and take her out onto the
dance floor. She hadn't danced with him often, but
each time was indelibly imprinted in her mind. She
could close her eyes and see him, touch him. She sighed
miserably. Well, she might as well stop looking back.
She had to go on, and King wanted no part of her. His
absence from this most special of all parties said so.

"I think it'll do," she replied after a minute. She gave
him a warm smile. "Come on and I'll show you the way
I've decorated the rest of the house."

TIFFANY WORE A long silver-sequined dress for the party, with a diamond clip in her short hair. She'd learned how to walk, how to move, how to pose, and even people who'd known her for years were taken aback at her new image.

Mark, at her side, resplendent in dark evening dress, drew feminine eyes with equal magnetism. His Italian ancestry was very evident in his liquid black eyes and olive complexion and black, black hair. One of Tiffany's acquaintances, a pretty little redhead named Lisa, seemed to be totally captivated by Mark. She stood in a corner by herself, just staring at him.

"Should I take pity on her and introduce you?" she asked Mark in a teasing whisper.

He glanced toward the girl, barely out of her teens, and she blushed as red as her hair. Seconds later, she rushed back toward her parents. He chuckled softly.

"She's very young," he mused. "A friend?"

She shook her head. "Her parents are friends of my father's. Lisa is a loner. As a rule, she doesn't care as much for dating as she does for horses. Her family has stables and they breed racehorses."

"Well, well. All that, and no beaux?"

"She's shy with men."

His eyebrows arched. He looked at the young woman a second time, and his eyes narrowed as they caught her vivid blue ones and held them relentlessly. Lisa spilled her drink and blushed again, while her mother fussed at the skirt of her dress with a handkerchief.

"How wicked," Tiffany chided to Mark.

"Eyes like hers should be illegal," he murmured, but he was still staring at Lisa just the same. He took

Tiffany's arm and urged her toward the group. "Introduce me."

"Don't…" she began.

"I'm not that much a rake." He calmed her. "She intrigues me. I won't take advantage. I promise." He smiled, although his eyes were solemn.

"All right, then." She stopped at Mrs. McKinley's side. "Will it stain?" she asked gently.

"Oh, I don't think so," the older woman said with a smile. "It was mostly ice. Lisa, you remember our Tiffany, don't you?" she added.

Lisa looked up, very flustered as her eyes darted nervously from Mark's to Tiffany. "H…hi, Tiffany. Nice to see you."

"Nice to see you, Lisa," Tiffany replied with a genuine smile. "I'm sorry about your dress. Have you met Mark Allenby? He works with me. We're both represented by the same modeling agency in New York. You might have seen him in the snack food commercials with the puppet…?"

"G…good Lord, was that you?" Lisa choked. "I thought he…you…looked familiar, Mr. Allenby!"

He smiled lazily. "Nice of you to remember it, Miss McKinley. Do you dance?"

She looked as if she might faint. "Well, yes…"

He held out a hand. "You'll excuse me?" he said to Tiffany and Lisa's parents.

Lisa put her hand into his and let him lead her onto the dance floor. Her eyes were so full of dreams and delight that Mark couldn't seem to stop looking down at her.

"He dances beautifully," Mrs. McKinley said.

"Not bad," her gruff husband agreed. "Is he gay?"

"Mark?" Tiffany chuckled. "No. Very straight. And quite a success story, in fact. His parents are Italian. He came to this country as a baby and his father held down two jobs while his mother worked as a waitress in a cafeteria. He makes enough to support both of them now, and his three young sisters. He's very responsible, loyal, and not a seducer of innocents, just in case you wondered."

Mrs. McKinley colored. "I'm sorry, but he was an unknown quantity, and it's very easy to see the effect he has on Lisa."

"I wouldn't worry," she said gently. "He's just broken up with his long-time girlfriend and his heart hurts. He's not in the market for an affair, anyway."

"That's a relief," the older woman said with a smile. "She's so unworldly."

Because she'd been as sheltered as Tiffany herself had. There were great disadvantages to that overprotection in today's world, Tiffany thought miserably. She stared into her champagne and wondered why King had declined the invitation to the party. Perhaps he was making the point that he could do nicely without Tiffany. If so, he'd succeeded beyond his wildest dreams.

She got through the long evening on champagne and sheer willpower. Mark seemed to be enjoying himself immensely. He hardly left Lisa all evening, and when she and her parents got ready to leave, he held on to her hand as if he couldn't bear to let it go.

They spoke in terse, quiet tones and as she left, her blue eyes brightened considerably, although Mrs. McKinley looked worried.

"I'm going over there tomorrow to see their horses. You don't mind?" he asked Tiffany as the other guests were preparing to leave.

She stared up at him curiously. "She's very young."

"And innocent," he added, his hands deep in his pockets. "You don't need to tell me that. I haven't ever known anyone like her. She's the sort of girl I might have met back home, if my parents hadn't immigrated to America."

She was startled. "I thought you were grinding your teeth over your girlfriend?"

He smiled vaguely. "So did I." His head turned toward the front door. "She's breakable," he said softly. "Vulnerable and sweet and shy." His broad shoulders rose and fell. "Strange. I never liked redheads before."

Tiffany bit her lower lip. She didn't know how to put into words what she was feeling. Lisa was the sort of girl who'd never get over having her hopes raised and then dashed. Did he know that?

"She dances like a fairy," he murmured, turning away, his dark eyes introspective and oblivious to the people milling around him.

Harrison joined his daughter at the door as the last guests departed.

"Your friend seems distracted," he murmured, his eyes on Mark, who was staring out a darkened window.

"Lisa affected him."

"I noticed. So did everybody else. He's a rake."

She shook her head. "He's a hardworking man with deep family ties and an overworked sense of responsibility. He's no rake."

"I thought you said he had a girlfriend."

"She dumped him for somebody richer," she said simply. "His pride was shattered. That's why he's here with me. He couldn't bear seeing her around town in all the nightspots with her new lover."

Harrison's attitude changed. "Poor guy."

"He won't hurt Lisa," she assured him, mentally crossing her fingers. She saw trouble ahead, but she didn't know quite how to ward it off.

He studied her face. "You're much more mature. I wouldn't have recognized you." He averted his eyes. "Pity King didn't get back in time for the party."

She froze over. "I didn't expect him, so it's no great loss."

He started to speak, and suddenly closed his mouth. He smiled at her. "Let's have a nightcap. Your friend can come along."

She took his arm with a grin. "That sounds more like you!"

THE NEXT DAY, Mark borrowed Harrison's sedan again and made a beeline for the McKinley place outside town. He was wearing slacks and a turtle-neck white sweater and he looked both elegant and expensive.

As Tiffany stood on the porch waving him off, a car came purring up the driveway. It was a black Lincoln. She fought down the urge to run. She didn't have to back away from King anymore. She was out of his reach. She folded her arms over the red silk blouse she was wearing with elegant black slacks and leaned against a post in a distinctive pose to wait for him. It surprised her just a little that he didn't have Carla with him.

King took the steps two at a time. He was wearing

dark evening clothes, as if he'd just come from a party. She imagined he was still wearing the clothes he'd had on the night before. Probably he didn't keep anything to change into at Carla's place, she thought venomously, certain that it explained his state of dress.

"Well, well, what brings you here?" she drawled, without any particular shyness.

King paused at the last step, scowling as he got a good look at her. The change was phenomenal. She wasn't the young girl he'd left behind months before. She was poised, elegant, somehow cynical. Her eyes were older and there was no welcome or hero-worship in them now. Her smile, if anything, was mocking.

"I came to see Harrison," he said curtly.

She waved a hand toward the front door. "Help yourself. I was just seeing Mark off."

He seemed suddenly very still. "Mark?"

"Mark Allenby. We work together. He came home with me for our holidays." She gave him a cool glance. "You've probably seen him in commercials. He's incredibly handsome."

He didn't say another word. He walked past her without speaking and went right into the house.

Tiffany followed a few minutes later, and found him with her father in the study.

Harrison glanced out the door as she passed it on her way to the staircase. "Tiffany! Come in here a minute, would you, sweetheart?"

He never called her pet names unless he wanted something. She wandered into the room as if King's presence made no difference at all to her. "What do you want, Dad?" she asked with a smile.

"King needs some papers from the safe at my office, and I promised I'd drive Lettie down to Floresville to visit her sister. Would you…?"

She knew the combination by heart, something her father had entrusted her with only two years before. But she sensed a plot here and she hesitated. King noticed, and his face froze over.

"You don't have anything pressing, do you?" Harrison persisted. "Not with Mark away?"

"I suppose not." She gave in. "I'll just get my jacket."

"Thanks, sweetheart!"

She only shrugged. She didn't even glance at King.

It was a short drive to the downtown office her father shared with King. It seemed a little strange to her that King didn't have the combination to Harrison's safe, since they were partners. She'd never really wondered why until now.

"Doesn't he trust you?" she chided as they went into the dark office together.

"As much as he trusts anyone," he replied. "But in case you wondered, he doesn't have the combination to my safe, either. Our respective lawyers have both. It's a safeguard, of a sort."

He turned on the lights and closed the door. The sprawling offices were vacant on this holiday and she was more aware than ever of being totally alone with him. It shouldn't have bothered her, knowing what she did about his relationship with Carla, but it did. It hadn't been long enough for her to forget the pleasure of his kisses, being in his arms.

She ignored her tingling nerves and went straight

to the concealed safe, opening it deftly. "What do you want out of here?" she asked.

"A brown envelope marked *Internet Proposals*."

She searched through the documents and found what he wanted. She closed the safe, replaced the painting that covered it, and handed the envelope to King.

"Is that all you needed me for?" she asked, turning toward the door.

"Not quite."

She hesitated a few feet away from him. Her eyes asked the question for her.

He wasn't smiling. The friendly man of years past was missing. His eyes were wary and piercing. He didn't move at all. He just stared at her until she felt her heartbeat accelerate.

She lifted her chin. "Well?"

"Was it deliberate?"

She blinked. "Was what deliberate?"

"Leaving us off the guest list for the New Year's Eve party."

She felt an uncomfortable tension in the air. She frowned. "You and Carla were invited," she said. "I faxed the list of invitations straight to the printers. The two of you were the first two names on the list. In fact, they went straight to my father's secretary from the printer's, to be mailed. Carla knows Rita, Dad's secretary. I'm sure she knew that you were on the list."

His eyes narrowed. "She said that she checked the list. Our names weren't there."

"Someone's lying," Tiffany said quietly.

He made a sound deep in his throat. "I don't need two guesses for a name."

"You think I did it. Why?"

He shrugged. "Spite?" he asked with a mocking smile. "After all, I sent you packing, didn't I?"

Months of conditioning kept her face from giving away any of her inner feelings. She pushed a hand into her jacket pocket and lifted an eyebrow. "You did me a favor, as it happens," she said. "You needn't worry, I'm no longer a threat to you. Mark and I are quite an item about town these days. We both work for the same agency. We see a lot of each other. And not only on the job."

His narrow gaze went over her, looking for differences. "You've changed."

Her shoulders rose and fell. "I've only grown up." Her smile never reached her eyes. "I have a bright future, they tell me. It seems that my body is photogenic."

Something flashed in his eyes and he turned away before she could see it. "I thought you were going on a holiday, not to find a job."

"I didn't have much choice," she said, turning back to the door. "There was nothing for me here."

His fist clenched at his side. He turned, about to speak, but she'd already opened the door and gone out into the hall.

He followed her, surprised to find her headed not for the exit, but for Rita's computer. She sat down behind the desk that her father's secretary used, turned on the computer, fed in a program, and searched the files for the invitation list. She found it and pulled it up on the screen. Sure enough, King's name wasn't on it. Neither was Carla's. But one of the agency models was a computer whiz and she'd been tutoring Tiffany on the side.

"I told you our names weren't there," he said gruffly from behind her.

"Oh, don't give up yet. Wait just a sec…" She put up another program, one designed to retrieve lost files, and set it searching. A minute later, she pulled up the deleted file and threw it up on the screen. There, at the top of the list, were King's and Carla's names.

King scowled. "How did you do that? I didn't see your hands typing on the keyboard."

"They didn't. This file was deliberately erased and replaced. I'm sure if I look for the fax, I'll discover that it's been redone as well." She saved the file, cut off the computer, and got to her feet. She met his eyes coldly. "Tell Carla nice try. But next time, she'd better practice a little more on her technique."

She retrieved her purse and went out the door, leaving King to follow, deep in thought.

"Why do you think Carla tampered with the list?" he asked on the way home.

"She's a girl with aspirations. Not that I'm any threat to them," she added firmly. "I have a life in New York that I'm learning to love, and a man to shower affection on. You might tell her that, before she dreams up any new ideas to put me in a bad light."

He didn't answer her. But his hands tightened on the steering wheel.

SHE WAS OUT of the car before he could unfasten his seat belt.

The house was empty, she knew, because Harrison was supposed to be out, and she was certain that Mark was still at Lisa's house. She didn't want King inside.

She paused on the lowest step. "I'll tell Dad you got the information you needed," she said firmly.

His narrow eyes went from her to the front of the house. "Is he in there waiting for you?" he asked coldly.

"If he is, it's nothing to do with you," she said solemnly. "As you said on that most memorable occasion, I wanted to play house and you didn't. For the record," she added with cold eyes, "I no longer want to play with you, in any manner whatsoever. Goodbye."

She went to the door, unlocked it, let herself in, and threw the bolt home after her. If he heard it, so much the better. She didn't want him within three feet of her, ever again!

CHAPTER SIX

TIFFANY WENT UPSTAIRS, almost shaking with fury at Carla's treacherous action, because certainly no one else could be blamed for the omission of those names on the guest list. Carla was playing to win and thought Tiffany was competition. It was funny, in a way, because King wanted no part of her. Why didn't Carla know that?

She went into her room and opened her closet. It was New Year's Day, and tomorrow she and Mark would have to fly back to New York and get ready to begin work again. It was going to be a hectic few weeks, with the spring showings in the near future, and Tiffany was almost certain that she'd be able to land a new contract. She was young and photogenic and her agent said that she had great potential. It wasn't as heady a prospect as a life with King, but it would have to suffice. Loneliness was something she was just going to have to get used to, so she...

"Packing already?"

The drawled question surprised her into gasping. She whirled, a hand at her throat, to find King lounging in the doorway.

"How did you get in?" she demanded.

"Kitty let me in the back door. She's cleaning the

kitchen." He closed the door firmly behind him and
started toward Tiffany with a strange glitter in his pale
blue eyes. "It isn't like you to run from a fight. You
never used to."

"Maybe I'm tired of fighting," she said through a
tight throat.

"Maybe I am, too," he replied curtly.

He backed her against the bed and suddenly gave
her a gentle push. She went down onto the mattress and
his lean, hard body followed her. He braced himself on
his forearms beside her head and stared into her eyes
at a breathless proximity.

"I'm expecting Mark..." She choked.

"Really? Kitty says he's at Lisa McKinley's house,
and very smitten, too, from the look of them at the
party last night." His hand smoothed away the lapels of
her jacket. His big hand skimmed softly over her breast
and his thumb lingered there long enough to make the
tip go hard. He smiled when he felt it. "Some things,
at least, never change."

"I don't know what you...oh!"

She arched completely off the bed when his mouth
suddenly covered her breast. Even through two layers
of cloth, it made her shiver with pleasure. Her hands
clenched at her ears and her eyes closed as she gave in
without even a struggle.

His hands slid under her clothing to the two fas-
tenings at her back. He loosened them and his hands
found the softness of her breasts. "Good God, it's like
running my hands over silk," he whispered as his head
lifted. "You feel like sweet heaven."

As he spoke, his hands moved. He watched her pu-

pils dilate, her lips part on whispery little sighs that
grew sharp when his thumbs brushed her hard nipples.

"The hell with it," he murmured roughly. He sat up,
drawing her with him, and proceeded to undress her.

"King…you can't…!"

"I want to suckle you," he said quietly, staring into
her shocked eyes as he freed her body from the clothes.

The words fanned the flames that were already devouring her. She didn't speak again. She sat breathing like a track runner while he tossed her jacket and
blouse and bra off the bed. Then his hands at her rib
cage arched her delicately toward him. He bent and his
mouth slowly fastened on her breast.

There was no past, no present. There was only the
glory of King's hard mouth on her body. She sobbed
breathlessly as the pleasure grew to unbelievable
heights.

He had her across his knees, her head falling naturally into the crook of his arm, while he fed on her
breasts. The nuzzling, suckling pressure was the
sweetest sensation she'd ever known. It had been so
long since he'd held her like this. She was alive again,
breathing again.

"Easy, darling," he whispered when she began to
sob aloud. "Easy, now."

"King…!" Her voice broke. She sounded as frantic
as she felt, her heartbeat smothering her, the pressure
of his hands all of heaven as he held her to his chest.

"Baby…" He eased her onto the bed and slid alongside her, his face solemn, his eyes dark with feeling.
His mouth found hers, held it gently under his while
his hands searched out the places where she ached and

began to soothe them…only the soothing made the tension worse.

She moaned, tears of frustration stinging her eyes as his caresses only made the hunger more unbearable.

"All right," he whispered, easing down against her. "It's too soon, Tiffany, but I'm going to give you what you want."

He shifted her and his hand moved slowly against her body. She stiffened, but he didn't stop. He kissed her shocked eyelids closed and then smothered the words of protest she tried to voice.

She had no control over her body, none at all. It insisted, it demanded, it was wanton as it sought fulfillment. Her eyes remained tightly closed while she arched and arched, pleading, whispering to him, pride shorn from her in the grip of a madness like none she'd ever experienced.

She opened her eyes all at once and went rigid as a flash of pleasure like hot lightning shot through her flesh. She looked at him in shock and awe and suddenly she was flying among the stars, falling, soaring, in a shuddering ecstasy that none of her reading had ever prepared her for.

Afterward, of course, she wept. She was embarrassed and shocked by this newest lesson in passion and its fulfillment. She hid her face against him, still shivering gently in the aftermath.

"I told you it was too soon," he whispered quietly. He held her close, his face nuzzling her throat. "I took it too far. I only meant to kiss you." His arms tightened. "Don't cry. There's no reason to be upset."

"Nobody…*ever*…" She choked.

His thumb pressed against her swollen lips. "I know." His mouth moved onto her wet eyelids and kissed the tears away slowly. "And that was only the beginning," he whispered. "You can't imagine how it really feels."

He carried her hand to his body and shivered as he moved it delicately against him. "I want you."

She pressed her lips to his throat. "I know. I want you, too."

His teeth nipped her earlobe gently and his breath caught. "Tiffany, your father is my business partner. There's no way we can sleep together without having him find out. It would devastate him. He doesn't really belong to this century."

"I know." She grimaced slightly. "Neither do I, I suppose."

He lifted his head and looked down at her soft hand resting so nervously against his body. He smiled gently even through the pleasure of her touch. His hand pressed hers closer as he looked into her eyes hungrily. "I'm starving," he whispered.

She swallowed, gathering her nerve. "I could...?"

He sighed. "No. You couldn't." He took her hand away and held it tightly in his. "In my way, I'm pretty old-fashioned, too." He grimaced. "I suppose you'd better come into town with me tomorrow and pick out a ring."

Her eyelids fluttered. "A what?"

"An engagement ring and a wedding band," he continued.

"You don't want to marry. You said so."

He looked down at himself ruefully and then back at her flushed face. "It's been several months," he said pointedly. "I'm not a man to whom abstinence comes naturally, to put it modestly. I need a woman."

"I thought you were having Carla," she accused.

He sighed heavily. "Well, that's one of the little problems I've been dealing with since you left. She can't seem to arouse my...interest."

Her eyes widened. This was news. "I understood that any woman can arouse a man."

"Reading fiction again, are we?" he murmured dryly. "Well, books and instruction manuals notwithstanding, my body doesn't seem to be able to read. It only wants you. And it wants you violently."

She was still tingling from her own pleasure. She grimaced.

"What?" he asked.

"I feel guilty. This was all just for me," she faltered, still a little embarrassed.

"I'll run around the house three times and have a cold shower," he murmured dryly. "No need to fret."

She laid back on the bed, watching him sketch her nudity with quick, possessive eyes. "You can, if you want to," she whispered with a wicked smile, never so sure of him as she was at the moment. "I'll let you."

His high cheekbones actually flushed. "With Kitty in the kitchen and aware that I'm up here?" He smiled mockingly and glanced at his watch. "I'd say we have about two minutes to go."

"Until what?"

"Until you have a phone call, or I have a phone call," he remarked. "Which will have strangely been disconnected the minute we pick up the receiver."

She giggled. "You're kidding."

"I'm not." He got up and rearranged his tie, staring down at her with pure anguish. "I want to bury myself in you!" he growled softly.

She flushed. "King!"

It didn't help that her eyes went immediately to that part of him that would perform such a task and she went even redder. She threw herself off the bed and began to fumble to put her clothing back on.

He chuckled. "All that magnificent bravado, gone without a whimper. What a surprise you've got in store on our wedding night," he murmured.

She finished buttoning her blouse and gave him a wry look. "You really are a rake."

"And you'll be glad about that, too," he added with a knowing look. "I promise you will."

She moved close to him, her eyes wide and eloquent. "It won't hurt after what we've done, will it?"

He hesitated. "I don't know," he said finally. "I'll be as careful and gentle as I can."

"I know that." She searched his eyes with a deep sadness that she couldn't seem to shake. "It's only because you want me that we're getting married, isn't it?"

He scowled. "Don't knock it. Sex is the foundation of any good marriage. You and I are highly compatible in that respect."

She wanted to pursue the conversation, but there was a sudden knock at the door.

"Yes, what is it, Kitty?" Tiffany called, distracted.

"Uh, there's a phone call for Mr. Marshall, Miss Tiffany," she called nervously.

"I'll take it downstairs, Kitty. Thanks!" he added with a roguish look in Tiffany's direction.

"You're welcome!" Kitty called brightly, and her footsteps died away.

"Your father puts her up to that," he mused.

"He's sheltered me."

"I know."

She pursed her lips and eyed him mischievously. "I've been saved up for you."

"I'll be worth the effort," he promised, a dark, confident gleam in his eyes.

"Oh, I know that." She went to open the door, pushing back her disheveled hair. "Are you coming to dinner tonight?"

"Is your male fashion plate going to be here?"

"I'm not sure. Lisa was very taken with him, and vice versa."

He smiled. "I started up here bristling with jealousy. I could have danced a jig when Kitty stopped me to tell me about your houseguest and Lisa."

"You were jealous?" she asked.

He lifted an eyebrow and his eyes slid over her like hands. "We both know that you've belonged to me since you've had breasts," he said blatantly. "I kept my distance, almost for too long. But I came to my senses in time."

"I hope you won't regret it."

"So do I," he said without thinking, and he looked disturbed.

"I'll try to make you glad," she whispered in what she hoped was a coquettish tone.

He grinned. "See that you do."

She opened the door and he followed her out into the hall.

MARK WAS MORE amused than anything when he discovered that his gal pal was engaged to her dream man. He and Lisa had found many things in common and a romance was blooming there, so he had only good wishes for Tiffany and her King. But there was something in the way King looked that made him uneasy. That man didn't have happily ever after in mind, and he wasn't passionately in love with Tiffany—and it showed. He wanted her; that was obvious to a blind man. But it seemed less than honest for a man to marry a woman only because of desire. Perhaps her father was the fly in the ointment. He couldn't see the dignified Mr. Blair allowing his only daughter to become the mistress of his business partner.

Of course! That had to be the reason for the sudden marriage plans. King had manipulated Tiffany so that she was done out of a fairy tale wedding, so that she was settling for a small, intimate ceremony instead. It was unkind and Mark wished he could help, but it seemed the only thing he could do for his friend was wish her the best and step aside. King didn't seem like a man who'd want a male friend in his virgin bride's life....

LIFE CHANGED FOR Tiffany overnight. She went to one of the biggest jewelers in San Antonio with King, where they looked at rings for half an hour before she chose a wide antique gold wedding band in yellow and white gold, with engraved roses.

King hesitated. "Don't you want a diamond?" he asked.

"No." She wasn't sure why, but she didn't. She let

the salesman try the ring on her finger. It was a perfect fit and she was enchanted with it.

King held her hand in his and looked down at it. The sentiment of the old-fashioned design made him strangely uneasy. It looked like an heirloom, something a wife would want to pass down to a child. His eyes met hers and he couldn't hide his misgivings. He'd more or less been forced into proposing by the situation, but he hadn't thought past the honeymoon. Here was proof that Tiffany had years, not months, of marriage in mind, while he only wanted to satisfy a raging hunger.

"Don't you like it?" she asked worriedly.

"It's exquisite," he replied with a determined smile. "Yes, I like it."

She sighed, relieved. "Don't you want to choose one?" she asked when he waved the salesman away.

"No," he said at once. He glanced down at her. "I'm not much on rings. I'm allergic to gold," he added untruthfully, thinking fast.

"Oh. Oh, I see." She brightened a little. It had hurt to think he didn't want to wear a visible symbol of his married status.

IN NO TIME at all, they were caught up in wedding arrangements. King didn't want a big society wedding, and neither did Tiffany. They settled for a small, intimate service in the local Presbyterian church with friends and family. A minister was engaged, and although traditionally the groom was to provide the flowers, Tiffany made the arrangements for them to be delivered.

Her one regret was not being able to have the elegant wedding gown she'd always imagined that she'd have. Such a dress seemed somehow out of place at a small service. She chose to wear a modern designer suit in white, instead, with an elegant little hat and veil.

She wished that her long-time best friend hadn't married a military man and moved to Germany with him. She had no one to be maid or matron of honor. There again, in a small service it wouldn't be noticeable.

King became irritable and withdrawn as the wedding date approached. He was forever away on business or working late at the office, and Tiffany hoped this wasn't going to become a pattern for their married life. She was realistic enough to understand that his job was important to him, but she wanted a big part in his life. She hoped she was going to have one.

The night before the wedding, King had supper with Tiffany and her father. He was so remote even Harrison noticed.

"Not getting cold feet, are you?" Harrison teased, and tensed at the look that raced across the younger man's face before he could conceal it.

"Of course not," King said curtly. "I've had a lot on my mind lately, that's all."

Tiffany paused with her glass in midair to glance at King. She hadn't really noticed how taut his face was, how uneasy he seemed. He'd never spoken of marriage in anyone's memory. In fact, he'd been quite honest about his mistrust of it. He'd had girlfriends for as long as Tiffany could remember, but there had never been a reason to be jealous of any of them. King never let himself become serious over a woman.

"Don't drop that," King murmured, nodding toward the loose grip she had on the glass.

She put it down deliberately. "King, you do want to marry me, don't you?" she asked abruptly.

His eyes met hers across the table. There was no trace of expression in them. "I wouldn't have asked you if I hadn't meant to go through with it," he replied.

The phrasing was odd. She hesitated for a few seconds, tracing patterns on her glass. "I could work for a while longer," she suggested, "and we could put off the ceremony."

"We're getting married Saturday," he reminded her. "I already have tickets for a resort on Jamaica for our honeymoon. We're scheduled on a nonstop flight Saturday afternoon to Montego Bay."

"Plans can be changed," she replied.

He laughed humorlessly. "Now who's got cold feet?" he challenged.

"Not me," she lied. She smiled and drained her glass. But inside, butterflies were rioting in her stomach. She'd never been more unsure of her own hopes and dreams. She wanted King, and he wanted her. But his was a physical need. Had she pushed him into this marriage after all, and now he was going to make the most of it? What if he tired of her before the honeymoon was even over?

She stopped this train of thought. It was absurd to have so little faith in her own abilities. She'd vamped him at her twenty-first birthday party, to such effect that he'd come home from his business trip out of his mind over her. If she could make him crazy once, she could do it twice. She could make him happy. She could fit in his world. It was, after all, hers, too. As for Carla, and the complications she might provoke, she could worry about that later. If she could keep King happy at home, Carla wouldn't have a prayer of splitting them up.

Her covetous eyes went over him as if they were curious hands, searching out his chiseled mouth, his straight nose, the shape of his head, the darkness of his hair, the deep-set eyes that could sparkle or stun. He was elegant, devastating to look at, a physical presence wherever he went. He had power and wealth and the arrogance that went with them. But was he capable of love, with the sort of loveless background he'd had? Could he learn it?

As she studied him, his head turned and he studied her, his eyes admiring her beauty, her grace. Something altered in the eyes that swept over her and his eyes narrowed.

"Am I slurping my soup?" she asked with an impish grin.

Caught off guard, he chuckled. "No. I was thinking what a beauty you are," he said honestly. "You won't change much in twenty years. You may get a gray hair or two, but you'll still be a miracle."

"What a nice thing to say," she murmured, putting down her soup spoon. "You remember that, in about six years' time. I'll remind you, in case you forget."

"I won't forget," he mused.

Harrison let out a faint sigh of relief. Surely it was only prenuptial nerves eating at King. The man had known Tiffany for years, after all, there wouldn't be many surprises for them. They had things in common and they liked each other. Even if love was missing at first, he knew it would come. It would have to. Nothing short of it would hold a man like King.

Tiffany glanced at her father's somber expression and lifted an eyebrow. "It's a wedding, not a wake," she chided.

He jerked and then laughed. "Sorry, darling, I was miles away."

"Thinking about Lettie?" she teased.

He glared at her. "I was not," he snapped back. "If they ever barbecue her, I'll bring the sauce."

"You know you like her. You're just too stubborn to admit it."

"She's a constant irritation, like a mole at the belt line."

Tiffany's eyes widened. "What a comparison!"

"I've got a better one," he said darkly.

"Don't say it!"

"Spoilsport," he muttered, attacking his slice of apple pie as if it were armed.

King was listening to the byplay, not with any real interest. He was deeply thoughtful and unusually quiet. He glanced at Tiffany occasionally, but now his expression was one of vague concern and worry. Was he keeping something from her? Perhaps something was going on in his life that she didn't know about. If she could get him alone later, perhaps he'd tell her what it was.

But after they finished eating, King glanced quickly at his watch and said that he had to get back to the office to finish up some paperwork.

Tiffany got up from the table and followed him into the hallway. "I thought we might have a minute to talk," she said worriedly. "We're getting married tomorrow."

"Which is why I have to work late tonight," he replied tersely. "It's been a very long time since I've given myself a week off. Ask your father."

"I don't have to. I know how hard you work." She looked up at him with real concern. "There's still time to back out, if you want to."

His eyebrows shot up. "Do you want to?"

She gnawed the inside of her lip, wondering if that was what he wanted her to admit. It was so difficult trying to read his thoughts. She couldn't begin to.

"No," she said honestly. "I don't want to. But if you do…"

"We'll go through with it," he said. "After all, we've got plenty in common. And it will keep the business in the family."

"Yes, it will go to our children…" she began.

"Good God," he laughed without mirth, "don't start talking about a family! That's years away, for us." He scowled suddenly and stared at her. "You haven't seen a doctor, have you?"

"For the blood test," she reminded him, diverted.

"For birth control," he stated flatly, watching her cheeks color. "I'll take care of it for now. But when we get back from our honeymoon, you make an appointment. I don't care what you choose, but I want you protected."

She felt as if he'd knocked her down and jumped on her feetfirst. "You know a lot about birth control for a bachelor," she faltered.

"That's why I'm still a bachelor," he replied coldly. He searched her eyes. "Children will be a mutual decision, not yours alone. I hope we've clarified that."

"You certainly have," she said.

"I'll see you at the church tomorrow." His eyes went over her quickly. "Try to get a good night's sleep. We've got a long day and a long trip ahead of us."

"Yes, I will."

He touched her hair, but he didn't kiss her. He laughed again, as if at some cold personal joke. He left her in the hallway without a backward glance. It was a foreboding sort of farewell for a couple on the eve of their wedding, and because of it, Tiffany didn't sleep at all.

CHAPTER SEVEN

THE NEXT DAY dawned with pouring rain. It was a gloomy morning that made Tiffany even more depressed than she had been to start with. She stared at her reflection in the mirror and hardly recognized herself. She didn't feel like the old devil-may-care Tiffany who would dare anything to get what she wanted from life. And she remembered with chilling precision the words of an old saying: *be careful what you wish for; you might get it.*

She made up her face carefully, camouflaging her paleness and the shadows under her eyes. She dressed in her neat white suit and remembered belatedly that she hadn't thought to get a bouquet for the occasion. It was too late now. She put on her hat and pulled the thin veil over her eyes, picked up her purse, and went out to join her father in the downstairs hall. The house seemed empty and unnaturally quiet, and she wondered what her late mother would have thought of this wedding.

Harrison, in an expensive dark suit with a white rose in his lapel, turned and smiled at his daughter as she came down the staircase.

"You look lovely," he said. "Your mother would have been proud."

"I hope so."

He came closer, frowning as he took her hands and found them ice-cold. "Darling, are you sure this is what you want?" he asked solemnly. "It's not too late to call it off, you know, even now."

For one mad instant, she thought about it. Panic had set in firmly. But she'd gone too far.

"It will work out," she said doggedly, and smiled at her father. "Don't worry."

He sighed impotently and shrugged. "I can't help it. Neither of you looked much like a happy couple over dinner last night. You seemed more like people who'd just won a chance on the guillotine."

"Oh, Dad," she moaned, and then burst out laughing. "Trust you to come up with something outrageous!"

He smiled, too. "That's better. You had a ghostly pallor when you came down the stairs. We wouldn't want people to mistake this ceremony for a wake."

"God forbid!" She took his arm. "Well," she said, taking a steadying breath, "let's get it over with."

"Comments like that are so reassuring," he muttered to himself as he escorted her out the door and into the white limousine that was to take them to the small church.

Surprisingly, the parking lot was full of cars when they pulled up at the curb.

"I don't remember inviting anyone," she ventured.

"King probably felt obliged to invite his company people," he reminded her. "Especially his executive staff."

"Well, yes, I suppose so." She waited for the chauffeur to open the door, and she got out gingerly, keenly aware that she didn't have a bouquet. She left her purse in the limo, in which she and King would be leaving for the airport immediately after the service. A reception hadn't been possible in the time allocated. King would probably have arranged some sort of refreshments for his office staff, of course, perhaps at a local restaurant.

Tiffany entered the church on her father's arm, and they paused to greet two of King's vice presidents, whom they knew quite well.

King was standing at the altar with the minister. The decorations were unsettling. Instead of the bower of roses she'd hoped for, she found two small and rather scruffy-looking flower arrangements gracing both sides of the altar. Carelessly tied white ribbons festooned the front pews. Family would have been sitting there, if she and King had any close relatives. Neither did, although Tiffany claimed Lettie as family, and sure enough, there she sat, in a suit, and especially a hat, that would have made fashion headlines. Tiffany smiled involuntarily at the picture her fashionable godmother made. Good thing the newspapers weren't represented, she thought, or Lettie would have overshadowed the bride and groom for splendor in that exquisite silk dress. And, of course, the hat.

The minister spotted Tiffany in the back of the church with her father and nodded to the organist who'd been hired to provide music. The familiar strains of the "Wedding March" filled the small church.

Tiffany's knees shook as she and her father made their way down the aisle. She wondered how many couples had walked this aisle, in love and with hope and joy? God knew, she was scared to death of what lay ahead.

And just when she thought she couldn't feel any worse, she spotted Carla in the front pew on King's side of the church. With disbelief, she registered that the woman was wearing a white lacy dress with a white veiled hat! As if she, not Tiffany, were the bride!

She felt her father tense as his own gaze followed hers, but neither of them were unconventional enough to make any public scene. It was unbelievable that King would invite his paramour here, to his wedding. But, then, perhaps he was making a statement. Tiffany would be his wife, but he was making no concessions in his personal life. When confronted by the pitiful floral accessories, and her lack of a bouquet, she wasn't particularly surprised that he'd invited Carla. She and her dress were the final indignity of the day.

King glanced sideways as she joined him, her father relinquishing her and going quickly to his own seat. King's eyes narrowed on her trim suit and the absence of a bouquet. He scowled.

She didn't react. She simply looked at the minister and gave him all her attention as he began the ceremony.

There was a flutter when, near the end of the service, he called for King to put the ring on Tiffany's finger. King searched his pockets, scowling fiercely, until he found it loose in his slacks' pocket, where he'd placed it earlier. He slid it onto Tiffany's finger, his face hardening when he registered how cold her hand was.

The minister finished his service, asked if the couple had any special thing they'd like to say as part of the ceremony. When they looked uneasy, he quickly pronounced them man and wife and smiled as he invited King to kiss the bride.

King turned to his new wife and stared at her with narrowed eyes for a long moment before he pulled up the thin veil and bent to kiss her carelessly with cold, firm lips.

People from the front pews surged forward to offer congratulations. Lettie was first. She hugged Tiffany warmly, acting like a mother hen. Tiffany had to fight tears, because her new status would take her away from the only surrogate mother she'd ever known. But she forced a watery smile and started to turn to her father when she saw a laughing Carla lift her arms around King's neck and kiss him passionately, full on the mouth.

The minister looked as surprised as Tiffany and her father did. Harrison actually started forward, when Lettie took his arm.

"Walk me to my car, Harrison," Lettie directed.

Seconds later, King extricated himself and shook hands with several of his executives. Tiffany gave Carla a look that could have fried an egg and deliberately took her father's free arm.

"Shall we go?" she said to her two elderly companions.

"Really, dear, this is most…unconventional," Lettie faltered as Tiffany marched them out of the church.

"Not half as unconventional as forgetting which woman you married," she said loudly enough for King, and the rest of the onlookers, to hear her.

She didn't look at him, although she could feel furious eyes stabbing her in the back.

She didn't care. He and his lover had humiliated her beyond bearing, and on her wedding day. She was tempted to go home with her father and get an annulment on the spot.

As she stood near the limousine with Harrison and Lettie, debating her next move, King caught her arm and parceled her unceremoniously into the limousine. She barely had time to wave as the driver took off.

"That was a faux pas of the highest order," he snapped at her.

"Try saying that with less lipstick on your mouth, darling," she drawled with pure poison.

He dug for a handkerchief and wiped his mouth, coming away with the vivid orange shade that Carla had been wearing.

"My own wedding," she said in a choked tone, her hands mangling her small purse, "and you and that… creature…make a spectacle of the whole thing!"

"You didn't help," he told her hotly, "showing up in a suit, without even a bouquet."

"The bouquet should have come from you," she said with shredded pride. "I wasn't going to beg for one. Judging by those flower arrangements you provided, if you'd ordered a bouquet for me, it would have come with dandelions and stinging nettle! As for the suit, you didn't want a big wedding, and a fancy gown would have been highly inappropriate for such a small ceremony."

He laughed coldly, glaring at her. "You didn't say you wanted a bouquet."

"You can give Carla one later and save her the trouble of having to catch mine."

He cursed roundly.

"Go ahead," she invited. "Ruin the rest of the day."

"This whole damned thing was your idea," he snapped at her, tugging roughly at his constricting tie. "Marriage was never in my mind, until you started throwing yourself at me! God knew, an affair was never an option."

She searched his averted profile sadly. As she'd feared, this had been, in many ways, a shotgun wedding. She mourned for the old days, when they were friends and enjoyed each other's company. Those days were gone forever.

"Yes. I know," she said heavily. She leaned back against the seat and felt as if she'd been dragged behind the car. She'd lost her temper, but it wasn't really his fault. He was as much a victim as she was, at the moment. "I don't know why I should have expected you to jump with joy," she said when she'd calmed a little. "You're right. I did force you into a marriage you didn't want. You have every right to be furious." She turned to him with dead eyes in a face like rice paper. "There's no need to go on with this farce. We can get an annulment, right now. If you'll just have the driver take me home, I'll start it right away."

He stared at her as if he feared for her sanity. "Are you out of your mind?" he asked shortly. "We've just been married. What the hell do you think it will say to my executives and my stockholders if I annul my marriage an hour after the ceremony?"

"No one has to know when it's done," she said reasonably. "You can fly to Jamaica and I'll go back to New York with Lettie until this all blows over."

"Back to modeling, I suppose?" he asked curtly.

She shrugged. "It's something to do," she said.

"You have something to do," he returned angrily. "You're my wife."

"Am I?" she asked. "Not one person in that church would have thought so, after you kissed Carla. In fact, I must say, her dress was much more appropriate than mine for the occasion, right down to the veil."

He averted his eyes, almost as if he were embarrassed. She leaned back again and closed her own eyes, to shut him out.

"I don't care," she said wearily. "Decide what you want, and I'll do it. Anything at all, except," she added, turning her head to stare at him with cold eyes, "sleep with you. That I will not do. Not now."

His eyebrows arched. "What the hell do you mean?"

"Exactly what I just said," she replied firmly. "You can get…that…from Carla, with my blessings." She almost bit through her lip telling the flat lie. Pride was very expensive. She closed her eyes again, to hide the fear that he might take her up on it. "I've been living in a fool's paradise, looking for happily ever after, dreaming of satin and lace and delicious nights and babies. And all I've got to show for it is a secondhand lust without even the gloss of friendship behind it and an absolute edict that I'm never to think of having a child."

He sat back in his own seat and stared straight ahead. Yes, he'd said that. He'd been emphatic, in fact, about not having children right away. He'd withdrawn from her in the past two weeks, so deliberately that he'd given the impression of a man being forced to do something he abhorred. He'd arranged a quick ceremony, but he hadn't let his secretary—Carla—arrange the flowers. He'd left that duty to another subordinate. He wondered what the hell had gone wrong. Only two sparse and not-very-attractive flower arrangements had graced the church and Tiffany had been denied a bouquet. He knew that it was deliberate, that Carla was somehow involved, but there was no way to undo the damage. By the time he saw the flowers it was far too late to do anything. Carla's dress and the kiss had been as much a surprise to him as it had to Tiffany. She wouldn't believe it, though. She was thinking of the things he'd denied her.

She'd been denied more than just flowers, at that. She hadn't had a photographer, a ring bearer, flower girls and attendants, a reception—she'd lacked all those as well. And to top it all off, it looked as if he'd wanted to kiss his secretary instead of his new bride, in front of the whole assembly.

His eyes sought her averted face again, with bitter regret. He'd fought marrying her from the start, hating his weakness for her, punishing her for it. This had been a travesty of a wedding, all around. She was bitter and wounded, and it was his fault. He studied her drawn countenance with haunted eyes. He remembered Tiffany all aglitter with happiness and the sheer joy of living, teasing him, laughing with him, tempting him, loving him. He could have had all that, just for himself. But he'd let his fears and misgivings cloud the occasion, and Tiffany had suffered for them.

He drew in a long breath and turned his eyes back to the window. This, he thought wearily, was going to be some honeymoon.

IN FACT, it was some honeymoon, but not at all the sort Tiffany had once dreamed about having. Montego Bay was full of life, a colorful and fascinating place with a long history and the friendliest, most welcoming people Tiffany could ever remember in her life.

They had a suite at an expensive resort on the beach, and fortunately it contained two rooms. She didn't ask King what he thought of her decision to sleep in the smaller of the two rooms; she simply moved in. She paid him the same attention she'd have paid a female roommate, and she didn't care what he thought about that, either. It was her honeymoon. She'd had no real wedding, but she was going to have a honeymoon, even if she had to spend it alone.

King had brought along his laptop with its built-in fax-modem, and he spent the evening working at the small desk near the window.

Tiffany put on a neat beige trouser suit and fixed her hair in a soft bun atop her head. She didn't even worry with makeup.

"I'm going to the restaurant to have supper," she announced.

He looked up from his monitor, with quiet, strangely subdued eyes. "Do you want company?"

"Not particularly, thanks." She went out the door while he was getting used to being an unwelcome tourist.

She sat alone at a table and ate a seafood salad. She

had a piña colada with her meal, and the amount of rum it contained sent her head spinning.

She was very happy, all of a sudden, and when a steel band began to play to the audience, she joined in the fun, clapping and laughing with the crowd.

It wasn't until a tall, swarthy man tried to pick her up that she realized how her behavior might be misinterpreted. She held up her left hand and gave the man a smile that held just the right portions of gratitude and regret. He bowed, nonplussed, and she got up to pay her bill.

King was out on the patio when she returned, but he looked at her curiously when she stumbled just inside the closed door and giggled.

"What the hell have you been doing?" he asked.

"Getting soused, apparently," she said with a vacant smile. "Do you have any idea how much rum they put in those drinks?"

"You never did have a head for hard liquor," he remarked with a faint smile.

"A man tried to pick me up."

The smile turned into a cold scowl. He came back into the room slowly. He'd changed into white slacks and a patterned silk shirt, which was hanging open over his dark-haired chest. He looked rakish with his hair on his forehead and his eyes glittering at her.

"I showed him my wedding ring," she said to placate him. "And I didn't kiss him. It is, after all, my wedding day."

"A hell of a wedding day," he replied honestly.

"If I hadn't gone all mushy, we'd still be friends,"

she said with a sad little sigh as the liquor made her honest. "I wish we were."

He moved a little closer and his chest rose and fell roughly. "So do I," he admitted tersely. He searched her sad eyes. "Tiffany, I...didn't want to be married."

"I know. It's all right," she said consolingly. "You don't have to be. When we get back, I'll go and see an attorney."

He didn't relax. His eyes were steady and curious, searching over her slender body, seeking out all the soft curves and lines of her. "You shouldn't have grown up."

"I didn't have much choice." She smothered a yawn and turned away. "Good night, King."

He watched her go with an ache in his belly that wouldn't quit. He wanted her, desperately. But an annulment would be impossible if he followed her into her room. And she'd already said that she didn't want him. He turned back to the cool breeze on the patio and walked outside, letting the wind cool his hot skin. He'd never felt so restless, or so cold inside.

TIFFANY AWOKE WITH a blinding headache and nausea thick in her throat. She managed to sit up on the side of the bed in her simple white cotton gown. It covered every inch of her, and she was glad now that she'd decided not to pack anything suggestive or glamorous. She looked very young in the gown and without her makeup, with her dark hair in a tangle around her pale face.

King knocked at the door and then walked in, hesitating in the doorway with an expression of faint surprise when he saw the way she looked. His brows drew together emphatically.

"Are you all right?" he asked curtly.

"I have a hangover," she replied without looking at him. "I want to die."

He breathed roughly. "Next time, leave the rum to the experts and have a soft drink. I've got some tablets in my case that will help. I'll bring you a couple. Want some coffee?"

"Black, please," she said. She didn't move. Her head was splitting.

When he came back, she still hadn't stirred. He shook two tablets into her hand and gave her a glass of water to swallow them with. She thanked him and gave back the glass.

"I'll bring the coffee in as soon as room service gets here," he said. "I don't suppose you want breakfast, but it would help not to have an empty stomach."

"I can't eat anything." She eased back down on the bed, curled up like a child with her eyes closed and a pillow shoved over her aching head.

He left her against his better judgment. A caring husband would have stayed with her, held her hand, offered sympathy. He'd fouled up so much for her in the past few weeks that he didn't think any overtures from him would be welcomed. She didn't even have to tell him why she'd had so much to drink the night before. He already knew.

Minutes later, he entered the room with the coffee and found Tiffany on the floor, gasping for breath. She couldn't seem to breathe. Her face was swollen. Red-rimmed eyes looked up at him with genuine panic.

"Good God." He went to the phone by her bed and called for a doctor, in tones that made threats if one wasn't forthcoming. Then he sat on the floor beside her, his expression one of subdued horror, trying to reassure her without a single idea what to do. She looked as if she might suffocate to death any minute.

The quick arrival of the doctor relieved his worry, but not for long.

Without even looking at King, the doctor jerked up the telephone and called for an ambulance.

"What did she eat?" the doctor shot at him as he filled a syringe from a small vial.

"Nothing this morning. She had a hangover. I gave her a couple of aspirins a few minutes ago…"

"Is she allergic to aspirin?" he asked curtly.

"I…don't know."

The doctor gave him a look that contained equal parts of contempt and anger. "You are her husband?" he asked with veiled sarcasm, then turned back to put the needle directly into the vein at her elbow.

"What are you giving her?" King asked curtly.

"Something to counteract an allergic reaction. You'd better go out and direct the ambulance men in here. Tell them not to lag behind."

King didn't argue, for once. He did exactly as he was told, cold all over as he took one last, fearful glance at Tiffany's poor swollen face. Her eyes were closed and she was still gasping audibly.

"Will she die?" King choked.

The doctor was counting her pulse. "Not if I can help it," he said tersely. "Hurry, man!"

King went out to the balcony and watched. He heard the ambulance arrive an eternity of seconds later. Almost at once ambulance attendants came into view. He motioned them up the stairs and into Tiffany's bedroom.

They loaded her onto a gurney and carried her out. Her color was a little better and she was breathing much more easily, but she was apparently unconscious.

"You can ride in the ambulance with her, if you like," the doctor invited.

King hesitated, not because he didn't want to go with her, but because he'd never been in such a position before and he was stunned.

"Follow in a cab, then," the other man rapped. "I'll ride with her."

He muttered under his breath, grabbed his wallet and key, locked the door, and went down to catch a cab at the front of the hotel. It was a simple exercise, there was always a cab waiting and a doorman to summon it.

MINUTES LATER, he was pacing outside the emergency room waiting for the doctor to come out. Strange how quickly his priorities had changed and rearranged in the past few minutes. All it had taken was seeing Tiffany like that. He knew that as long as he lived, the sight of her on the floor would come back to haunt him. It had been so unnecessary. He'd never bothered to ask if she was allergic to anything. He hadn't wanted to know her in any intimate or personal way.

Now he realized that he knew nothing at all, and that his ignorance had almost cost her her life this morning. Nothing was as important now as seeing that she had the best care, that she got better, that she never had to suffer again because of a lack of interest or caring on his part. He might not have wanted this marriage, but divorce was not feasible. He had to make the best of it. And he would.

CHAPTER EIGHT

BUT THE THING that hadn't occurred to him was that Tiffany might not care one way or the other for his concern. When she was released from the hospital later that day, with a warning not to ever touch aspirin again in any form, her whole attitude toward her husband had changed. Every ounce of spirit seemed to have been drained out of her.

She was quiet, unusually withdrawn on the way back to the hotel in the taxi. Her paleness hadn't abated, despite her treatment. The swelling had gone, but she was weak. He had to help her from the taxi and into the hotel.

"I never asked if you had allergies," King said as he supported her into the elevator. He pushed the button for their floor. "I'm sorry this happened."

"The whole thing was my fault," she said wearily. "My head hurt so bad that it never occurred to me to question what you were giving me. I haven't had an aspirin since I was thirteen."

He studied her as she leaned back against the wall of the elevator, looking as if she might collapse any minute. "One way or another, you've had a hell of a wedding."

She laughed mirthlessly. "Yes, I have."

The elevator jerked to a stop and the doors opened. King abruptly swung her up into his arms and carried her to their room, putting her down only long enough to produce the key and open the door.

She let her head rest on his broad shoulder and closed her eyes, pretending that he loved her, pretending that he wanted her. She'd lived on dreams of him most of her life, but reality had been a staggering blow to her pride and her heart. They were married, and yet not married.

He carried her into the sitting room and deposited her gently on the sofa. "Are you hungry?" he asked. "Do you think you could eat something?"

"A cold salad, perhaps," she murmured. "With thousand island dressing, and a glass of milk."

He phoned room service, ordering that for her and a steak and salad and a beer for himself.

"I didn't know you ever drank beer," she mused when he hung up.

He glanced at her curiously. "We've lived in each other's pockets for as long as I can remember," he said. "Amazing, isn't it, how little we actually know about each other."

She pushed back her disheveled hair with a sigh and closed her eyes. "I don't think there's a drop of anything left in my poor stomach. I couldn't eat last night. I didn't even have breakfast this morning."

"And you don't need to lose weight," he stated solemnly. He scowled as he searched over her body. "Tiffany, you've dropped a few pounds lately."

"I haven't had much appetite for several months," she said honestly. "It wasn't encouraged when I was modeling. After I came home, and we…decided to get married, I was too busy to eat a lot. It's been a hectic few weeks."

He hadn't missed the hesitation when she spoke of their decision to marry. He hated the way she looked. The change in her was so dramatic that anyone who'd known her even a year before wouldn't recognize her.

His heavy sigh caught her attention.

"Do you want to go home?" she asked.

The sadness in her eyes hurt him. "Only if you do," he said. "There are plenty of things to see around here. We could go up and walk around Rose Hall, for example," he added, mentioning a well-known historical spot.

But she shook her head. "I don't feel like sightseeing, King," she told him honestly. "Couldn't we go home?"

He hesitated. She was worn-out from the rushed wedding, the trip over here, her experience with the allergic reaction. He wanted to tell her that a night's sleep might make all the difference, but the sight of her face was enough to convince him that she'd do better in her own environment.

"All right," he said gently. "If that's what you want. We'll leave at the end of the week. I'll try to get tickets first thing in the morning."

She nodded. "Thank you."

Room service came with their orders and they ate in a strained silence. Tiffany finished her salad and coffee and then, pleading tiredness, got up to go to bed.

She started for her own room.

"Tiffany."

His deep voice stopped her at the doorway. She turned. "Yes?"

"Sleep with me."

Her heart jerked in her chest. Her eyes widened.

"No," he said, shaking his head as he got to his feet. "I don't want you that way yet, honey," he said softly, to lessen the blow of the statement. "You don't need to be alone tonight. It's a king-size bed, and you won't need to worry that I'll take advantage."

It was very tempting. He'd hardly touched her in almost a month. And although he didn't know it, any fear of having him take advantage of the situation was nonexistent. She sometimes felt that she'd have given six months of her life to have him throw her down onto the nearest available surface and ravish her to the point of exhaustion. She wondered what he'd say if she admitted that. Probably it would be just one more complication he didn't want. And there was still Carla, waiting back home.

"All right," she said after a minute. "If you don't mind…"

"Mind!" He bit off the word and turned away before she could see his strained face. "No," he said finally. "I don't…mind."

He was behaving very oddly, she mused as she showered and then put on another of her white embroidered gowns. The garment was very concealing and virginal, and there was a cotton robe that matched it, with colorful pastel embroidery on the collar and the hem, and even on the belt that secured it around her trim waist.

When she walked into the other room and approached

King's, through the slightly open door she heard him talking on the telephone.

"...be home tomorrow," he was saying. "I'll want everything ready when I get to the office. Yes, we'll talk about that," he added in a cold, biting tone. "No, I wouldn't make any bets on it. You do that. And don't foul things up this time or it will be the last mistake you make on my payroll. Is that clear?"

He put down the receiver with an angry breath and ran a hand through his own damp hair. He was wearing an incredibly sexy black velour robe with silver trim. When he turned, Tiffany's knees went weak at the wide swath of hair-roughened chest it bared to her hungry eyes.

He was looking at her, too. The gown and robe should have been dampening to any man's ardor, because she looked as virginal as he knew she was. But it inflamed him. With her face soft in the lamplight, her eyes downcast, she made him ache.

"Which side of the bed do you want?" he asked curtly.

"I like the left, but it doesn't matter."

He waved her toward it. Trying not to notice that he was watching her obsessively, she drew off the robe and spread it across the back of a nearby chair before she turned down the covers and, tossing off her slippers, climbed under the sheet.

He looked at her with darkening, narrowed eyes. She could see his heartbeat, it was so heavy. While she watched, his hand went to the loop that secured the belt of his robe and loosened it, catching the robe over one arm to toss it aside. He stood there, completely nude, completely aroused, and let her look.

Her lips parted. It was a blatant, arrogant action. She didn't know what to do or say. She couldn't manage words. He was…exquisite. He had a body that would have made the most jaded woman swoon with pleasure. And, remembering the heated mastery of his lovemaking, her body throbbed all over. It was in her eyes, her flushed face, her shaking heartbeat.

"Take it off," he said in a husky soft tone. "I want to look at you."

She wasn't able to think anymore. She clammered out from under the sheet and onto her knees, struggling to throw off the yards of concealing cotton. At last, she tugged it over her head and threw it onto the floor. Her body was as aroused as his. He knew the signs.

He moved around the bed. As he came closer, he caught the rose scent of her. Forgotten was the rocky start to their honeymoon, the accusations, the sudden illness. He approached her like a predator.

She made a helpless little sound and abruptly reached beside her to sweep both pillows off the bed and onto the floor as she surged backward, flat on the sheet, her legs parted, her arms beside her head. She trembled there, waiting, a little afraid of the overwhelming masculinity of him, but hungry and welcoming despite it.

He came onto the bed, slowly, stealthily, as if he still expected her to bolt. One lean, powerful leg inserted itself between both of hers, his chest hovered above hers, his arms slid beside her, his fingers interlaced with her own and pinned them beside her ears.

"It's…pagan." She choked.

He understood. He nodded slowly, and still his eyes

held hers, unblinking, as his leg moved against the inside of hers in a sinuous, sensual touch that echoed the predatory approach of his mouth to her parted lips.

It was like fencing, she thought half-dazed. His body teased her, his mouth teased her, every part of him was an instrument of seduction. It was nothing like their earlier lovemaking, when he'd kissed her, touched her, even pleasured her. This was the real thing, a prowling, tenderly violent stalking of the female by the male, a controlled savagery of pleasure that enticed but never satisfied, that aroused and denied all at the same time.

Her body shook as if with a fever and she arched, pleaded, pulled, twisted, trying to make him end it. The tension was at a level far beyond any that he'd ever subjected her to.

He touched her very briefly and then, finally—finally!—moved down into the intimacy that she'd begged for. But even as it came, it frightened her. She stiffened, her nails digging into his muscular arms, her teeth biting at her lower lip.

He stilled. His heart was beating furiously, but his eyes, despite their fierce need, were tender.

"First times are always difficult," he whispered. He held her eyes as he moved again, very gently. "Can you feel me, there?" he murmured wickedly, bending to brush his smiling lips against hers. They rested there as he moved again. "Talk to me."

"Talk?" She gasped as she felt him invading her. "Good… Lord…!"

"Talk to me," he chided, laughing as she clutched him. "This isn't a ritual of silence. We're learning each other in the most intimate way there is. It shouldn't be an ordeal. Look down my body while I'm taking you. See how it looks when we fit together like puzzle pieces."

"I couldn't!" she gasped.

"Why?" He stilled and deliberately lifted himself for a few seconds. "Look, Tiffany," he coaxed. "It isn't frightening, or sordid, or ugly. We're becoming lovers. It's the most beautiful thing a man and woman can share, especially when it's as emotional as it is physical. Look at us."

It was a powerful enticement, and it worked. But her shocked eyes didn't linger. They went quickly back to his, as if to seek comfort and reassurance.

"You're my wife," he whispered softly. He caught his breath as his next movement took him completely to the heart of her, and his eyes closed and he shivered.

Seeing him vulnerable like that seemed to rob her of fear and the slight discomfort of their intimate position. One of her hands freed itself and moved hesitantly to touch his drawn face, to sift through his thick, cool black hair. His eyes opened, as if the caress startled him.

It was incredible, to look at him and talk to him with the lights on while they fused in the most shocking way. But he didn't seem at all shocked. In fact, he watched her the whole time. When his hips began to move lazily against hers and the shock of pleasure lifted her tight against him, and she gasped, he actually laughed.

"For...shame!" She choked, shivering with each movement as unexpected pleasure rippled through her.

"Why?" he taunted.

"You laughed!"

"You delight me," he whispered, bending to nibble her lips as his movements lengthened and deepened. "I've never enjoyed it like this."

Which was an uncomfortable reminder that he was no novice. She started to speak, but as if he sensed what she was going to say, he suddenly shifted and she was overwhelmed by the most staggering pleasure she'd ever felt.

It possessed her. She couldn't even breathe. She arched up, helpless, her mouth open, her eyes dazed, gasping with each deliberate movement of his body. She was trying to grasp something elusive and explosive, reaching toward it with every thread of her being. It was just out of her reach, almost, almost, tantalizingly close...

"Oh...please!" she managed to say in a shuddering little cry.

He looked somber, almost violent in that instant. He said something, but she didn't hear him. Just as the tension abruptly snapped and she heard her own voice sobbing in unbearable pleasure, his face buried itself in her soft throat and his own body shuddered with the same sweet anguish.

For a long time afterward, his breathing was audible, raspy and unsteady at her ear. She gasped for air, but she was still clinging to him, as if she could retain just a fragment of that extraordinary wave of pleasure that had drowned her for endless seconds.

"It doesn't last," she whispered shakenly.

"It couldn't," he replied heavily. "The human body can only bear so much of it without dying."

Her hands spread on his damp shoulders with a sort of wonder at the feel of him so deep in her body. She moved her hips and felt the pleasure ripple through her unexpectedly.

She laughed at her discovery.

He lifted his dark head and his eyes, sated now, searched hers. "Experimenting?"

She nodded, and moved gently again, gasping as she found what she was searching for. But along with it came a new and unfamiliar stinging sensation and she stilled.

He brushed back her damp hair gently. "Your body has to get used to this," he murmured. "Right now, you need rest more than you need me." He moved very slowly and balanced himself on his hands. "Try to relax," he whispered. "This may be uncomfortable."

Which was an understatement. She closed her eyes and ground her teeth together as he lifted away from her.

He eased over onto his back with a heavy breath and turned his head toward her. "And now you know a few things that you didn't, before," he mused, watching her expressions. "Want a bath or just a wet cloth?"

The matter-of-fact question shouldn't have shocked her, but it did. Her nudity shocked her, too, and so did his. Without the anesthetic of passion, sex was very embarrassing. She got to her feet and gathered up her gown, holding it over her front.

"I… I think I'd like a shower," she stammered.

He got out of bed, completely uninhibited, and took the gown from her fingers, tossing it onto the bed.

"None of that," he taunted softly. "We're an old married couple now. That means we can bathe together."

Her expression was complicated. "We can?"

"We can."

He led her into the bathroom, turned on the shower jets, and plopped her in before him.

It was an adventure to bathe with someone. She was alternately embarrassed, intrigued, amused, and scandalized by it. But she laughed with pure delight at this unexpected facet of married life. It had never occurred to her that she might take a shower with King, even in her most erotic dreams.

Afterward, they dried each other and he carried her back to bed, placing her neatly under the covers, nude, before he joined her and turned off the lights.

He caught her wandering hand and drew it to his hairy chest with a chuckle.

"Stop that," he murmured. "You're used up. No more for you tonight, or probably tomorrow, either."

She knew he was right, but she was still bristling with curiosity and the newness of intimacy.

His hand smoothed her soft hair. "We have years of this ahead of us," he reminded her quietly. "You don't have to rush in as if tonight was the last night we'd ever have together."

She lay against him without speaking. That was how it had felt, though. There was a sort of desperation in it, a furious seeking and holding. She didn't understand her own fears, except that she was fatally uncertain of Kingman Marshall's staying power. Carla still loomed in the background, and even if he'd found Tiffany enjoyable in bed, he was still getting used to a married

status that he'd never wanted. She didn't kid herself
that it was smooth sailing from now on. In fact, the
intimacy they'd just shared might prove to be more of
a detriment than an advantage in the cold light of day.

The worry slowly drifted away, though, as she lay
in her husband's warm arms and inhaled the expensive scent of his cologne. Tomorrow would come, but
for tonight, she could pretend that she was a much-
loved wife with a long happy marriage ahead of her.
King must know that she hadn't had time to see a doctor about any sort of birth control. But he apparently
hadn't taken care of it as he'd said he would. He'd been
too hungry for her to take time to manage it himself.

She thought of a child and her whole body warmed
and flushed. He didn't want children, but she did, desperately. If he did leave her for Carla, she'd have a
small part of him that the other woman could never
take from her.

FROM PIPE DREAMS to reality was a hard fall. But she
woke alone the next day, with her gown tossed haphaz-
ardly on the bed with her. King was nowhere in sight,
and it was one o'clock in the afternoon!

She put on the gown and her slippers and robe and
padded slowly out into the sitting room of the suite.
It was empty, too. Perturbed, she went across into her
own room and found some white jeans and a red-and-
blue-and-white jersey to slip into. She tied her hair back
in a red ribbon, slipped on her sneakers, and started to
go out and look for King when she saw the envelope
on the dresser.

Her name was on the front in a familiar bold black slash. She picked up the envelope and held it, savoring for a moment the night before, because she knew inside herself that whatever was in that envelope was going to upset her.

She drew out a piece of hotel stationery and unfolded it.

Tiffany,
I've left your passport, and money for a return
ticket and anything else you need in your purse.
I've paid the hotel bill. An emergency came up
back home. I meant to tell you last night that
I had to leave first thing this morning, but it
slipped my mind. I managed to get the last seat
on a plane to San Antonio. We'll talk later.
King.

She read it twice more, folded it, and put it into the envelope. What sort of emergency was so pressing that a man had to leave his honeymoon to take care of it?

That was when something niggled at the back of her mind, and she remembered the snatch of conversation she'd overheard before they'd gone to bed. King had said that he'd be home tomorrow—today. She drew in a harsh breath. *Carla.* Carla had phoned him and he'd left his wife to rush home. She'd have bet her last dollar that there was no emergency at all, unless it was that he was missing his old lover. Apparently, she thought with despair, even the heated exchange of the night before hadn't been enough for him. And why should it? She was a novice, only a new experience for him. Carla was probably as expert as he was.

With wounded pride stiffening her backbone, she picked up the telephone and dialed the international code and her father's private office number.

"Hello?" he answered after a minute.

The sound of his voice was so dear and comforting that she hesitated a few seconds to choke back hurt tears. "Hi, Dad," she said.

"What the hell's going on?" he demanded. "King phoned me from the airport and said he was on his way into the city to sort out some union dispute at one of the branch offices. Since when do we have a union dispute?" he asked irritably.

"I don't know any more than you do," she said. "He left me a note."

He sighed angrily. "I could have dealt with a dispute, if there had been one. I've been doing it longer than he has, and I'm the senior partner."

He didn't have to say that. She already knew it. "I'm coming home tomorrow," she told him. "I, uh, sort of had a bout with some aspirin and I'm feeling bad. I was ready to leave, but there was only one seat available on the morning flight. We agreed that I'd follow tomorrow," she lied glibly.

It sounded fishy to Harrison, but he didn't say a word about it. "You're allergic to aspirin," he said pointedly.

"I know, but King didn't. I had a splitting headache and he gave me some. He had to take me to the hospital, but I'm fine now, and he knows not to give me aspirin again."

"Damnation!" her father growled. "Doesn't he know anything about you?"

"Oh, he's learning all the time," she assured him. "I'll talk to you tomorrow, Dad. Can you have the car meet me at the airport? I'm not sure if King will remember me, if he's involved in meetings." *Or with Carla*, she thought. King hadn't said anything about her coming home at all in his terse little note. She was going to be a surprise.

There was an ominous pause. "I'll remember you. Phone me when you get in. Take care, darling."

"You, too, Dad. See you."

He put down the receiver, got out of his chair, and made the door in two strides. He went past his secretary and down the hall to King's office, pushed open the door on a startled Carla, and slammed it back.

She actually gasped. "Mr.….Mr. Blair, can I do something for you?"

"You can stop trying to sabotage my daughter's marriage, you black-eyed little pit viper," he said with furious eyes. "First you fouled up the flowers, then you wore a dress to the ceremony that even to the most unprejudiced person in the world looked like a wedding gown. You kissed the groom as if you were the bride, and now you've managed to get King back here on some tom fool excuse, leaving his bride behind in Jamaica!"

Carla's eyes almost popped. "Mr. Blair, honestly, I never meant…"

"You're fired," he said furiously.

She managed to get to her feet and her cheeks flamed.

"Mr. Blair, I'm King's secretary," she said through her teeth. "You can't fire me!"

"I own fifty-one percent of the stock," he told her with pure contempt. "That means I can fire whom I damned well please. I said, you're fired, and that means you're fired."

She drew an indignant breath. "I'll file a complaint," she snapped back.

"Go right ahead," he invited. "I'll call the tabloids and give them a story that you'll have years to live down, after they do a little checking into your background."

It was only a shot in the dark, but she didn't know that. Her face went paper white. She actually shivered.

"Your severance pay will be waiting for you on the way out," he said shortly.

He went out the office door, almost colliding with King.

"I've just fired your damned secretary!" Harrison told King with uncharacteristic contempt. "And if you want a divorce from my daughter so you can go chasing after your sweet little paramour, here, I'll foot the bill! The two of you deserve each other!"

He shouldered past King and stormed away down the hall, back into his own office. The walls actually shook under the force with which he slammed the door.

King gave Carla a penetrating look. He walked into the office, and closed the door. Harrison had beaten him to the punch. He was going to fire Carla, but first he wanted some answers.

"All right," he said. "Let's have it."

"Have what?" she faltered. She moved close to him,

using every wile she had for all she was worth. "You aren't going to let him fire me, are you?" she teased, moving her hips gently against his body. "Not after all we've been to one another?"

He stiffened, but not with desire, and stepped back. "What we had was over long before I married Tiffany."

"It never had to be," she cooed. "She's a child, a little princess. What can she be to a man like you? Nothing more than a new experience."

"You phoned and said there was a labor dispute," he reminded her. "I can't find a trace of it."

She shrugged. "Tom said there were rumors of a strike and that I'd better let you know. Ask him, if you don't believe me." She struck a seductive pose. "Are you going to let him fire me?" she asked again.

He let out a harsh breath. Harrison was breathing fire. Apparently he'd got the wrong end of the stick and Carla had done nothing to change his mind.

"You've made an enemy of him," King told her. "A bad one. Your behavior at the wedding is something he won't forget."

"You will," she said confidently. "You didn't want to marry her. You didn't even check about the flowers or a silly bouquet, because you didn't care, and she embarrassed you by wearing a suit to get married in." She made a moue of distaste. "It was a farce."

"Yes, thanks to you." He stuck his hands into his pockets and glowered at her. He wondered how far out of his mind he'd been to get involved with this smiling boa constrictor. She'd been exciting and challenging, but now she was a nuisance. "I'll see what I can do about getting you another job. But not here," he added quietly. "I'm not going against Harrison."

"Is that why you married her?" she asked. "So that you could be sure of inheriting the whole company when he dies?"

"Don't be absurd."

She shrugged. "Maybe it's why she married you, too," she said, planting a seed of doubt. "She'll have security now, even if you divorce her, won't she?"

Divorce. Harrison had said something about a divorce. "I have to talk to Harrison," he said shortly. "You'll work your two weeks' notice, despite what he said, and I'll see what's going at another office."

"Thank you, sweet," she murmured. She moved close and reached up to kiss him. "You're a prince!"

He went out the door with a handkerchief to his mouth, wiping off the taste of her on his way to his partner's office.

CHAPTER NINE

HARRISON JUST GLARED at King when he went into the office and closed the door behind him.

"I don't care what you say, she's history," Harrison told the younger man. "She's meddled in my daughter's affairs for the last time!"

King scowled. He didn't like the look of his partner. "I haven't said a word," he said softly. "Calm down. If you want her to go, she goes. But let her work out her notice."

Harrison relaxed a little. His eyes were still flashing. He looked deathly pale and his breathing was unusually strained. He loosened his tie. "All right. But that's all. That silly woman," he said in a raspy voice. "She's caused… Tiffany…no end of heartache already, and now I've got…to cause her…more…" He paused with a hand to his throat and laughed in surprise. "That's funny. My throat hurts, right up to my jaw. I can't…" He grimaced and suddenly slumped to the floor. He looked gray and sweat covered his face.

King buzzed Harrison's secretary, told her to phone the emergency services number immediately and get some help into Harrison's office.

It was terribly apparent that Harrison was having a heart attack. His skin was cold and clammy and his lips were turning blue. King began CPR at once, and in no time, he had two other executives of the company standing by to relieve him, because he had no idea how long he'd have to keep it up before the ambulance came.

As it happened, less than five minutes elapsed between the call and the advent of two EMTs with a gurney. They got Harrison's heartbeat stabilized, hooked him up to oxygen and rushed him down to the ambulance with King right beside them.

"Any history of heart trouble in him or his family?" the EMT asked abruptly as he called the medical facility for orders.

"I don't know," King said irritably. For the second time in less than a week, he couldn't answer a simple question about the medical backgrounds of the two people he cared for most in the world. He felt impotent. "How's he doing?" he asked.

"He's stabilized, but these things are tricky," the EMT said. "Who's his personal physician?"

Finally, a question he could answer. He gave the information, which was passed on to the doctor answering the call at the medical center.

"Any family to notify?" the man relayed.

"I'm his son-in-law," King said grimly. "My wife is in Jamaica. I'll have to get her back here." He dreaded that. He'd have to tell her on the phone, and it was going to devastate her. But they couldn't afford the loss of time for him to fly down there after her. Harrison might not live that long.

The ambulance pulled up at the hospital, and Harrison, still unconscious, was taken inside to the emergency room. King went with him, pausing just long enough to speak with the physician before he found a pay phone and called the hotel in Jamaica. But more complications lay in store. Mrs. Marshall, he was told, had checked out that very morning. No, he didn't know where she'd gone, he was sorry.

King hung up, running an angry hand through his hair. Playing a grim hunch, he telephoned Harrison's house instead of his own. A maid answered the call.

"This is Kingman Marshall. Is my wife there?" he asked.

"Why, yes, sir. She got in about two hours ago. Shall I get her for you?"

He hesitated. "No. Thank you."

This was one thing he couldn't do on the phone. He told the doctor where he was going, hailed a taxi and had it drive him to Harrison's home.

TIFFANY WAS UPSTAIRS, UNPACKING. She paled when she saw King come in the door. She hadn't expected her father to be at home, since it was a working day. She hadn't expected to see King, either.

"Looking for me?" she asked coolly. "I've decided that I'm going to live here until the divorce."

Divorce! Everything he was going to say went right out of his mind. He'd left her after the most exquisite loving of his life. Hadn't he explained the emergency that had taken him from her side? It wasn't as if he hadn't planned to fly right back. He'd had no idea at all that Carla had manufactured the emergency.

"Tiffany," he began, "I flew back because there was an emergency…"

"Yes, and I know what it was," she replied, having

phoned the office just a while ago. "My father fired your secretary, and you had to rush back to save her job. I've just heard all about it from the receptionist, thanks."

"The receptionist?"

"I wanted to know if you were in. She talked to someone and said I should call back, you were in the middle of some sort of argument with my father..."

He let out a short breath. "We'll talk about that later. There's no time. Your father's had a heart attack. He's in the emergency room at city general. Get your purse and let's go."

She grasped her bedpost. "Is he alive? Will he be all right?"

"He was seeing the doctor when I left to fetch you," he replied. "Come on."

She went out with him, numb and shocked and frightened to death. Her life was falling apart. How would she go on if she lost her father? He was the only human being on earth who loved her, who needed her, who cared about her.

Through waves of fear and apprehension, she sat motionless as he drove her Jaguar to the hospital. When he pulled up at the emergency entrance and stopped, she leapt out and ran for the doors, not even pausing to wait for him.

She went straight to the clerk, rudely pushing in front of the person sitting there.

"Please." She choked, "My father, Harrison Blair, they just brought him in with a heart attack...?"

The clerk looked very worried. "You need to speak with the doctor, Miss Blair. Just one minute..."

King joined her in time to hear the clerk use her maiden name. Under different circumstances, he'd have been furious about that. But this wasn't the time.

The clerk motioned Tiffany toward another door. King took her arm firmly and went with her, sensing calamity.

A white-coated young doctor gestured to them, but he didn't take them into the cubicle where King had left her father. Instead, he motioned them farther down the hall to a small cluster of unoccupied seats.

"I'm sorry. I haven't done much of this yet, and I'm going to be clumsy about it," the young man said solemnly. "I'm afraid we lost him. I'm very sorry. It was a massive heart attack. We did everything we possibly could. It wasn't enough."

He patted her awkwardly on the upper arm, his face contorted with compassion.

"Thank you," King said quietly, and shook his hand. "I'm sure it's hard for you to lose a patient."

The doctor looked surprised, but he recovered quickly. "We'll beat these things one day," he said gently. "It's just that we don't have the technology yet. The worst thing is that his family physician told us he had no history of heart problems." He shook his head. "This was unexpected, I'm sure. But it was quick, and painless, if that's any comfort." He looked at Tiffany's stiff, shocked face and then back at King. "Bring her along with you, please. I'll give you something for her. She's going to need it. Any allergies to medicines?" he asked at once.

"Aspirin," King said. He glanced down at Tiffany, subduing his own sorrow at Harrison's loss. "Are you allergic to anything else, sweetheart?" he added tenderly.

She shook her head. She didn't see, didn't hear, didn't think. Her father was dead. King had argued with him over Carla. Her father was dead because of King.

She pushed his hand away. Her eyes, filled with hatred, seared into his mind as she looked up at him. "This is your fault." She choked. "My father is dead! Was keeping Carla worth his life?"

He sucked in a sharp breath. "Tiffany, that wasn't what happened…"

She moved away from him, toward the cubicle where the doctor was waiting. She was certain that she never wanted to speak to her husband again for as long as she lived.

THE NEXT FEW days were a total black void. There were the arrangements to be made, a service to arrange, minor details that somehow fell into place with King's help. The Blair home became like a great empty tomb. Lettie came to stay, of course, and King did, too, in spite of her protests. He slept in a bedroom down the hall from Tiffany's, watching her go through life in a trance while he dealt with friends and lawyers and the funeral home. She spoke to him only when it became necessary. He couldn't really blame her for the way she felt. She was too upset to reason. There would be plenty of time to explain things to her when she'd had time to recover. Meanwhile, Carla was on her way out of the office despite her plea to work out her notice. On that one point, King had been firm. She had her severance pay and a terse letter of recommendation. If

only he could have foreseen, years ago, the trouble it
was going to cause him when he put her out of his life,
all this anguish with Tiffany might have been avoided.
But at that time, Carla had been an exciting companion and he'd never considered marrying anyone. Now
he was paying the price for his arrogance.

UNDAUNTED BY HER FIRING, Carla showed up at the funeral home, only to be escorted right back out again
by King. She made some veiled threat about going to
the tabloids with her story, and he invited her to do her
worst. She was out of his life. Nothing she did would
ever matter to him again, and he said so. She left, but
with a dangerous glint in her cold eyes.

She didn't come to the funeral service, Tiffany
noted, or to the graveside service. Apparently she'd
been told that it wasn't appropriate. Some people, Lettie had said huffily, had no breeding and no sensitiv-
ity. She said it deliberately, and within King's hearing.
He didn't react at all. Whatever he felt, he was keeping it to himself.

The only chip in his stony front came the night of
the funeral, when he sat in Harrison's study with only
a lamp burning and downed a third of a bottle of Harrison's fine Scotch whiskey.

Lettie intruded long enough to ask if he wanted
anything else from the kitchen before the housekeeper
closed it up.

He lifted the glass toward her. "I'm drinking my
supper, thanks," he drawled.

Lettie closed the door behind her and paused in front

of the big antique oak desk, where his booted feet were propped on its aged, pitted surface.

"What are you going to do about the house?" she asked abruptly. Her eyes were red. She'd cried for Harrison almost as much as Tiffany had. Now her only concern was the girl's future.

"What do you mean, what am I going to do?" he asked. "It belongs to Tiffany."

"No, it doesn't," Lettie said worriedly. "Harrison was certain right up until the wedding ceremony that you weren't going to go through with the marriage. He wanted Tiffany provided for if something happened to him, and he didn't want her to have to be dependent on you. So he went to see his personal accountant about having everything he owned put in trust for her, including the house and his half of the business." She folded her hands at her waist, frowning worriedly. "But the accountant couldn't be located. Then Harrison found out that the man had been steadily embezzling from him for the past three years." She lifted her hands and spread them. "Just this week, he learned that a new mortgage had been taken out on the house and grounds and the money transferred to an account in a Bahamian bank." She grimaced as King lowered his feet to the floor and sat up. "He'd hired a private detective and was to see his attorney this afternoon after filing a lawsuit against the man before he skips the country with what's left of Harrison's fortune. If you can't stop him, Tiffany will be bankrupt."

"Good God!" King got to his feet, weaving a little. "No wonder he was so upset! Lettie, why the hell didn't you say something before this?"

"Because I wasn't sure that I had the right to involve you, except where the business is concerned," she said flatly. "You must know that Tiffany doesn't want to continue your marriage."

His face was drawn taut like a rope. "I know it."

She shrugged. "But there's no one else who can deal with this. I certainly can't. I can't even balance my checkbook. I wouldn't know how to proceed against the man."

King leaned forward with his head in his hands. "Get me a pot of strong coffee," he said through heavy breaths. "Then I want every scrap of information you have on the man and what Harrison planned."

Lettie brightened just a little. "We'll all miss him," she said gently as she turned toward the door. "But Tiffany most of all. He was both parents to her, for most of her life." She hesitated. "She needs you."

He didn't reply. She didn't seem to expect him to. She went out and closed the door behind her.

Tiffany was sitting on the bottom step of the staircase, looking pale and worn. Her eyes were red and she had a crumpled handkerchief in her hand. The long white gown and robe she was wearing seemed to emphasize her thinness.

"Child, you should be in bed," Lettie chided softly.

"I can't sleep." She stared at the study door. "Is he in there?"

Lettie nodded.

"What's he doing?"

"Getting drunk."

That was vaguely surprising. "Oh."

"I want to know why my father had a heart attack,"

she said grimly. "The receptionist wouldn't let me speak with King the day Daddy died because he and my father were arguing. Then at the funeral, one of his coworkers said it was a pity about the blow-up, because it was only seconds later when he collapsed. I know he fired Carla. Was that why King argued with him?"

"I don't know. Tiffany," she said, approaching the girl, "this is a vulnerable time for all of us. Don't say anything, do anything, that you'll have cause to regret later. King's hurt, too. He respected Harrison. Even if they did argue, they were friends as well as business partners for a long time."

"They were friends until I married King." Tiffany corrected her. "My father thought it was a mistake. He was right."

"Was he? It's early days yet, and some marriages can have a rocky beginning. It's no easy thing to make a life with another person. Fairy tales notwithstanding, even the most loving couples have to adjust to a shared coexistence."

"It helps if both partners work at it," Tiffany said.

"I agree. Get in there and do your part," her godmother prodded, jerking her red head toward the closed study door. "If you want answers, he's the only person who's got them."

Tiffany stared at the carpet for a minute and then got slowly to her feet.

"That's the idea," Lettie said. "I'm going to make him a pot of coffee. We have a few complications. Get him to tell you about them. Shared problems are another part of building a marriage."

Tiffany laughed, but without mirth. She went to the door after Lettie vanished down the hall and opened it.

King glanced at her from behind the desk as she came into the room. "I didn't plan to strand you in Montego Bay," he said pointedly. "I would have been on my way back that night."

"Would you?" She went to the chair in front of the desk, a comfortable burgundy leather armchair that she'd occupied so many times when she and her father had talked. She sighed. "The whole world has changed since then."

"Yes. I know."

She leaned back, sliding her hands over the cold leather arms, over the brass studs that secured it to the frame. "Tell me how he died, King."

He hesitated, but only for a second. His chiseled mouth tugged into a mocking smile. "So they couldn't wait to tell you, hmm? I'm not surprised. Gossip loves a willing ear."

"Nobody told me anything. It was inferred."

"Same difference." He spread his hands on the desk and stood up. "Okay, honey, you want the truth, here it is. He fired Carla and they had a royal row over it. I walked in and he started on me. I followed him to his office and got there just in time to watch him collapse."

She let out the breath she'd been holding. Her nails bit into the leather arms of the chair. "Why did you follow him? Were you going to talk him out of it?"

"No. But there's more to this than an argument over Carla," he added, searching for the right way to explain to her the tangled and devastating fact of her father's loss of wealth.

"Yes, there is. We've already agreed that I maneuvered you into a marriage you didn't want," she said curtly. "We can agree that what happened in Montego Bay was a form of exorcism for both of us and let it go at that," she added when he started to speak. "Charge me with desertion, mental cruelty, anything you like. Let me know when the papers are ready and I'll sign them."

His eyes flashed like black fires. "There won't be a divorce," he said shortly.

She was surprised by the vehemence in his tone, until she remembered belatedly just what her status was. As her father's heir, by a quirk of fate she was now his business partner. He couldn't afford to divorce her. What an irony.

She cocked her head and looked at him with cold curiosity. "Oh, yes, I forgot, didn't I? We're business partners now. How nice to have it all in the family. You won't even have to buy me out. What's mine is yours."

The look on his face was a revelation. Amazing how he could pretend that the thought had never occurred to him.

"That's a nice touch, that look of surprise," she said admirably. "I expect you practiced in front of a mirror."

"Why are you downstairs at this hour of the night?" he asked.

"I couldn't sleep," she replied, and was suddenly vulnerable. She hated having it show. "My father was buried today," she drawled, "in case you forgot."

"We can do without the sarcasm," he said. "Wait a minute." He reached into her father's top desk drawer and extracted a bottle. "Come here."

She stopped with the width of the desk between them and held her hand out. He shook two capsules into her hand and recapped the bottle.

"Don't trust me with the whole bottle?" she taunted.

That was exactly how he felt, although he wasn't going to admit it. She'd had one too many upsets in the past few weeks. Normally as sound as a rock, even Tiffany could be pushed over the edge by grief and worry. He couldn't add the fear of bankruptcy to her store of problems. That one he could spare her. Let her think him a philanderer, if it helped. When she was strong enough, he'd tell her the truth.

"Take those and try to sleep," he said. "Things will look brighter in the morning."

She stared at the capsules with wounded wet eyes. "He was my rudder," she said in a husky whisper. "No matter how bad things got, he was always here to run to."

His face hardened. Once, he'd been there to run to, before they married and became enemies. "You'll never know how sorry I am," he said tightly. "If you believe nothing else, believe that I didn't cause him to have that heart attack. I didn't argue with him over Carla."

She glanced at him and saw the pain in his eyes for the first time. It took most of the fight out of her. She seemed to slump. "I know you cared about my father, King," she said heavily.

"And in case you're wondering," he added with a mocking smile, "she's gone. She has her severance pay and some sort of reference. You won't see her again."

She studied him silently. "Why?"

"Why, what?"

"Why did my father fire her?"

It was like walking on eggshells, but he had to tell her the truth. "Because she dragged me home from Jamaica with a nonexistent emergency, just to interfere with our honeymoon, and he knew it. He said he'd had enough of her meddling."

"So had I," she returned.

"Not half as much as I had," he said curtly. "Harrison beat me to the punch by five minutes."

"He did?"

"Come here."

He looked faintly violent, and he'd been drinking. She hesitated.

He got up and came around the desk, watching her back away. "Oh, hell, no, you don't," he said in a voice like silk. His arms slid under her and he lifted her clear of the floor. "I've listened to you until I'm deaf. Now you can listen to me."

He went back to his chair and sat down with Tiffany cradled stiffly in his arms.

"No need to do your imitation of a plank," he chided, making himself comfortable. "Drunk men make bad lovers. I'm not in the mood, anyway. Now, you listen!"

She squirmed, but he held her still.

"Carla wasn't supposed to have anything to do with the flowers for our wedding," he said shortly. "I gave that task to Edna, who heads the personnel department, because she grew up in a florist's shop. But I was out of the office and Carla went to her with a forged letter that said I wanted Carla to do it instead."

Tiffany actually gasped.

He nodded curtly. "And she didn't get those arrangements from a florist, she did them herself with wilted flowers that she either got from a florist, or from a florist's trash can! She never had any intention of bringing you a bouquet, either. The whole thing was deliberate."

"How did you find out?"

"I went to see Edna when I flew back from Jamaica and found there was no emergency. I gave her hell about the flowers," he said. "She gave it back, with interest. Then she told me what had really happened. I was livid. I'd gone straight to my office to have it out with Carla when I found your father there."

"Oh."

He searched her stunned eyes. "You don't think much of me, do you?" he asked quietly. "Regardless of how I felt about the wedding, I wouldn't have deliberately hurt you like that."

She grimaced. "I should have known."

"You wore a suit to be married in," he added. "That was a blow to my pride. I thought you were telling me in a nonverbal way that you were just going through the motions."

"And I thought that you wouldn't mind what I wore, because you didn't want to marry me in the first place."

The arm behind her shoulders contracted, and the big, warm hand at the end of it smoothed over her upper arm in an absent, comforting motion. "I drew away from you at a time when we should have been talking about our insecurities," he said after a minute. "We had too many secrets. In fact, we still have them." He took a quick breath. "Tiffany, your father's personal accountant just did a flit with the majority of your inheritance. I'll bet that's what really set your father off, not Carla, although she helped. He was upset because he knew he'd have to tell you what had happened when you came home."

Tiffany's eyes widened. "You mean, Daddy was robbed?"

"In a nutshell," he agreed. He smiled faintly. "So, along with all your other woes, my wife, you may have bankruptcy looming unless I can find that accountant and prosecute him."

"I'm broke?" she said.

He nodded.

She sighed. "There goes my yacht."

"What do you want with one of those?"

She kept her eyes lowered demurely. Her heart was racing, because they were talking as they'd never talked before. "I thought I'd dangle it on the waterfront for bait and see if I could catch a nice man to marry."

That sounded like the girl he used to know. His eyes began to twinkle just faintly and he smiled. "What are you going to do with the husband you've already got?"

She studied his lean face with pursed lips. "I thought you were going to divorce me."

One eyebrow levered up. His eyes dropped to her slender body and traced it with arrogant possession. "Think again."

CHAPTER TEN

THE LOOK IN his eyes was electric and Tiffany watched him watching her for long, exquisite seconds before his head began to bend.

She lay in his arms, waiting, barely breathing as he drew her closer. It seemed like forever since he'd kissed her, and she wanted him. She reached up, barely breathing, waiting…

The sudden intrusion of Lettie with a tray of coffee and cookies was as explosive as a bomb going off. They both jerked.

She hesitated just inside the door and stared at them. "Shall I go away?" she asked, chuckling.

King recovered with apparent ease. "Not if those are lemon cookies," he said.

Tiffany gasped, but he got up and helped her to her feet with a rakish grin. "Sorry, honey, but lemon cookies are my greatest weakness."

"Do tell," she murmured with her hands on her hips.

He gave her a thorough going-over with acquisitive eyes. "My *second* greatest weakness," he said, correcting her.

"Too late now," she told him and moved a little self-consciously toward Lettie as King swept forward and took the heavy tray from her.

He put it on the coffee table and they gathered around it while Lettie poured coffee into thin china cups and distributed saucers and cookies.

"I'm going to be poor, Lettie," Tiffany told Lettie.

"Not yet, you're not," King murmured as he savored a cookie. "I'll get in touch with the private detective your father hired to trail your elusive accountant, not to mention Interpol. He'll be caught."

"Poor Daddy," Tiffany sighed, tearing a little as she thought of her loss. "He must have only found out."

"About two days before the heart attack, I think," Lettie said heavily. She leaned over to pick up her coffee. "I tried to get him to see a doctor even then. His color wasn't good. That was unusual, too, because Harrison was always so robust—" She broke off, fighting tears.

Tiffany put an arm around her. "There, there," she said softly. "He wouldn't want us to carry on like this."

"No, he wouldn't," King added. "But we'll all grieve, just the same. He was a good man."

Tiffany struggled to get in a deep breath. She bit halfheartedly into a cookie and smiled. "These are good."

"There's a bakery downtown, where they make them fresh every day," Lettie confided.

"I know where it is," King mused. "I stop by there some afternoons to buy a couple to go with my coffee."

Tiffany glanced at him a little shyly and smiled. "I didn't know you liked cookies."

He looked back at her, but he didn't smile. "I didn't know you were allergic to aspirin."

He sounded as if not knowing that fact about her really bothered him, too.

"It's the only thing," she replied. She searched his drawn features. "King, you couldn't have known about Daddy's heart. I didn't even know. You heard what the doctor said. There was no history of heart trouble, either."

He stared at his half-eaten cookie. "It didn't help to have him upset…"

She touched his hand. "It would have happened anyway," she said, and she was sure of it now. "You can only control so much in life. There are always going to be things that you can't change."

He wouldn't meet her eyes. His jaw was drawn tight.

"Yes, I know, you don't like being out of control, in any way," she said gently, surprising him. "But neither of us could have prevented what happened. I remember reading about a politician who had a heart attack right in his doctor's office, and nobody could save him. Do you see what I mean?"

He reached out his free hand and linked it with hers. "I suppose so."

Lettie sipped coffee, lost in her own thoughts. She missed Harrison, too. The house was empty without him. She looked up suddenly. "Good Lord, you only had a one-day honeymoon," she exclaimed.

"It was a good day," King murmured.

"Yes, it was," Tiffany said huskily, and his fingers contracted around hers.

"We'll finish it when we solve our problems here," King replied. "We have all the time in the world."

Tiffany nodded.

"It will be a shame if you can't catch that crook," Lettie said, looking around her at the beauty of the study. "This house is the beginning of a legacy. Harrison had hoped to leave it to his grandchildren."

Tiffany felt King stiffen beside her. Slowly, she unlinked her hand with his and put both hands around her coffee cup.

"We have years to talk about children," she told Lettie deliberately. "Some couples don't ever have them."

"Oh, but you will, dear," Lettie murmured dreamily. "I remember how we used to go shopping, and the nursery department was always the first place you'd stop. You'd touch little gowns and booties and smile and talk about babies…"

Tiffany got to her feet, hoping her sudden paleness wouldn't upset Lettie. She had no way of knowing that King didn't want a child.

"I'm so tired, Lettie," she said, and looked it. She smiled apologetically. "I'd like to try to go back to sleep, if you don't mind."

"Of course not, dear. Can you sleep now, do you think?"

Tiffany reached into the pocket of her robe and produced the two capsules King had given her. She picked up her half-full cup of coffee and swallowed them. "I will now," she said as she replaced the cup in the saucer. "Thank you, King," she added without looking directly at him.

"Will you be all right?" he asked.

She felt that he was trying to make her look at him. She couldn't bear to, not yet. She was thinking about the long, lonely years ahead with no babies. She didn't dare hope that their only night together would produce fruit. That one lapse wasn't enough to build a dream on. Nobody got pregnant the first time. Well, some people did, but she didn't have that sort of luck. She wondered if King remembered how careless he'd been.

"I hope you both sleep well," she said as she went from the room.

"You, too, dear," Lettie called after her. She finished her coffee. "I'll take the tray back to the kitchen."

"I'll do it," King murmured. He got up and picked it up, less rocky on his feet now that he'd filled himself full of caffeine.

"Are you going to try to sleep?"

He shook his head. "I've got too much work to do. It may be the middle of the night here, but I can still do business with half the world. I have to wrap up some loose ends. Tomorrow, I'm going to have my hands full tracing that accountant."

Lettie went with him to the kitchen and sorted out the things that needed washing.

King paused at the door, his face solemn and thoughtful. "Stay close to Tiffany tomorrow, will you?" he asked. "I don't want her alone."

"Of course, I will." She glanced at him. "Are you worried about Carla?"

He nodded. "She's always been high-strung, but just lately she seems off balance to me. I don't think she'd try to do anything to Tiffany. But there's no harm in taking precautions."

"I wish…" she began and stopped.

"Yes. I wish I'd never gotten involved with her, either," he replied, finishing the thought for her. "Hindsight is a grand thing."

"Indeed it is." She searched his bloodshot eyes. "You aren't sorry you married Tiffany?"

"I'm sorry I waited so long," he countered.

"But there are still problems?" she probed gently.

He drew in a long breath. "She wants babies and I don't."

"Oh, King!"

He winced. "I've been a bachelor all my life," he said shortly. "Marriage was hard enough. I haven't started adjusting to it yet. Fatherhood…" His broad shoulders rose and fell jerkily. "I can't cope with that. Not for a long time, if ever. It's something Tiffany will have to learn to live with."

Lettie bit down on harsh words. She sighed worriedly. "Tiffany's still very young, of course," she said pointedly.

"Young and full of dreams," King agreed. He stared at the sink. "Impossible dreams."

Outside the door, the object of their conversation turned and made her way slowly back upstairs, no longer thirsty for the glass of milk she'd come to take to bed with her. So there it was. King would never want a child. If she wanted him, it seemed that she'd have to give up any hopes of becoming a mother. Some women didn't want children. It was a pity that Tiffany did.

SHE DIDN'T HAVE to avoid King in the days that followed. He simply wasn't home. Business had become overwhelming in the wake of Harrison Blair's death. There were all sorts of legalities to deal with, and King had a new secretary who had to learn her job the hard way. He was very seldom home, and when he was, he seemed to stay on the telephone.

Lettie was still in residence, because Tiffany had begged her to stay. The house was big and empty without Harrison, but Lettie made it bearable. And on the rare occasions when King was home, their meals weren't silent ones. Lettie carried on conversations with herself if no one else participated, which amused Tiffany no end.

She hadn't paid much attention to the date. She'd grieved for two long weeks, crying every time she saw familiar things of her father's, adjusting to life without him. But just as she was getting used to the lonely house, another unexpected complication presented itself.

Tiffany suddenly started losing her breakfast. She'd never had any such problems before, and even if it was too soon for tests, deep inside she knew that she was pregnant. She went from boundless joy to stifling fear in a matter of seconds as she realized how this news was going to affect her husband. Her hands went protectively to her flat stomach and she groaned out loud.

She couldn't tell him. He wouldn't want the baby, and he might even suggest…alternatives. There wasn't an option she was willing to discuss. She was going to have her baby, even if she had to leave him and hide it away. That meant that she had to keep her condition secret.

At first it was easy. He was never home. But as the demands of business slowed a couple of weeks later, he began to come home earlier. And he was attentive, gentle with Tiffany, as if he were trying to undo their rocky beginning and start over.

It wounded her to the quick to have to withdraw from those sweet overtures, because she needed him now more than at any time in their shared past. But it was too great a risk to let him come close. Her body was changing. He wasn't stupid. If he saw her unclothed, there were little signs that even a bachelor might notice.

Her behavior surprised him, though, because they'd become much closer after Harrison's death. He'd had business demands that had kept him away from home, and he'd deliberately made very few demands on Tiffany just after her father's death, to give her time to adjust. But now, suddenly, she was talking about going back to modeling in New York, with Lettie to keep her company.

King worried about her attitude. He'd been kept busy with the transfer of authority and stocks and the implementation of Harrison's will, not to mention tracking down the elusive accountant. Perhaps she'd thought he wasn't interested in her feelings. That wasn't true. But when he tried to talk to her, she found dozens of excuses to get out of his vicinity.

Even Lettie was puzzled and remarked about Tiffany's coldness to the man, when he'd done so much for them. But Tiffany only smiled and ignored every word she said. Even from Lettie, the bouts of nausea were carefully concealed. No one was going to threaten her baby, Tiffany told herself. Not even Lettie, who might unwittingly let the cat out of the bag.

She talked about going to New York, but all the

while, she was checking into possible escape routes. She could fly anywhere in the world that she wanted to go. Even without her father's fortune, she had a legacy from her mother, which guaranteed her a tidy fixed sum every month paid into her personal checking account. She could live quite well and take care of her child. All she needed was a place to go.

King found her one afternoon poring over travel brochures, which she gathered with untidy haste and stuffed back into a folder as if she'd been caught stealing.

"Planning a trip?" he asked, scowling as he stood over her.

She sat forward on the sofa. "Who, me? No!" She cleared her throat. "Well, not immediately, at least. I thought..." She hesitated while she tried to formulate an answer that would throw him off the track.

"Heard from your friend Mark?" he asked abruptly.

"Mark?" She'd all but forgotten her modeling friend, although she saw Lisa occasionally, and Lisa certainly heard from him. They were becoming an item. "I believe he's in Greece," she added. "Doing a commercial for some swimwear company."

"Yes, he is," King replied thoughtfully. "I saw Lisa's father at a civic-club meeting this week. He said that the two of them are quite serious."

"I'm glad," Tiffany said. "Mark's had a hard life. So has Lisa, in some ways. She's always had money, but her father is a very domineering sort. I hope he isn't planning to throw a stick into their spokes."

"Apparently Lisa's threatened to run away if he

does," he mused, and smiled. "Love does make a woman brave, I suppose."

She could have made a nasty remark about Carla, but she let it go and made some careless remark.

"Don't you eat breakfast anymore?" he asked abruptly.

She jumped. "I… Well, no, I don't, really," she stammered. "I've gotten into bad habits since Daddy died," she added with a nervous laugh. "Breakfast reminds me too much of him."

"Which is still no reason to starve yourself, is it?"

She shifted, tracing a flower in the pattern on her skirt. "I'm not starving myself. I just don't like eating breakfast at the table. I have it in my room."

He stood there without speaking, frowning, jingling the loose change in his pocket.

She glanced at the clock and then at him. "Aren't you home early?" she asked.

"Yes." He moved to the armchair beside the sofa and dropped into it. "I thought you might like to know that we've found the runaway accountant."

"Have you really!"

He chuckled at her radiance. "Vengeful girl. Yes, he thought he'd gotten clean away. He was passing the time in luxurious splendor on a private island in the Bahamas when some rogue popped a bag over his head, trussed him up like a duck, and carted him off to a sailboat. He was hauled onto the beach in Miami and summarily arrested."

"Do we know rogues who would do such a thing?" she asked.

He chuckled. "Of course we do!"

"Does he still have any money?"

"All but a few thousand," he replied. "He confessed wholeheartedly when faced with a long prison term for his pains. He offered to give the money back without any prompting. To do him credit, he was sorry about Harrison."

"My father might still be here, if it hadn't been for that skunk. I won't shed any tears for him," she muttered. "I hope he isn't going to get off with a slap on the wrist."

"Not a chance," he replied. "He'll serve time. And he'll never get another job of trust."

"I suppose that's something. But it won't bring Daddy back."

"Nothing will do that."

She crossed her legs and glanced at King. He was restless and irritable. "What's wrong?" she asked.

"I wish I didn't have to tell you."

She sat up, bracing herself for anything. After what she'd just come through, she felt that she could take it on the chin, though, whatever it was. She was stronger than she'd ever been.

"Go ahead," she said. "Whatever it is, I can take it."

He looked at her, saw the new lines in her face, the new maturity. "How you've changed, Tiffany," he murmured absently.

"Stop stalling," she said.

He let out a hollow laugh. "Am I? Perhaps so." He leaned forward, resting his forearms across his knees. "I want you to see a doctor."

Her eyebrows arched. "Me? What for?"

"Because we're married," he replied evenly. "And I've gone without you for as long as I can. That being the case, you have to make some sort of preparation about birth control. We can't have any more lapses."

Steady, girl, she told herself. You can't give the show away now. She swallowed. "You said that you'd take care of it," she hedged.

"Yes, I did, didn't I?" he reflected with a laugh. "And you remember how efficiently I did it, don't you?" he asked pointedly.

She flushed. "It was…unexpected."

"And exquisite," he said quietly. "I dream about how it was. I've tried to wait, to give you time to get over the trauma of losing Harrison. But, to put it bluntly, I'm hurting. I want you."

She felt her cheeks go hot. She still wasn't sophisticated enough for this sort of blunt discussion. "All right," she said. "I'll see the doctor."

"Good girl." He got up and moved toward the sofa, reaching down to pull her up into his arms with a long sigh. "I miss you in my bed, Tiffany," he murmured as he bent to her mouth. "I want you so badly…!"

His mouth opened on hers and she moaned harshly at the pleasure of his embrace. She reached up and held him around the neck, pressing her body to his, moving provocatively, involuntarily.

He groaned harshly and his hands went to her waist to pull her closer. Then, suddenly, he stilled. Holding her rigidly, he lifted his head. His breath seemed to catch in his throat. His eyes looked straight into hers. And while she was trying to decide what had made him stop, his hands smoothed with deliberation over her thick waist and, slowly, down over the faint swell of her stomach.

His face changed. She knew the instant he began to suspect. It was all there, the tautness, the shock, the horror.

She jerked away from him, her face stiff with pain. The breath she drew was painful.

He let his arms fall to his sides. The look he sent to her belly would have won a photo contest.

"No, I won't." She choked out the words before he could speak. She backed toward the door. "I won't do anything about it, I don't care what you say, what you do! It's mine, and I'm going to have it! Do you hear me, I'm going to have it!"

She whirled and ran toward the staircase, desperate to reach the sanctuary of her room. She could lock the door and he couldn't get in, she could outrun him! But out of the corner of her eye, she saw him racing toward her. She'd never make the staircase, not at the speed he was running.

She turned at the last second and went toward the front door, panic in her movements, nausea in her throat. She jerked open the front door and forgot the rain that had made the brick porch as slick as glass. Her feet went out from under her and she fell with a horrible, sickening thud, right on her back.

"Tiffany!"

King's exclamation barely registered. She knew every bone in her body was broken. She couldn't even breathe, much less talk. She had the breath knocked completely out of her. She stared at his white face and didn't really see it at all.

"My...baby," she moaned with the only bit of breath she could muster.

King knelt beside her, his hands running over her gently, feeling for breaks while he strangled on every breath he took. There was a faint tremor in his long fingers.

"Don't try to move," he said uneasily. "Dear God…!" He got up and went back to the doorway. "Lettie! Lettie, get an ambulance, she's fallen!"

"Is she all right?" Lettie's wail came out the door.

"I don't know. Call an ambulance!"

"Yes, dear, right now…!"

King knelt beside Tiffany and took her cold, nerveless hand in his. The rain was coming down steadily beyond the porch, like a curtain between the two of them and the world.

Tiffany sucked in shallow breaths. Tears ran down her cheek. One hand lifted to her stomach. She began to sob. "My baby," she wept. "My baby!"

"Oh, God, don't!" he groaned. He touched her wet cheeks with the backs of his fingers, trying to dry the tears. "You're all right, sweetheart, you're going to be fine. You're going to be fine… Lettie! For God's sake!"

Lettie came at a run, pausing at the slick porch. "I've phoned, and they're on the way right now." She moved onto the wet surface and looked down at Tiffany. "Oh, my dear," she groaned, "I'm so sorry!"

Tiffany was beyond words. She couldn't seem to stop crying. The tears upset King more than she'd ever seen anything upset him. He found his handkerchief and dried her wet eyes, murmuring to her, trying to comfort her.

She closed her eyes. She hurt all over, and she'd probably lost the baby. She'd never get another one.

He'd make sure that she took precautions from now on, she'd grow old without the comfort of a child, without the joy of holding her baby in her arms...

The sobs shook her.

King eased down beside her, regardless of the wet floor, and his big hand flattened gently over her flat stomach, pressing tenderly.

"Try not to worry," he whispered at her lips. He kissed her softly, and his hand moved protectively. "The baby's all right. I know he is."

CHAPTER ELEVEN

TIFFANY COULDN'T BELIEVE what she'd just heard. Her eyes opened and looked straight into his.

"You don't want it," she whispered.

He drew in a rough breath and his hand spread even more. "Yes, I do," he said quietly. "I want both of you."

She could barely get enough breath to speak, and before she could find the words, the ambulance drowned out even her thoughts as it roared up at the front steps and two EMTs disembarked.

She was examined and then put into the ambulance. King went with her, promising Lettie that he'd phone the minute he knew anything.

Tiffany felt him grasp her hand as the ambulance started up again. "You're forever taking me away in ambulances," she whispered breathlessly.

He brought her hand to his mouth and kissed the palm hungrily. "Wherever you go, I go, Tiffany," he said. But his eyes were saying other things, impossible things. They took the rest of her breath away.

She was taken to the local emergency room and checked thoroughly, by the family physician who was doing rounds.

Dr. Briggs chuckled at her when he'd finished his tests and had the results, over an hour later. "I heard about your wild ride in Montego Bay. Now, here you are in a fall. Maybe marriage doesn't agree with you," he teased, having known her from childhood.

"It agrees with her," King murmured contentedly, watching her with open fascination. "So will having a baby to nurse." He glanced at Briggs. "Is she?"

He nodded, smiling complacently at Tiffany's gasp and radiant smile. "I don't imagine we'll have much trouble computing a delivery date," he added wickedly.

Tiffany flushed and King chuckled.

"One time," he murmured dryly. "And look what you did," he accused.

"What I did!" she exclaimed.

"I only plant. I don't cultivate."

She burst out laughing. She couldn't believe what she was hearing. All that talk about not wanting babies, and here he sat grinning like a Cheshire cat.

"He'll strut for a while," the doctor told her. "Then he'll start worrying, and he won't do any more strutting until after the delivery. You'll have to reassure him at frequent intervals. Expectant fathers," he said on a sigh, "are very fragile people."

"She'll have to have an obstetrician," King was murmuring aloud. He glanced at Briggs. "No offense."

"None taken," the doctor mused.

"A good obstetrician."

"I don't refer pregnant women to any other kind," he was assured.

"We'll need to find a good college, too—"

Tiffany started to protest, but King was at the window, talking to himself and Dr. Briggs held up a hand.

"Don't interrupt him," he told Tiffany. "He's considering all the other appropriate families in town who have baby daughters. He'll have to have the right wife—"

"It could be a girl," she interjected.

"Heresy!" the doctor said in mock alarm.

"Shouldn't we point that out?" she continued, glancing at King.

Dr. Briggs shook his head. "A man has to have dynastic dreams from time to time." He smiled. "You're fine, Tiffany. A few bruises, but nothing broken and that baby is firmly implanted. Just don't overdo during the first trimester. Call me Monday and I'll refer you to an obstetrician. I do not," he added, "deliver babies. I like sleeping at night."

"Are babies born at night?"

"From what I hear, almost all of them," he said with a chuckle.

King took her home, still reeling with his discoveries. He carried her inside, cradling her like a treasure.

Lettie met them at the door, wringing her hands. "You didn't phone," she said accusingly.

"He was too busy arranging the wedding," Tiffany replied.

Lettie looked blank. "Wedding?"

"Our son's."

"Son." Lettie still looked blank. Then her face flushed with glorious surprise. "You're pregnant!"

"Yes," she said.

Lettie gnawed her lip and shot a worried glance at King.

"I know," he said wearily. "I'll have to eat boiled crow for the next month, and I deserve to." He shrugged, holding Tiffany closer. "I didn't know how it was going to feel," he said in his own defense, and he smiled with such tenderness that electricity seemed to run through her relaxed body. "What an incredible sensation."

Tiffany smiled and laid her cheek against his shoulder. "I'm sleepy," she said, yawning.

King glanced at Lettie. "I'm going to put her to bed."

"That's the best place for her," Lettie said with a warm smile. "Let me know if you need anything, dear," she told Tiffany, and bent to kiss the flushed cheek.

"I'll be fine. Thank you, Lettie."

King was grinning from ear to ear all the way up the staircase, and he never seemed to feel her weight at all, because he wasn't even breathing hard by the time they reached the top.

"You don't want children," she murmured drowsily. "You said so."

"We're all entitled to one stupid mistake." He carried her to his room, not hers, and laid her gently on the coverlet. His eyes were solemn as he looked down at her. "For what it's worth, I do want this child. I want it very much. Almost as much as I want you."

She flushed. "King, Dr. Briggs said—" she began cautiously.

He put a finger over her lips. "He said that the first trimester is tricky," he replied. He nodded. "We won't make love again until the baby is at home." He bent and kissed her with aching tenderness. "But we'll sleep in each other's arms, as we should have been doing from the first night, when you were a virgin bride— my beautiful princess bride. If you're cold, I'll warm you. If you're afraid, I'll cuddle you." He pushed back her soft hair. His eyes looked deeply, hungrily into hers. "And if you want to be loved, I'll love you. Like this." His lips drew softly against her mouth, cherishing, tasting. His cheek rested on hers and he sighed. "I'll love you with all my heart," he whispered a little roughly. "For all my life."

Her caught breath was audible. "You love me?"

"As much as you love me," he agreed. He lifted his head and searched her eyes. "Didn't you think I knew?"

She sighed. "No. Not really."

"That's the only thing I was ever sure of, with you. And sometimes, I wondered why you loved me. I've been a lot of trouble. Still want to keep me, in spite of everything?"

She smiled slowly. "More than ever. Somebody has to teach the baby how to take over corporations when he or she is old enough."

He chuckled. "Well, you're stuck with me, whether you want me or not." He touched her cheek and looked at her with pale eyes that mirrored his awe and delight. "I never dreamed that it would feel like this to belong to someone, to have someone who belonged to me." He sighed. "I didn't think I could."

"I know why," she replied, tracing his mouth with her fingertip. "But we're not like your parents, King. We won't have their problems. We'll have each other and our child."

He began to smile. "So we will."

She drew him down to her lips and kissed him with pure possession. "Now, try to get away," she challenged under her breath.

He chuckled as he met her lips with his. "That works both ways."

She thought what a wonderful godmother Lettie would be to the new arrival, and how proud her father would have been. It made her a little sad to think of him.

But then her husband's warm, strong arms tightened gently around her and reminded her that in life, for each pain, there is a pleasure. She closed her eyes and her thoughts turned to lullabies as the rain beat softly on the roof.

* * * * *